Also from Mickey Hoffman
& Indigo Sea Press

School of Lies

www.indigoseapress.com

DEADLY TRAFFIC

BY

MICKEY HOFFMAN

Stiletto Books
Published by Indigo Sea Press
Winston-Salem

Stiletto Books
Indigo Sea Press
302 Ricks Drive
Winston-Salem, NC 27103
This book is a work of fiction. Names, characters,
locations and events are either a product of the author's
imagination, fictitious or used fictitiously. Any resemblance
to any event, locale or person, living or dead, is purely
coincidental.

First Stiletto Books edition published
January, 2016
Stiletto Books, Moon Sailor and all production design
are trademarks of Indigo Sea Press, used under license.

For information regarding bulk purchases of this book,
digital purchase and special discounts, please contact the publisher
at indigoseapress@gmail.com

Cover design by Stacy Castanedo
Manufactured in the United States of America
ISBN 978-1-63066-359-9

Dedicated to the love of my life (you know who you are, I hope) for your support and boundless patience with my ranting and raving.

—Mickey Hoffman

Acknowledgements:

Special thanks to author Dave Freas for sharing his knowledge about writing and for his superb editing.

Also, a tip of my Yankee cap to Lynette Hall Hampton and several other members of the Mystery Writers' Forum for your valuable help.

Last, but not least, my thanks to the wonderful folks at Indigo Sea Press for the skills you put to solving the problems I create.

Chapter 1

Saturday, October 9

Kendra retreated farther beneath the yellow awning and opened a bottle of cold water. The temperature had risen steadily since 8 a.m. when she'd arrived at the park. At the end of the day, would she end up with new customers or just with a case of heat stroke? Hopefully, after the canine fashion show and agility events came to an end there would be a line of customers at her booth. She settled onto a large ice chest embossed with the Waggy Tails logo and fanned herself with a brochure.

This annual Doggie Day event had long been a favorite with higher income dog owners, so she'd jumped at the chance to promote her pet sitting business which had fallen off at the end of summer. While on a leave of absence from her regular job, she counted on the income, but so far the day had been a wash. Along with her competitors, vendors had come to sell everything from grooming services to pet portraits. Kendra's booth partner had drifted off an hour ago to distribute flyers for Waggy Tails shelter—or more likely, to socialize—leaving her bored, restless, and second-guessing her idea to attend.

A bleat of microphone feedback brought Kendra back to her feet. The organizer thanked everyone for participating and suggested they spend time browsing the booths. Almost immediately, the aisle in front of her teemed with boisterous children, their sweating parents and a wide variety of canines in various states of arousal.

For the next half hour Kendra did double duty, fielding questions about the shelter and publicizing her own dog walking business. At the first lull, she picked up her purse and headed for the ice cream stand. She was waylaid by a bony man wearing shorts and a T-shirt with Bridges printed across the chest in large italics. He handed her a leaflet, saying, "Appreciate your help," then quickly moved on.

She glanced at the sheet of goldenrod paper, expecting to see an advertisement, but the headline brought her to a full stop. And when she saw the two headshots, the cheerful clamor around her receded as if this piece of paper had carved out a dark and lonely space of its own. After skimming the Spanish text, she turned to the English section to make sure she fully comprehended. Under the words, REWARD FOR INFORMATION, the text read:

The Arbor City Mayor's office has authorized a $10,000 reward for information leading to the arrest and prosecution of the person(s) responsible for the death of Imelda Perez.

On Monday, October 4, at 2:00 a.m., the nude body of the victim, aged 16, was discovered near the corner of Southbridge and 8th Street. The Medical Examiner has ruled this death a homicide.

Also, approximately 2 hours later, the body of a second victim, an unidentified white female approximately 20 years of age, was found at the side of the Interstate near the 18th Street on-ramp. These incidents may be related.

Anyone with information regarding this crime, or who saw either victim earlier in the day is urged to contact one of the following:
Arbor City Police Department: 555-2677 (555-COPS)
Citizens' Crime Alert Line: 555-8477 (555-TIPS)
Bridges Multicultural Teen Center: 555-4357 (555-HELP)
All information will be held in confidence.

Kendra rushed to catch up to the Bridges man. "Excuse me, I might have some information about Imelda."
The man ran his eyes over her. An eyebrow went up. Was he questioning what a Caucasian, middle-class looking young female in her twenties could possibly know about the life of someone like Imelda? At another time, Kendra might have challenged his narrow perspective, but this wasn't about her.
The man asked, "Do you have any knowledge of her activities on October 3rd or 4th?"
"This girl—she went to Standard High, is that right?"

2

Deadly Traffic

"Yes."

Imelda dead! The immediacy of the death hit her like a punch to the gut. And the second girl's photo rang a bell; was she also enrolled last spring in the Special Ed. program? If so, like Imelda, she'd been truant more often than not.

The man sensed her distress and asked, "Are you all right, Miss?"

Kendra nodded as she straightened. "I just—I knew her."

"You a friend?"

"I'm a teacher. My name's Kendra Desola. She was in my Vocational Skills class. How—"

"Someone strangled her, then dumped her on the street like a piece of trash. If you know who she hung out with, that might help us find who did this to her."

Kendra shook her head. "No, sorry. I haven't seen her since last June, but I can give you a few people to call. Maretta Edwards, especially, should be able to tell you more." She took the offered pen and quickly wrote down several teachers' phone numbers. She'd call Maretta herself when she got home.

"Well, if you do think of anything, you have our flyer. I'll get back to it, then. See you."

She stood dumbfounded until a large poodle bumped her back into the moment. As she swept her head to look around, the sun burned into her eyes and she fled back to the shade beneath her canopy. After frantically rooting through her pocketbook for her prescription eye drops, she finally spilled the entire contents to the ground before resigning herself to four more hours of discomfort. Zipping the purse up again she remembered putting the medicine in her dog walking pack—before making a last minute decision to bring her purse instead.

"Are you all right? I didn't mean to upset you."

It was Bridges again. Blinking away the pain, she shook her head. "I'm fine, just too much sun. What can I do for you?"

He held out his clipboard and gave her a self-conscious grin "Sorry to bug you again. I should have gotten your personal information as well, if you wouldn't mind?"

"Of course." She bent to the form. When she looked up to hand back the clipboard, the Bridges man had stepped away and was handing out more leaflets. He gave one to a man coming

3

toward her booth with a large dog at his side. Although her faulty vision made people watching a chore, something about him immediately caught her interest. Maybe it was the way he and his large dog threaded effortlessly through the churning crowd without as much as a leash tangle. Was he a professional athlete? When he stepped up to her booth, she had only a second to collect herself enough to make sure her tongue wasn't hanging out. Golden hair, blue eyes, symmetrical features, and a smile that intimated that he'd invented it just for her.

At that moment, Bridges darted back for his clipboard, apologized for the intrusion and went on his way. Meanwhile, the Olympic god in front of her was reading his copy of the Bridges handout. The smile vanished from his face, replaced by something close to contempt. He crushed the paper into a ball and with an agile movement shot it into a trashcan several yards away. His dog reacted by jumping up for a game of go fetch, but was quickly commanded to heel.

"It's just horrible what goes on these days," he said. "No one's really safe anymore. I don't know what's happened to this town."

Kendra felt her own smile fail. This is his reaction to news about two brutally murdered teenage girls? Perhaps he belonged to the class of people who spent their lives living in a bubble. The silence felt awkward, so she put on her most businesslike smile and, hoping she wouldn't have to go through the entire spiel again, asked, "Are you familiar with Waggy Tails shelter?"

"Sure am," he said. His eyes passed from the dog collars the shelter was selling to Kendra's business cards. "Ah, I could use a dog walker. Do you know if she's any good?"

"That's my card, actually, and yes, I am," Kendra said. "Is this the dog you want walked?"

The man gave his pet a reassuring pat. "He's a good mutt— except for eating my shoes. I got him from a shelter, not Waggy Tails, another one. They couldn't give me much history except someone dumped him outside their office with wounds covering his body. He's a real love when he gets to know you."

"What a terrible life he must have had! But he looks like he's getting good care now."

The dog seemed to know he was the subject of conversation and tilted his head toward his master. "He's quite spoiled, actually, prances around like he's a pedigree or something but his ears are kind of funky, see? He must be only half Lab and who knows what the other half is? But we don't care, do we boy?"

"I can see that." Kendra hoped the remark encompassed everything.

The man aimed a look at her that made her knees go weak. She cursed herself when her pulse quickened in defiance of directives from her higher brain.

"We certainly could use someone like you for walks. Let me introduce myself. My name's Roger Rhus and this here is Jackson." He pressed his business card into her hand.

Roger Rhus, Attorney at Law. She should have gotten a clue about his profession from the way he'd been speaking to her, slowly enunciating each word as if he assumed she lacked intelligence. One of the hardest things about her current stint as a pet sitter was adjusting to being treated like an unintelligent, high school dropout who couldn't get a different sort of job. But then, how would Mr. Rhus ever imagine she was really a Special Ed. teacher on a leave of absence?

She rounded the table and slowly approached the chocolate brown Lab, but when she got within arm's reach, the animal shied away.

"I'm afraid he doesn't like being touched by strangers," Roger explained.

Kendra wasn't sure she wanted a skittish pet for a client. She could handle students with issues, but she didn't have the training or experience to deal with neurotic dogs. Still, she needed customers and this guy's Rolex told her that he could afford to pay top dollar. Then again, some of the wealthiest people turned out to be the stingiest clients.

Perhaps she could charge him more if she gave him the routine where she pretended to be so busy and exclusive she'd take only certain clientele. What a crock, but she'd learned how the business world worked. In that respect, she couldn't wait to return to teaching. "I'd have to see if I can fit you into my schedule. What exactly were you wanting, daily walks or pet care for a vacation or…?"

"I've been working long hours recently. Jackson hasn't been getting enough exercise. Would you be able to walk him once a day for, let's say, an hour? I hope you don't charge the same hourly rate we lawyers do." He grinned at his joke.

She decided to double down and quote him an exorbitant fee, one that would cover taxi fare in case he lived away from the bus lines. She had no intention of telling him she couldn't see well enough to drive, even if it was temporary. "My fee is forty dollars an hour, payment due at time of service," she answered firmly and waited for him to refuse or try to talk her down.

"No problem. Do you have references?"

She handed him a Kendra's Critter Service packet to take with him, although she expected this would be the last she ever heard from him.

"I'll look over your material and be in touch," he said.

"I'll have to make sure Jackson won't be afraid of me when I visit him at home alone. I may have to spend an hour or two with him the first time before I can get him on a leash."

"Of course, I understand."

The Lab heard the word home, shook himself and pulled away. "I think my boy wants to go home now. I'll call you as soon as I check your references. Nice to meet you."

Chapter 2

Sandi found Win leaning on the bar counter, waiting for her when she came out of the Ladies' room. A greenish glow from the wine bottles above the bar accented the planes of his handsome face. The young bartender smiled as she returned his change. A hostess led a party of three toward a table along the wall. He frowned at the receipt in his hand and stored it in his wallet. She couldn't see him turning it in to his boss; since when did petty criminals ask for meal allowances? More likely, it would be kept to demonstrate how well he treated her, right after he told her she didn't deserve dinner at such an expensive restaurant.

He plucked a toothpick from a shot glass near the cash register and used it like a wand to direct her toward the door. Sandi winced as a punishing blast of hot air struck her face, giving a longing look back at the cool interior of the restaurant. Win slid a stiffened palm to the small of her back to make sure they stayed hip to hip as he chose a pace that suited his long legs.

As they walked, Sandi kept her eyes fixed straight ahead, on a distant point that existed only in her mind, so she could pretend not to see the shock on people's faces when their eyes landed on her, the ungainly girl at his side. He, as usual, basked in the attention he drew from passersby. Impervious to the heat, he wore all black, chosen, she knew, to complement his hair and highlight the three diamond studs that sparkled in his left ear. A manicurist, outside for a smoke, paused mid-puff and stared in admiration, as if Sandi's companion had stepped straight off the glossy cover of one of the People magazines in her salon. Sandi wished she could hold that fantasy cover in her hands and shred him to bits, starting with his complacent smile. Why didn't anyone ever see him for what he really was?

Of course, Win got a kick out of seeing her humiliation. The way he played up his resemblance to Bruce Lee only served to accentuate her inadequacies—skinny legs with thick ankles, a sway back, and pudgy cheeks that refused to go away no matter how much weight she lost. The only thing that marred his perfection was a gold tooth that showed when he smiled. But women didn't consider it a flaw, they liked it, said it gave him character.

Sandi tracked away, pretending she wanted to avoid a bike rack, but he steered her back to his side as they joined a group waiting for a traffic light at a busy intersection. On the far corner, a steady stream of customers went in and out of the Arbor City Gourmet Deli. A wiry blond man stepped toward the curb, sipping at a large coffee. He barely caught her attention until she saw him retrieve a dog from where he'd tied it to a street sign. In a flash of recognition, she quickly sidestepped into the recessed doorway of a clothes boutique.

"Where do you think you're going?" barked Win in Burmese, catching up to her in two strides.

"Hah! Not really 'all American' yet, are you?" she replied in English. She pressed her nose to the glass, feigning interest in the merchandise. She needed to do something to gain more time. Playing to his vanity, she said, "Look here, these leather jeans would look good on you." As he checked out the jeans, she chanced a look down the block, starting to breathe again when she saw that her "uncle" hadn't seen her. He was leading his dog in the opposite direction.

Win opened the shop door, but stepped away as a red-haired woman came out. She brazenly brushed against him, the filmy cloth of her skirt teasing at his leg, then looked over her shoulder to throw him a suggestive look before proceeding into the adjacent shoe store. Sandi hoped he'd follow the woman, but he didn't respond to the lure. Instead, he was staring at the wall clock inside the boutique.

"Let's go in and you can try the pants on," Sandi suggested.

She had a moment of hope while he appeared to consider it, but he frowned and said, "Not now, I have to get you back."

He took her arm in a firm grip and set a fast pace back toward where they'd parked. She saw with dismay that in spite of her dawdling, they were in danger of catching up to the demon now only a block ahead and paused in front of an art gallery, sipping his coffee while his dog sniffed around an outdoor sculpture.

Sandi prayed for a distraction and for once the gods listened. From across the street, at a table set under the awning of an outdoor café, a triad of raucous coeds noticed Win and began to wave. How she loathed those women. They embodied everything she hoped to be when she reached their age, but would never become. She envied their carefree laughter, hated them for their self-assurance, but silently thanked them for being flirty. She felt the grip on her arm relax.

"Hey there!" Win called out to the women, moving slowly toward them while framing them in the camera of his cell phone.

Sandi dropped back a few paces and eyed the alley up ahead, on the near side of the parking lot where they were headed. It had to be now or she'd lose her chance. The alley was a dimly lit canyon where she felt she could lose him, especially if he didn't immediately figure out where she'd gone.

A few more steps to increase the distance between them...good, now he would lose sight of her as soon as she ran between the tall buildings. She curled her toes so her sandals wouldn't flop off and darted to the right. Suddenly, a bicyclist rounded the corner and swerved in front of her. She shrieked reflexively, losing the advantage of surprise, but she kept going. She heard his boots hit the pavement as he ran hard after her, shouting her name. She pushed down her fear and kept moving, into the alley and toward her goal, the little park beyond where she planned to disappear among the throngs of people gathered for a 10K charity run. She ran not for charity, only for her life.

She lost one shoe, heard him closing the distance. She spotted a line of dumpsters and flung herself into the darkness behind, landing hard. She inched backward, feeling the way with her hands. Then the ground beneath her tilted and she slid backwards until she hit a wall. Upended wooden pallets ringed her like a three-sided cage. Her pursuer let out a yelp of pain and his footsteps halted. Was he hurt? If she ran again, would he be able to chase her? Her answer came quickly.

"Don't move! You've got two choices, you can let me get you out of there before the rest of those things fall and crush you, or you can wait and leave in a body bag."

She froze, sprawled on the broken planks, skirt rucked up, legs askew. She felt a sharp, hot wetness on the palm of her hand and she licked at the blood. There wasn't enough to really taste, not like when she cut herself. Her ankle was twisted, the sole of her remaining sandal caught in a crevice between two pallets. She slid a hand down to free her foot and found her wristband; it must have unsnapped during the slide.

"Why...are you...running from me?" Win labored to catch his breath.

"You brought me to downtown to hand me over to him, didn't you!"

"Who's him? What's wrong with you?"

Sandi wanted to scream back, "What's wrong with you?" but she already knew the answer. She sat there in despair, relishing the pain of the wooden splinters in her skin as penance for her own stupidity.

He leaned in, stretching a hand toward her. She recoiled and, in spite of the shadows, pulled down her skirt to conceal the pattern of partially healed bruises on her thighs. When she felt the touch of his fingers on her foot, she threw her wristband at him. He swore at her as it bounced against his head, but managed to grab on to her ankle and reeled her in. She made a last attempt to shake loose, but his arms clamped around her so tightly she could hardly breathe. She'd lost.

"You won't run off again?" he asked, but it really wasn't a question.

"Not so you'll catch me," she said under her breath.

From a near distance came a muffled cry.

"Someone's coming," said Win. "Keep quiet or I'll make sure you can't scream." With a new urgency, he half-carried her through the alley emerging a mere block from the park that no longer was her refuge. Somewhere along the way she lost her other shoe. Eyes cast to the pavement, she numbly let him walk her back to the parking lot.

"You're bleeding. I think there's tissue in the car."

Sandi wanted to believe the concern in his voice but she no longer trusted anyone. For that, maybe she should blame herself. She was angry, but also ashamed, and she couldn't tell him or ask for help. Not anymore.

When they reached the car, he pushed her into the passenger seat, then got in the driver's side and reached over to fasten her seat belt. Sure, she thought, don't damage the valuable cargo. Why doesn't he just throw me into the trunk like he does with the others and be done with it? Or do the other girls just go along with him?

Win found a package of Kleenex under the seat, took one out and put it in her lap. She picked it up and bunched it in her fist, wondering what he'd do if she rubbed the blood from her wound all over his handsome face.

"We'll talk when you calm down. I don't have to tie you up, do I?" he asked in a tone indicating it was an option.

"You'd like that, wouldn't you," she spat. "Then you can charge extra for delivering me."

"You're sick. I'm taking you home. I don't even know who you are anymore." He turned the key in the ignition.

She gave him a look of scorn. "You never did, brother."

Chapter 3

Kendra shortened the dog's retractable leash and checked to make sure the locking mechanism held. Another ten minutes of this and Curtis would pull her arm out of the socket. Luckily, he was a Greyhound and not a more muscular breed, because she topped the scales at 120 even after a junk food binge. From now on, she'd keep him to side streets where she at least wouldn't have to worry as much about his overreaction to stimuli such as traffic and other pedestrians. Curtis's owner, like many of her pet sitting clients, hadn't bothered with leash training. Kendra couldn't help but appreciate the irony; she'd gone from dealing with students whose parents didn't parent, to pet owners who didn't train their pets. There must be a karmic meaning in this absurd twist to her life.

Curtis paused to let an elderly couple pet him, forcing Kendra to bake a few extra moments in the Arbor City heat. Wasn't the sun supposed to be less strong in October? Even the extra-dark glasses she wore weren't enough to keep her injured, light sensitive eyes from tearing. She used her free hand to shove up the sunglasses and wipe at her eyes. She fumbled in her fanny pack for the drops the doctor insisted were the best cure for the adverse reaction she was having from recent Lasik surgery. She couldn't wait until she got better and could see 20/20. Right now she dubbed it 20/glare.

She was relieved when the dog hurried under a canopy to sniff at a planter box, excited by something he'd detected among the geranium leaves. She reeled in the leash to stand beside him and waited for her eyes to make sense out of the jumble under his nose. She yanked him back just before his jaws closed around a greasy take-out bag.

"No! Sorry, but trans fats are bad for your figure," she said, as she redirected the reluctant Greyhound to the middle of the sidewalk where he'd be less likely to treasure hunt. When they rounded the corner on to a major street, she heard off-key female voices singing Happy Birthday and squinted toward the café across the street. From the sound of things, the partiers were well into a pitcher of beer, probably enjoying the café's specialty meal, sausage panini. The smell made her hungry, even though she didn't usually eat sausage anything; who really knew what went into a sausage? One of Curtis' relatives? She made a mental note to pick up something special, vegetarian maybe, after this dog walk.

"We have to speed it up and get you back," she told Curtis. "Your thirty minutes are almost up. I have three more doggies to visit today. Of course, they're not as cute as you, my lovely, but business is business."

Since taking a leave of absence from Standard High School, the half-hour time segment had become her new way of ordering the day. Normally, at about this time, she'd have been straightening up her classroom, preparing for the last two afternoon classes and fretting over the lesson planning and paper grading that she'd have to finish at home that night.

She'd expected the long summer break to restore her after last semester's double whammy—being a murder suspect, followed by the calamitous end of her relationship with Brian—but by mid-August she knew she wasn't ready to face the fall semester at Standard High and a fresh wave of gossip and blowback from her role in the police investigation there. So, she applied for a semester leave, and to her relief, the district granted it. Special Education teachers might not be appreciated, but they were desperately needed nonetheless.

A sharp jerk to her wrist brought her back to the here and now, only to find the leash played out to its fullest, and that she was being pulled into a narrow and dark alley. Not good. Alleys were where the trendy and cosmopolitan veneer of downtown came to a screeching halt. Kendra heard voices and thought she saw someone, maybe two people, moving erratically at the far end. She dug in her heels, but the dog had momentum on his side, dragging her forward, into the shadows. She used her free hand to flip up her sunglasses, but it was too late. Her left foot stumbled on a piece of debris and she fell painfully to all fours. Then the leash went slack. The unruly quadruped had lowered himself to his haunches and was happily sniffing at something. Why was that darn dog always one step ahead of her? Or was it four steps?

"All good for you," she grumbled at Curtis.

A faint scraping sound reminded her where she was. Fearfully, she glanced toward where she'd seen the shadowy figures, but it appeared they'd moved on. No longer afraid, she could at least console herself that no one had witnessed her embarrassing clumsiness. She moved to right herself and found a plastic sandal lying between her feet. Slowly, she stood and moved each leg gingerly to test for damage. Reaching down to brush the dirt from her jeans so she wouldn't emerge from the alley giving the appearance she'd slept there, she found she'd picked up the shoe. The large, cheery sunflower mounted on the V strap seemed to be mocking her clumsiness and inept dog skills. She hurled the thong away, where it bounced with a satisfying thud to rest against the filthy brick of the adjacent warehouse.

Kendra took a calming breath and maneuvered the suddenly pliant Greyhound to face in the opposite direction.

"We're going back to the street," Kendra commanded. "If you like alleys this much, there's one right in back of your house we can visit tomorrow." She led the prancing Curtis back to their original path, happy to trade the gloomy alley for the sunlit sidewalk. Then she saw it. No wonder he'd given up so quickly.

"Okay, what are you chewing on? Can I see?" She reached down and grabbed the slender object dangling from Curtis's mouth, but he jumped away, thinking they were playing tug of war. Kendra quickly dug a treat out of her pack and when Curtis opened his mouth to get the bacon bone, she won the round.

Under the dog's reproachful gaze, she brought his treasure closer to her eyes to examine it, praying there were no sharp edges or toxic substances on it. It proved to be a white leather wristband decorated with tiny studs. She wondered what story there might be behind this cast off item, its only flaw a small tear she attributed to dogteeth. Curtis made another play for his chew toy and she held it up higher to keep it from him while she got a better view. One blink later, she dropped it and hurried Curtis away. If she was right, those dark markings were bloodstains.

Chapter 4

Sunday, October 10

Roger frowned at the surface of the Formica table and wiped away a thumb-sized congelation with his napkin. He examined his glass of ice tea more closely and decided to stir it with his straw instead of the spoon. Shifting his weight, he slid to the edge of the booth's vinyl bench to avoid sinking into a deep hollow, an archived history of diners' backsides.

Even though he wore jeans and a faded, loose pullover—an outfit he'd hoped would make him blend in with the other diners at Emma's Pancake House—he noted that all the adult females within sight were ignoring their Sunday brunch and were either checking him out or texting their friends. From experience, he knew they were reporting the proximity of a "hottie" who resembled an iconic TV star. Well, if his presence made dining in this depressing place more pleasant for them, he was happy to be of service, as long as none of the ladies actually came over. At 41, Roger diligently worked out at the gym to make sure he kept in shape, but at the moment he didn't want distractions. Perhaps he should have picked a more upscale eatery for the meeting, one where the women wouldn't act foolishly. Unfortunately, he knew his dining companion would have stuck out in his favorite Euro Café like a freshly severed finger on an entrée of their Belgian waffles.

Thus far, though, no one had approached but the waitress, and things were going as planned. Roger looked with distaste at the man sitting across the table. He'd just concluded the preamble to their informal meeting by congratulating Elias on his early release from prison. Now the real conversation could begin, should he manage to hold the guy's attention.

Elias licked one of his fingers provocatively as the waitress topped off his coffee. She pretended to ignore him, all the while leaning her huge plateau of breast toward his nose. Roger impatiently watched her sashay over to serve a booth near the cash register, wondering how any male over the age of twelve could possibly be enchanted by such a saggy mound of flesh. Perhaps a few months in prison lowered a man's standards.

"So, Mr. Carmona, as long as you follow the conditions of your parole, you'll be fine. I don't want to have to go back into court with you again." Roger hoped the word parole would get Elias to focus.

"Hey, Mr. Rhus, I really owe you for getting me the early release," said Elias, finally showing some interest in Roger.

"Because I represented West Ridge I felt I should act as your attorney as well," Roger said disingenuously. West Ridge Retirement Center was a major client at the law firm where Roger specialized in immigration law. He'd been retained by West Ridge after a series of raids by Immigration and Customs Enforcement.

Elias jumped in, "West Ridge used me so they could claim the company didn't know about any undocumented workers in their employment. What bullshit! They knew what went on. They kept telling me to find them more workers as fast as I could for the kitchens and housekeeping. Worked out good for them, but I went to jail."

In Roger's experience, employers often found it convenient to look the other way. Elias could be telling the truth. In any case, either by lack of oversight or by design, West Ridge had a record of hiring people who did not have legal status.

"I got you the lightest sentence possible. But don't put all the blame on the company. You should have taken the earlier raids as a warning. West Ridge got off paying fines of $10,000 on the two earlier citations, but I warned them someone would go to jail the next time it happened."

"Yeah, me." Elias adjusted the collar of his polo shirt, giving Roger an unwanted view of his abundant chest hair.

"You were supervising the kitchens for a year. You did the hiring."

"Human Resources told me they'd take care of all the paperwork."

Roger suppressed a smile. This guy might be even dumber than he looked? Unlikely, given those heavily lidded, goldfish eyes and the thick lips that reminded Roger of those edible waxy, Halloween disguises.

"Look, Elias, let's not get bogged down with the past. The reason I asked you here is to give you a heads-up. West Ridge has hired me to monitor their hiring on a continuing basis. They don't want any more bad publicity."

"Like I care? They ain't gonna hire me back."

"Remember, before you went to prison, I told you I'd help you out? Well, West Ridge has agreed to rehire you, just not as a supervisor. You don't have to start until the end of the week. Gives you a few days to get acclimated again."

Elias became more animated. "No kidding? Great, then I got time—"

"Wait. Before you start thinking you can go back to doing what you did before, I have to tell you I'm going to be double-checking the documentation of all the employees. So, in other words, I'll be watching you."

"What is this, some kind of a set up?"

"On the contrary, it's a way for you to make money."

"Like how?"

"Since I went to bat for you, I'd like to see you succeed. But if I help you, it's not a free pass. Remember, if I choose to, I can have you put back inside. However, if you cooperate, we can solve the staffing problem at West Ridge and increase your net income at the same time."

"Net income? What are you talking about? Do I look like an accountant? You know I don't have no college." Elias frowned and turned his attention back to the waitress, watching avidly as she worked at the coffee maker.

Roger summoned the patience of his legal training and waited until she moved behind the counter and on into the kitchen before he took up the conversation again. "Let me explain. I can get foreign workers over here legally with H1 and H2B visas. The 2B visas are perfect for the domestic, landscaping, and kitchen help they need at West Ridge."

"If you want to start up an employment agency, I got no interest there, man." Elias ran his fingers over the stubble on his head, like he expected his long hair to still be there. "Shaved it, better than their stupid prison cut," he told Roger proudly.

"Yes, very nice." Roger closed his eyes briefly and attacked the subject again. "Let me finish. There are plenty of foreign workers anxious to come here, but there are very few visas. Most of them are so happy to get one they don't bother to read all the fine print. The HB visa lists the person's workplace right on the permit. Once a person from a foreign country gets here, the person is allowed to work only for that employer. If they leave the job for any reason, they're not legal anymore and they can be arrested and deported."

Elias stirred restlessly. "Sounds like a lawyer's gig. What's your point?"

"Point one, they come in legally with visas so no one's watching them. I did research and out of a group of over 90,000 workers recruited with H1 visas, only about 250 employers ever got checked. So, if we import workers my way, nobody's looking at them and no one's looking at you either." Or me, thought Roger smugly.

"Okay, no hassle from Immigration, but where's the money in this?"

Roger rubbed away the tension developing in his neck. Subtlety was lost on this one." Before the workers even arrive, they are willing to pay a big, up front recruitment fee, as much as 10K, to whoever can get them a visa. You're dealing with a different class of people here; they wouldn't risk sneaking in illegally in the first place, and once they're here, they'll do anything to keep their legal status, hoping they can upgrade their visa into permanent residence."

Elias dumped more cream into his coffee and stared at the turbid surface, as if a divination floated there. Roger decided to try one more time; after all, he wasn't meeting with Elias because of the guy's intellect. "I'll give you an example. Say I find five foreign workers for West Ridge and collect 10K from each of them for my work on their visas." He chose not to tell Elias the fee would double if he fudged some of the client's personal information the way they wanted. "After they arrive and start working, they find out they have to pay a monthly fee to manage the visa."

"And what if they say, 'fine, take the visa and shove it?' What then?"

"They won't. They won't want to return home and lose all the money they paid for the visas. In most cases they got their whole

18

family to chip in for the 10K and if they go home they lose the means to repay them, leaving their relatives back home in a very bad way. They'll stick it out here, viewing the monthly payments as a temporary burden on their road to a Green Card. Trust me, these workers are not going to make waves."

"Yeah, I get it. I see how they'd be willing to put up with some crap to stay here." Elias grinned like a man who takes a seat on a bus and finds a fat wallet he doesn't intend to return. "10K ain't bad, but where do I come in?

"Here's my proposal. I get the visas, then after the workers arrive, we confiscate their documents and tell them they're going to have to make payments until they've paid us enough to get the papers back. We'll set up a fee schedule and collect every month."

"That's what you lawyers call it, a fee schedule?" Elias gave a sharp laugh, then abruptly sat straight and shot Roger a suspicious look. "You got everything worked out so good why even tell me about this?"

"We form a partnership. You'll be my point man. I need someone to manage the clients, make sure they understand how it is, and you obviously have the hands-on experience."

"Seems to me I'd be taking most of the risk."

Roger knew the conversation had reached a critical stage. He countered the hard look in Elias's eyes with a casual smile. "What risk? These employees are legal, no one will check on them. And you'll have a job right away, at West Ridge, a better one than you could get on your own given the circumstances. Once we have the operation running there, we'll branch out and both of us can stop working with West Ridge. I have several, more highly skilled workers in the pipeline who'll pay even more. But for now, West Ridge is a good place to test the waters, and you'll be right there to keep an eye on things."

Rhus saw the man's resistance fading and moved to close the deal. "To show my good faith since you'll be on the front lines, so to speak, I went ahead and prepared a special contract." Roger slid an 8 x 10 document folder across the table.

Elias undid the string ties and peered in. His eyebrows rose at the neatly stacked hundred dollar bills. The folder quickly disappeared under his jacket. "All right, Mr. Rhus, I'm in."

"Good. We'll work out details next week. My new assistant

will be the go-between. Don't contact me directly unless there's an emergency."

"Who's your assistant?"

"You know him, Win Ni. He used to work part time for you at West Ridge."

Elias gave away his surprise with a double blink. "Win. Mr. Earrings. Yeah, I know him. I hired his mother as a cook, and later, I let the kid come work a few hours a week doing food prep. Is he in on this?"

"He knows only enough to be useful and he doesn't ask questions. I just got his family some of those bright and shiny new visas. He and his mother are overjoyed to have them and as you might expect, very, very grateful."

Elias suddenly became very interested in reading the label on the steak sauce bottle. The prolonged silence left Roger wondering if he'd wandered into unknown territory. Was Elias somehow more involved with Win and his mother than he let on? Roger said carefully, "I thought you'd be okay with Win being a part of this. I won't tell him you're back for a few days if you want some time to yourself, but he's going see you soon enough when you show up for work at West Ridge. Win's not going to be a problem, he's been very helpful to me, and loyal. So is his mother."

"That woman's fine. I wouldn't mind a taste of—."

"I'm afraid she's taken," said Rhus brusquely. "I'm sure after being in prison, you're not feeling too fussy anyway."

"Who's got my old job?" asked Elias. "Does the new supervisor know I'm on parole? As soon I show up for work, won't everyone be watching me?"

"The new guy's name is Grant, Mose Grant, and I don't think you have to worry on his account. He's not very experienced. I heard he's in way over his head. He won't have the time or energy to spend on you. Just keep a low profile and I'll be in touch."

Chapter 5

Monday, October 11

A line of poplar trees cast long bands of shadow across the driveway by the time Win pulled the car to a stop just inside the wrought iron gate. A high stucco wall encircled the property, providing security to an angular, three-story house and beautifully landscaped grounds. The lights were on in Mr. Rhus's study in the flat-roofed turret that made up the top floor. He almost expected to see Mr. Rhus's silhouette in the window, watching for them.

He glanced at the dashboard clock and back to the woman in the passenger seat. Even in profile, he could read Thida's anger from the stubborn set of her jaw. She sat there, motionless, staring straight ahead. He knew if he didn't get her inside soon, Mr. Rhus would be angry, and Win didn't want to do anything to jeopardize the good relationship he had with his boss.

"Here we are. We can talk more tomorrow, okay?"

His mother seldom shared her thoughts, but he usually could read her moods. He'd sensed her distress during the drive home from the casino. Instead of asking him how he'd spent his time there, she'd been preoccupied and sullen, endlessly weaving her fingers through the strands of her long hair. When they reached the city limits, she'd finally spoken her mind, telling him she didn't want to go home—but not why. Whatever her problem was, if she screwed up her relationship with Mr. Rhus, his mother would not only make things hard on herself, she'd ruin his plans as well.

"Mom, you have to go in. I am sick of arguing. You can't stay overnight at my place. Look at the time. We were supposed to be back hours ago and Mr. Rhus is going to ask questions if I show up without you. What are you going to do while I return the car keys, hide in the bushes? What am I supposed to tell him, that he was hallucinating your presence? Give me a break. He's probably watching us sitting here. Whatever you two have going on, why do you have to bring me into it?"

"You did that by bringing me back here. I said not to."

21

"What's wrong with here all of a sudden? Mr. Rhus found out the hard way about Sandi. Do I have to tell him you're a whack job too?"

"When did you learn to talk to me like that?"

"Shh, keep your voice down. He'll hear you." Win glanced toward the house and switched from English to their native Burmese. "I'm fed up. I'm an adult now and I won't let you keep making decisions that screw up my life."

"I didn't like it, but I didn't try to stop you from working for Mr. Rhus. At least you told me that is what you're doing now."

"How can you criticize me for being tight with him when you're the one who hooked up with him in the first place? I'll admit I didn't like the idea at first, not until he asked us to move in and I saw this place. If Sandi would have been nice to him, she'd still be living here instead of at the foster home and maybe he'd help her out in the future with a job, like he's helping me."

Thida replied in such in a low voice Win could only hear the words, "…what I am afraid of."

"What did you say?"

"Nothing. Things are complicated. I need a day to think things over. Take me to a hotel if you won't let me stay with you."

"Hotel? Don't talk crazy. Mr. Rhus treats us good. Like, he let me borrow this car again and he even gave me gas money, a good thing because you made me drive you all the way out to the middle of nowhere." Win watched her closely, hoping to see something in her face that might explain her unexplained change to their afternoon plans. "I thought we'd see a movie, eat out somewhere, but you wanted to spend the afternoon in a casino. When did you get into gambling, anyway?"

She shrugged. "The women in the kitchens were always saying they had a good time up there."

"Okay, it's your money, your day off. I'm just glad the place had a sports bar. You know, I went into the card room to ask if you wanted to try the buffet and couldn't find you. Where did you go, anyway?"

She shifted her feet. "I tried the slots a little."

"Must have been more than a little. Your poker buddies were asking for you. Whatever you did, I thought you had a good time, but you've been acting strange the whole drive home. Did you lose too much money, or did something weird happen to you in the casino?"

Thida pulled on the charm at the end of her necklace. "Nothing happened. I—I just—I want to stay somewhere else tonight, think things through. I don't think I can live here anymore."

"Mom, you have a great set up here and anyway, you don't have another place to live. You can't stay in my apartment. I'm not getting involved." He heard her let out a harsh breath and knew he'd sounded too self-serving. "And what would you do for money?"

"Let me worry about it."

"You aren't thinking straight. Remember, even if you're sick of working here, you can't change jobs. Our visas, the ones Mr. Rhus got us in case you forget, only let us work at the place listed on the visa. For you, that means right here as his housekeeper. You change jobs, you get deported."

"I don't believe they can tell us where to work. This is a free country. You're lying because you care more about him, or at least his money, than you care about me."

"Sure, I care about him. If not for Mr. Rhus, we wouldn't have our visas. Don't you want to stay in America? If you mess this up, he'll have us all sent back to Thailand."

"Oh, we would not be staying in Thailand," she said with venom. "We would be sent right out of there, right back to a work camp in Myanmar…."

"Whatever. Thailand, Myanmar, I'm not going back to that world again. Yeah, I care about Rhus's money, but we owe him a lot, too. Maybe you don't like him or your job so much anymore, but for now, we have no choice." Win rested his head back on the seat and sighed. "Like it or not, you can't always do things your own way."

"My way got us over the border into Thailand, didn't it?"

"But then what? All those years, running, moving from place to place. Finally, we settled down when Dad got a job as a dive instructor."

"Dive instructor? He just carried air tanks and gear for the rich, lazy guests."

"Kho Phi Phi island survived on those rich tourists. They even

23

bought shells and driftwood from me. I didn't see you complaining when I gave you the money."

"Okay, you liked living there. I am the one who had to clean guest rooms while you and Sandi played on the beaches."

Win let out a breath. "If not for the tsunami, we might still be there. And Dad would be alive."

Win's memories of the months following the Tsunami were a collage of mud covered ruins, constant hunger, and the cries of the bereaved. Somehow, his family had avoided the large refugee camps, moving instead from one temporary shelter to the next. Much later, when Win reached adolescence, Thida told him how she'd been cleaning the manager's office when the waves began to rise and while everyone else fled the oncoming wall of water, she'd stopped long enough to empty the cash drawers before leading him and Sandi in a mad scramble uphill. Thida used her "found" money to keep them out of the refugee camps, then to buy passage on a ship to Mexico, and from there, a ride over the border into the United States.

Yeah, he had to give his mother credit for raising him and keeping him safe, but he'd come to despise her unrelenting, single-minded quest for what she called "a better life." Win didn't even remember her stopping to mourn her own husband. Win deeply felt the loss of his father, but his mother hardly mentioned him. He wanted a better life, sure, but he still had feelings.

Thida seemed to read his thoughts. "I saved us and you blame me. Sandi does not."

"Sandi lives in her own world. I didn't see her cry once until after we got to L.A. She hated that we had to keep moving every few months to avoid being picked up by Immigration."

"And you liked moving all the time because it made it easier for you to cut school and spend time on the streets."

"I learned more by not going to school, especially about how this country works."

"What you learned is how to lie and get away with it—until high school where they didn't just pass you to the next grade because of good manners and a nice smile. Now you don't even have a high school diploma."

"It doesn't matter. I learned what counts. My English is much better than yours and I know how the system works here." Win reached back, grabbed Thida's purse from the back seat and set in on her lap. "Okay, time for you to get moving."

She hunched defensively into the leather seat. "Maybe if I go see the nice counselor from Sandi's school, Miss Goodman, she can find me somewhere to stay."

"You even know where she lives?"

"No, I could call her at the school tomorrow...."

"You can't wait out on the street all night," Win said firmly. He went on, pressing his case. "Don't be selfish. If you walk out on Rhus, what happens the next time Sandi gets into trouble? He sure won't help us then."

"I did not think of that."

He heard the weariness in his mother's voice and decided to take charge of the situation. "Come on, I'll walk you in. I'll return the keys and stick around long enough to make sure there are no monsters waiting to get you." He got out of the car, choosing to ignore the conflicted look on Thida's face. "You go change clothes, cook up a nice dinner, relax, and don't think so much."

Thida looked toward the house and up at the third floor balcony. She suddenly seemed to notice for the first time that the outside lighting had come on. "Dinner, it is late. Mr. Rhus will be angry."

Win gripped the steering wheel in exasperation. "So, big deal. Dinner is late, he might not be happy. I'm sure you can turn his mood around." Win tried to take her hand but she pulled it away. "Maybe things aren't going for you like you planned, Mom, but the Boss says with my brains I can really go far and he's going to help me."

"You can't put someone else's promises in the bank. Go back to school where you belong. There's still a lot you have to learn."

"I'll think about it," he said. Win knew when to stop. His mother would come around. And when he started pulling in some real money, she'd respect him.

Chapter 6

Roger watched the sky change from cerulean to violet with the last rays of the setting sun. On a clear autumn night like this, he liked to take a break and enjoy a glass of wine on the tiny balcony just outside his home office. Beneath him, artfully placed landscape lights accented the winding paths, rock formations and plantings he'd used to create a Chinese garden on the double sized lot. Once his new corporation, RR Global Manpower took off, he'd buy a rural property where he couldn't see his neighbors and could fulfill his dream of duplicating an entire Song Dynasty garden.

Tonight, Roger found himself unable to enjoy his dominion. He leaned on the railing and peered down at his SUV and the two people inside. Five more minutes, then he'd call Win's cell. He downed the last of the wine and forced himself to return to his desk where he flipped through case files he'd brought home from the law office. A complex litigation on behalf of West Ridge Retirement Village was entering the final stages. An American citizen had been caught up in one of the previous sweeps for undocumented workers and was suing. The case had been a factor in West Ridge's decision to have Roger verify their employees' citizenship and take advantage of his skill at obtaining visas.

He swiveled his chair to face the window. What were Win and Thida doing down there with the SUV stopped at the far end of the driveway? The two of them were late, yet obviously not in a rush. Roger wasn't about to go down to get them. Not his style. His stomach growled impatiently, seeming somehow to take a cue from Thida's return. He expected a hot meal every weeknight and she knew it. He'd been more than fair, letting her take the day off to go out with her son even though she'd forgotten to take his shirts to the cleaners on Friday, something he hadn't become aware of until he started to get dressed for work this morning.

Maybe he should have given more thought to this change in her normally dutiful behavior and cancelled her day off. Now it seemed she'd taken advantage of him, staying out past time. He'd definitely settle up about this later. Perhaps he was partially to blame for not keeping better track of her. The past few months he'd been extremely busy, setting up RR Global while simultaneously having to keep up with the demands of his job at the law firm. Fortunately, he'd found young Win to be exceedingly helpful and a quick learner.

Roger heard the engine rev and watched as the car finally pulled up to the garage. Win came around and protectively draped a sweater over his mother's shoulders. Not for the first time, he wondered if he should have started a modeling business instead; he could probably make a fortune with those two, but he doubted Win could stand still long enough and Thida was too valuable to him the way she was. Had it really been eighteen months since he'd first laid eyes on her?

On that spring day, he'd been waiting for an elevator in the lobby at West Ridge and was idly looking out the floor to ceiling windows when he spotted her crossing the parking lot. He was intrigued by her posture, head held high, and the delicate swing of her arms as she walked. When she pushed the lobby door open, their gaze met. She flushed and cast her eyes down in confusion. Excited by the momentary flash of electricity that passed between them, he watched her go down the hall and into the dressing room used by the kitchen staff. He took a place by the kitchen entrance and waited. She soon reappeared, coming from an interior door that led directly into the kitchen, and went over to the wall ovens, where she began to remove heavily laden trays and slide them one by one on to cooling racks.

He couldn't stop looking at the tiny, very sexy birthmark to one side of her full upper lip. In contrast to his own Nordic coloring, her dark ebony hair shone as if it reflected the stainless steel surfaces around her. Although she was slightly built, he noted an unexpected strength in her easy handling of the large trays. The mix of delicate and strong excited him. The fact she was Asian added another enticement because he was an avid fan of all things Asian. He'd seen first hand how males dominated in most Asian cultures and he, likewise, preferred his women to be submissive. At that moment, he decided to add her to his oriental collection.

As soon as he approached her, he guessed by her nervous demeanor she must be another of Elias's supposedly unnoticed,

Mickey Hoffman

undocumented hires. She certainly was one he wouldn't expose. He knew her precarious situation would make her easy to manipulate. And so it had, especially after he befriended her son.

Roger had recognized Win's cleverness and saw promise in the boy's strong drive to become rich without worrying about how he got there. When Roger brought it up, the kid had jumped at the chance to be his personal assistant. Tonight, for the first time, he wondered if he'd been too nice to the kid. He'd have to watch him more closely from now on in case Win was taking their relationship for granted.

When he heard the clankity-clank of keys dropping to the marble table in the foyer, Roger pushed back from his desk and quickly descended to the ground floor. Thida had already disappeared into the kitchen and Win had gone outside, headed toward his motorcycle. Roger caught up with him near at the koi pond just past the front entrance.

"Thanks for letting me borrow the car again," said Win. "I filled up the tank."

"That's two loans in four days," Roger said with a faint smile. "Next time I dock your pay for car rental. Listen, I have some news for you. Your old boss is out."

"Already? How's that?" asked Win, flashing a momentary look of discomfort Roger thought might need following up.

"Out early for good behavior, or maybe because of prison overcrowding. Don't worry. I won't fire you. I made you my assistant to teach you business skills. When Elias gets settled, he can do the hands on stuff."

"What if he wants to, um, go back to—you know. Elias really might not want to stop what he was doing before. He was making a lot of money."

"I will make arrangements with Elias." Roger waved a hand to indicate they were finished with the subject. Then, he smiled at Win and asked, "So, how's life in the apartment?"

"Great! Thanks so much for helping me rent the place," Win lowered his voice, "and for telling my mom I'm renting a room in your cousin's house. We can tell her the truth when she gets used to me living on my own. I'm not sure a landlord would have rented such a nice place to someone like me without the reference from you. And getting me an ID saying I'm twenty-four sure helped."

28

Deadly Traffic

In actuality, Roger agreed to set up Win in an apartment to keep Thida from getting wind of what her son was helping him with. "I only added three years to your age, not a big deal. I could tell you were ready to be my personal assistant and mature enough to live on your own." He clasped Win's shoulder, then quickly let his hand drop. *He's really filled out the last few months. I have to remember he's not a child anymore, not so easily led.* "Well, I'll let you go now, see you tomorrow."

Roger took a few steps toward the house and then, as if it was an afterthought, asked, "I'd invite you to stay for dinner, but I'm not even sure there will be any. You got back late, did you run into traffic or something?"

"Um, no not exactly. I lost the parking ticket and the idiot working there wanted me to pay for 24 hours. I made him call the manager and it took forever. Sorry, Mr. Rhus, it won't happen again."

"If it does, you won't be borrowing one of my cars again."

He watched Win's motorcycle shoot out of the graveled courtyard. The kid really loved his acid blue, Honda Rebel, and was assiduously keeping up with the payments. At the moment, though, Roger almost regretted the loan he'd given him for the down payment. No, it wasn't fair to blame Win for the tardy arrival; those things happened. Overall, Win treated him with respect and did exactly what he was asked. His mother, on the other hand, might need another reminder. He went inside to check on Thida, who he hoped to find in the kitchen with dinner well underway.

Chapter 7

Thida stared into a pot of boiling pasta, watching the strands of spaghetti writhe in consort with her emotions. She heard her boss's footsteps in the passageway and turned her back, as if that would deflect the barrage of criticism she expected. The cold marble and steel surfaces of the kitchen reinforced her presentiment that this would be a hard night. Roger used her badly, yet he'd also done a lot for her and her family in the beginning.

How she'd savored their initial flirtation. He'd driven her crazy the way he strung out his brief contacts with her over a period of several weeks. By the time he finally gave her his business card, she'd been so excited she'd called him the next day.

Although she was a bit wary because of the difference in their social status, when she learned what he did for a living her final objections melted away. She hinted at her desire for a Green Card and that she would be willing to do almost anything to get it. Still, he held back until finally, when neither of them could stand it any longer, he took her. First gently, then rougher as time went on. And she acceded to everything he wanted as if she also couldn't get enough.

Gradually, she came to understand she was more of a symbol to him than a real person. He used her to satisfy his desire for the exotic, and, above all, his need to dominate. Before she knew it, she was under his control, both because of her family's tenuous legal status, and, if she was honest with herself, by virtue of an unhealthy mix of gratitude, fear and sexual attraction.

"Have a nice time out with your son?" Roger asked in a much too quiet voice as he came up behind her.

She played with the lid of the pasta box, afraid to meet his piercing blue eyes. "I am sorry we were late back. Do not blame Win, it is all my fault."

"I saw you parked out there. Get lost in the driveway?" His tone had turned sarcastic now.

"We...we have...to talk family business. I had to ask him about Sandi. I worry about her." She wished her command of the

Deadly Traffic

English language didn't suffer so much when she was under stress. If she used the wrong words here, Rhus might realize she was lying and become angrier.

Thida felt his breath on the back of her neck. She tensed for what would come next. He slid his right arm around her, holding her tightly to his chest, lifting her slight body off the floor while sliding his left hand under her skirt and up her leg. Finding the soft flesh of her inner thigh, he pinched and twisted until she whimpered. Letting out a grunt of pleasure, he let her slide down his body and suddenly let her go. She pitched forward into the cloud of steam billowing up from the boiling water. As it engulfed her face, she jerked away from the searing heat. Panting, and half blind with tears, she felt for the countertop to steady herself, then felt a linen handkerchief being pushed into her hand.

"Blow your nose, woman, that's disgusting."

Thida wiped at her face, using the moment to collect herself, listening to the hissing gas flame, the water crackling in the pot, and her own blood roaring harder than either.

"You should be thinking more about me, not your ungrateful daughter. I got you a visa as my live-in housekeeper and when you asked for visas for your children, I did that too. I welcomed all of you into my house."

"You are always very good to us, I know that. We are all grateful."

"Except Sandi," said Roger thoughtfully. "She can't accept me, or the idea her saintly, widowed mother would ever pair up with a new man."

"I am sorry she call you all those names, but you and Mrs. Goodman found a place where she can live and get some help."

"Let Carol Goodman and the Home worry about her. You need to be thinking about me."

He brought Thida closer and said, half to himself, "You're so beautiful, even with your mascara running everywhere." He cupped her chin with one hand and squeezed her jaw. When she blinked in pain, he gave a little grunt of satisfaction. "It's not too much for me to expect a little gratitude. If it wasn't for me, your family would be the 'illegal aliens' the politicians are always ranting about."

"I am grateful."

31

"You will show me tonight. Come to me at eleven o'clock." He pressed harder into her until she feared the edge of the stone countertop would snap her spine. "And until further notice, no more days off."

"Yes, sir," she gasped, watching his lips gloat with satisfaction.

"The pot's about to boil over," said Roger.

Then, without another word, he left her.

Chapter 8

Thida managed to twist off the burner before her knees buckled, then leaned on the counter until she felt steady enough to walk to the banquette. She longed for a hot bath to soothe the pain in her back, but the best she could do for now was to put her thoughts in order.

At least she'd caught the water before it boiled away and burned the pasta. Roger didn't know she only needed another minute or two to add sauce and set out the side dishes, so she had some time to reflect on her changed situation.

She now possessed the means to free herself and could stop Roger from dominating her mind, if not yet her body. He couldn't possibly know what she'd accomplished on her day off. She'd worried Win would find out, but he hadn't caught on to the real reason for her sudden interest in visiting a gaming resort. She'd been able to slip out of the card room while he was mesmerized by the text messages on his cell phone. Unfortunately, he was also mesmerized by Roger's wealth. Whose side would her son take if he knew the truth about her situation and her plans?

Thida quietly padded to the adjacent laundry room and brought a sewing kit out to the eating area. She slit open a side seam of the banquette cushion. This would be safe. She reached under the cushion and extracted two small objects from the makeshift hiding place where she'd quickly stashed them after saying goodbye to Win and rushing to the kitchen. She released the leather ties on a small pouch and stuck a finger inside, feeling the jagged stones. They'd come all the way from her past and were going to buy her a better future.

Thida worked the small pouch deep into the cushion's wadding, quickly restitched the seam and replaced the cushion. She thoughtfully ran a finger over the tiny device resting in her lap. If things didn't work according to plan and Daw double-crossed her, this would be her vindication, a way to win back Sandi's love, a way to explain why she hadn't told her children their father was alive. If Win didn't want to come with her, she'd have to leave him behind, but she couldn't leave Sandi.

She held her breath and listened for Roger, but the only sound was the whirr of the supersized, stainless steel fridge. Rhus had gone upstairs. She pushed the PLAY button and held the tape recorder to her ear. The voices were clear, a valuable, clandestine recording of this afternoon's meeting with her husband, the first meeting in many years.

They came face to face outside the loading dock of the resort's rustic hotel. He spoke first, greeting her awkwardly in English, then switched to Burmese, asking her to follow him. The recording went silent as they moved over springy pine needles to a secluded spot under the trees. After a long embrace, he held her at arm's length and looked her up and down. He wore a baggy custodial uniform but Thida could see he hadn't gone to fat like many of her compatriots when they adopted the American diet. His face was still so youthful, it made her hate him so much she almost wished he really was dead, like she'd long believed.

He released her and said, "I can see from your eyes that you might be having second thoughts. We can't live in the past. Now we are finally standing here together, say what you have to say."

"You didn't try very hard to find out if we were alive." Thida rasped.

"The dive boat almost capsized and several of the divers went overboard. We all nearly died. We were lucky to reach the shore near Phuket. There was no way I could get back to the island to check on you. Everything was chaos, the phones were out, and the soldiers were everywhere. I didn't want to be caught and sent to a camp. When the chance came, I took it, got myself smuggled to South America and—well, you know that already. Don't blame me for the years it took until we found each other again."

"Yes, years. I can understand. Things happen. But on the phone, you called me terrible names as if I betrayed you for another man."

"That was before you told me the details and I saw the advantages in keeping you there with your lawyer friend," said Daw. "But my patience is wearing out." He grabbed her by the shoulders. "You are my wife!"

"I have to be careful. Also, it will cost more than you told me to hire someone to do it."

"What I give you today better be enough. How can you live with a rich guy and not have money? Maybe you are just conning me." Daw's eyes narrowed.

"If I could get at his money, I would not still be living there. I think what really angers you is not the sex, but that I managed to get legal status and can't get it for you."

"You mean you don't want to get me a green card," he said. "You think if he never finds out about me he might marry you or something?"

Thida saw the anger and jealousy in Daw's eyes. Still, compared with what Rhus would do to her if he found out about Daw... "No, I mean I can't do it, just accept that. We agreed if we want to move forward we have to trust each other again."

He studied her face. "You trust me now because I thought of a way to make us both rich, but if you wait much longer your rich lawyer will toss you out for a younger woman before you make your move."

"I will take care of it. We have no time to stand here and argue. Win will wonder where I went. Before I go, I need to ask you something. Not for me, for Sandi. She is running away again, now from the foster home. I know this is a change of plans, but can you take her?"

"You changed your mind and told her I'm alive?"

"No, and I won't unless you agree to take her. I really don't know what's worse for her, thinking you're dead or knowing you deserted us."

"Don't play the victim, Thida. You did all right for yourself without me. Anyway, it will just be a few more weeks."

"You can take care of her for that long."

"Maybe it's not such a bad idea telling her I'm alive. I bet your rich lawyer would be willing to pay me not to come down, cause a fuss and ruin his reputation."

"Please, Daw, do not jump in and ruin the whole plan. Will you take Sandi?"

"I can't, Thida. I live in a dorm up here. We don't want her running off into the woods." Daw reached inside his shirt for a small cloth pouch suspended around his neck on a leather cord. Lifting it over his head, he shoved it into Thida's hands. "Here, take what you came for and go. I have only a few left, the rest I used to set us up. I still don't see why you can't get some money out of your rich boss man."

"He doesn't even give me wages anymore, just room and board."

Daw opened his mouth to say something, but only frowned and walked swiftly away. His parting words were barely audible, "Take care of our children, Thida."

Chapter 9

Tuesday, October 12

Kendra swiped a towel over the bathroom mirror and leaned closer to see her reflection through the fog. The problem, of course, came from her vision and not the mirror. Why look anyway when she knew last night's broken sleep had only added to the dark circles under her eyes? 9 a.m. shadow. Very fashionable. Right. Didn't they say that dreams last only a minute or two? Then how to account for this morning's twisted sheets and a very disgruntled cat? All available evidence led her to believe she'd spent another long night trying to run from her recurring nightmare, which always began mundanely enough in the classroom:

The bell rings, but she finds she's rooted to a chair in front of her computer. Unable to move or even close her eyes, she is forced to watch the monitor as a succession of sadistic, threatening emails pop open in separate, cascading windows until they fill the entire screen. The printer at her side clicks and hums and spits not pages, but typed words. They whiz into the air swarming, coalescing into irregular, pulsating shapes. She can only stare as the apparitions grow in size and coil around her head like menacing gargoyles, their sharp claws slashing at her face. With the clang of a bell, students and school administrators materialize in a ring to surround her, joining forces to jeer at her. For being a lousy teacher. An interfering do-gooder. A loser.

At that point, she always woke up, bathed in sweat. Kendra understood the dream to be a fantastical exaggeration of her own unresolved insecurities combined with images from computer games, but knowing that didn't seem to help.

Looking back, she'd been too slow to come to terms with a barrage of undeserved animosity from her coworkers, allowing the gossip to build for weeks before silencing it with an offer to actually do what they claimed she'd done: call the cops on them. Managing her professional problems still left the very raw damage her boyfriend Brian had done to her self-esteem. She still intended to make him pay somehow, especially for continuing to harass her after their break-up, even calling her friends—the ones who would still talk to him—to find out where she was living now.

Deep in thought, she jumped in fright when the bathroom door suddenly brushed against her arm. She relaxed when she registered the sensation of fur tickling her bare legs.

"Bobbins. Want the bathtub?" The cat replied with a purr-meow and leapt over the edge of the tub with a whoosh of the shower curtain. "Good you didn't bump into me when I was doing the eye drops. Didn't your pet human ever teach you to knock first?" She laughed. "Never mind, that would have been me."

She combed the tangles from her wet hair and reviewed her afternoon schedule. This afternoon would be hectic, five dog walks in succession with travel time between. She had spent a happy morning on line, taking her battle mage through a dungeon quest in Istaria: Chronicles of the Gifted, and drinking an entire pot of coffee, a combination that wiped her brain free of the last vestiges of her nightmare. Although she enjoyed having the leisure time, the leave of absence made her feel more useless and isolated than rejuvenated, especially since the fall term began. The night after Labor Day, a different dream replaced her usual nightmare; late for class, she wandered the halls in a panic, unable to find her classroom. When she awoke, an unreasonable guilt pressed down on her, telling her she needed to be at school, teaching, not pet sitting, and that nothing she did for the next six months would be more than a huge waste of time.

"Going in for a depression marathon, are we?" she asked the cat. "Maybe I should make myself something special for lunch instead. I haven't charred a grilled cheese sandwich in a while." Bobbins gave her a look that she interpreted as: If you must pursue your cooking debacles, I ask only that you don't feed any of it to me.

Lunch—another sign how her life had changed. When she was teaching, she had regularly missed lunch, either because she had unfinished work to do or a student emergency arose. Instead of pitying herself, she should be reveling in the opportunity to eat three meals a day.

She zipped up her jeans and slipped on a shirt with plenty of useful pockets. The cat chose that moment to stage an ambush from his place behind the shower curtain, shooting out to swat her ankle with one large, fuzzy paw. Kendra looked down in time to see a ball of gray fur streak down the hall toward the kitchen. She yelled, laughing, "Oh no you don't, that's not fair. Just wait till I catch you."

She was jogging toward the bedroom to get his favorite mouse toy when a sharp, brittle noise came from the kitchen, immediately followed by a loud thump that Kendra felt through the soles of her bare feet.

Her first instinct was to run toward the sound in case something had happened to Bobbins, but when she reached the kitchen entrance, she saw he wasn't there. A sense of caution took hold. What was that noise? She closed off the kitchen to keep Bobbins out and slowly inched toward a window where she could get a panoramic view of the yard. The trashcans were upright. The metal watering can was still perched on top of the decrepit birdbath. As far as she could tell the tiny yard was empty, not even a stray cat in sight.

But that didn't mean much, because she couldn't trust her eyesight. She waited a minute longer and hearing nothing, went right up to the window for a better look. Now she saw something, more like a reflection on the floor of the back porch. Glass? Kendra decided not to open the back door, but to investigate by going around from the front.

She slipped into a pair of clogs she kept in the front hall. The last thing she expected to see when she opened the door was a man standing on the top step of her porch. She shrank back in alarm.

The young man looked as startled as she was. "Don't scream, it's okay," he said. "I live next door. I heard a noise and came running."

The houses on this block were jammed close together; any of her neighbors could have heard something, but why this unexpected burst of community spirit? She looked him over, trying to assess the threat level, although his words, spoken with a foreign accent she couldn't place, were reassuring. He was obviously Asian, although taller than the stereotype, almost six feet. His skin tight T-shirt showed he wasn't overly pumped, but he had enough muscle to overpower her easily if he wanted to.

Still, with his spiky hair, ear studs, and green leather choker, he looked more like an androgynous computer hacker than a robber.

"Did you see anyone come out of my yard?" she asked.

"Nope. I heard a loud noise coming from this direction so I came running. By the time I got up front, there was no one around."

Kendra grabbed a key from inside and locked her door, then cautiously walked toward the back, with the guy following behind uninvited. Although she didn't know him, she did feel safer having someone along.

"No one here," he said, looking around the yard. "Yell if you need me," he added quickly, and left her as suddenly as he appeared.

"Need you for what?" she muttered. Then she heard a crunch underfoot. The sun was making her eyes tear so badly she could hardly make out that the ground was covered with shards of glass. The storm door had been shattered; the glass pane lay in pieces on the ground. A large river rock lay on the cement stoop.

She stepped carefully to avoid as much of the glass as possible and went to see if the wooden back door had been tampered with. A piece of decorative trim that bordered the upper panel had splintered where the rock had hit, but the wood held solid and the door remained firmly locked.

Okay, it's only broken glass, she told herself, but her eyes returned to the rock. Who did this? Is the person who threw it still around?

She suddenly needed to be inside her house, away from whoever did this to her. She fled toward the front, toward safety, and in her haste, collided with her newest acquaintance, inexplicably stepping down from the front porch. She felt more than saw a cascade of papers hit her feet. What the heck?

"I didn't think you'd still be here," she said, intending it more like an accusation than an apology.

"I was waiting to see if you needed anything and the mailman came by and handed your mail to me. I was just gonna put it into the box." He scrambled to pick up the mail. "Do you...you sure you're okay?"

How about going away and then I will be, she thought, but instead replied, "I'm sorry for being impolite. I guess I got stressed out. My name's Kendra. You live next door, right?"

He pointed to the large Victorian house that, like many in the area, had been chopped into apartments. "Yeah, apartment 2, down the side across from your back yard. My name's Win Ni."

He attempted to capture her mail in one hand while offering the other in a handshake, but wound up having to awkwardly juggle the letters before they hit the ground again. He put the mail into Kendra's hands with a sheepish grin.

"I'll see you around then," she said, and let herself inside without looking back at him.

Kendra dumped the mail on the built-in credenza in the entryway, and went to locate the cat. Bobbins had crammed his bulky body behind some shoeboxes on the floor of the bedroom closet, where he must have hidden after the rock hit. She gently coaxed him out and carried him to the couch.

"It's okay, sweet pea," she whispered. "Some low-life is branching out from the humdrum routine of smashing car windows to more challenging targets."

But another, worse thought came to mind. Perhaps Brian had found her and was letting her know he wasn't pleased she'd given him the slip all these months. No, she wasn't thinking clearly. This wasn't Brian's style. This was just random vandalism. She repeated the last phrase several times to convince herself.

She wistfully remembered her old neighborhood and the house she'd left to sever ties with Brian. The cheaper rent here was attractive while she was on leave and paying out of her savings, but this end of town had some decidedly rough edges.

After a while, the kitty settled into a nap and Kendra decided that she should go out and clean up the glass. The rental company wasn't going to like the broken storm door and even if they agreed to replace it, they wouldn't send anyone to clean up the mess. She carried a broom, dustpan, garbage bags, and her keys and sunglasses to the front door. As she turned the doorknob, the broom slipped from her grasp and upset the pile of mail on the credenza.

Cursing, she scooped up the scattering of bills and third class mail and was about to shove it all into a drawer when a patch of red caught her eye. One of the envelopes was printed with half-inch red lettering. She scooped it up and read the words on the bottom of the envelope: STATE DEPARTMENT OF CORRECTIONS MAIL.

Is that why her brother hadn't called her back? Was he in prison again? She squinted at the smaller print, then gave up and took the envelope over to the strong light of her desk lamp. She almost dropped the letter with relief when she saw that she wasn't the addressee. It was just a misdelivered piece of mail to someone she'd never heard of. But that made no sense because the house number and street were correct. How very odd. Maybe the last tenant of this house knew someone serving time? She examined the return address; the top line was a stamped cellblock number, and below that, the sender's name was scrawled in cursive, but only the first two letters of his name were remotely decipherable.

Anyway, it didn't matter because whoever sent it, this letter wasn't for her. Kendra no longer knew anyone in prison. Her brother Lincoln had been out for several years and wherever he'd gone, she had to believe he wasn't back inside.

She picked up a black marker, crossed out her address, drew a big arrow pointing to the return address and wrote in large letters, "RETURN TO SENDER." Then she rolled the envelope into her fanny pack to mail on her next round of dog walks.

Chapter 10

Wednesday, October 13

Carol Goodman bent to pick up an empty soda can and cursed under her breath at the wolf whistle coming from the basketball court behind her. As she tossed the can into one of the new campus recycling bins, she hazarded a look back. A male student raised his eyes from her ample buttocks, smacked his lips and said, "Not bad—better if you put a bag over your head."

The provocation was a challenge to test her authority. He wanted her to react with anger and order him to get to class, but nothing would persuade her to confront the notorious kid on her own, and he knew it. She heard him bouncing his basketball as she walked away.

The school bell rang, marking the end of her Wednesday yard duty. Although she could have returned to her office, she wanted to see what two female students were doing by the back fence and stop them before they slipped away behind the portables. From there, the bleachers beckoned. Carol didn't even want to imagine what might be taking place beneath those notorious hidey holes.

Months after a sweeping change of administration and a promise from the district to address Standard High's well-publicized security concerns, the school budget still didn't provide for sufficient security personnel. The supposed remedy was a policy requiring staff to rotate lunch duty, and to stand guard in the hallways during passing periods.

Carol could hear the girls giggle as they pressed against the high, chain link fence that separated them from a large man who stood on the street side. He dandled a long key chain suggestively in one hand, as if his fingers were caressing flesh instead of metal. In response, the girls rubbed against the fence like cats in heat.

Something in the man's appearance rang a bell, but she couldn't place him. She veered toward the right to get a better look before he noticed her, but sunglasses and a baseball cap with the brim pulled low made identification difficult. What was he doing

43

there? From the way the girls were behaving, none of the possibilities were likely to be good. Carol wanted to break up this little encounter as fast as possible, but she didn't want to get into an altercation with him, not without backup.

She need not have worried, because he saw her coming, swiftly retreated to a pickup truck and pulled away before she got a closer look at him. The girls bent heads together and whispered, pretending not to notice Carol. As a school counselor, she had the tools to deal with these situations. At times like this, her age was both an advantage and disadvantage: just young enough not to be their parents, but not old enough to be the authority figure some of them secretly wanted.

Carol approached, but instead of directly focusing on the girls, pretended to be watching a Pepsi truck unloading at the convenience store across the street. After a moment, she said casually, "Megan, Reyna. Lunch is over."

Reyna, a student in a Special Ed. class for kids with emotional disabilities was volatile at the best of times. Megan had a history of being uncooperative. They were fast friends, but Megan took the lead in everything except for fashion and makeup, where Reyna's graceful Latina beauty gave her the upper hand.

"Hey Mrs. G," said Megan, picking up her backpack and settling it on her shoulders. Carol nearly choked at the amount of breast that movement exposed. Megan was a few inches shorter than Reyna or Carol, maybe 5' 3", but weighed more than she and Reyna combined.

Meanwhile, Reyna had moved away, and was furtively stuffing a scrap of paper into the back pocket of her jeans. Carol would have liked to confiscate it and see what the man had given her, but she had no stomach to call for a body search, although given the skimpy clothing they wore in total defiance of the dress code, hidden body parts were few. Ironically, Reyna had chosen to cover her wrists, of all things, under leather bracelets, a growing fad on campus. Carol tried to keep up with things like that, with what the kids were up to.

There had been quite a buzz around campus lately about recent dropouts falling into drug use, turning tricks and actively trying to recruit their friends still attending school. Carol didn't know Megan well, but Reyna was definitely at risk for taking up that sort

Deadly Traffic

of activity, with her truancies mounting and a voiced intention to run away from her foster placement. Should she make an attempt to find out what these girls had been up to, or just get them to their next class without incident? Best to wait and speak to Reyna alone.

"You're not going to make it to class in time, girls. If you don't want a detention, I can walk you over to your class," said Carol, plastering a smile on her face to make the offer more palatable.

Fortunately, the girls seemed willing to go with her as long as she wasn't prying into their behavior. Relieved, Carol started to walk them toward the main building. To the untrained eye, such leniency might look irrational, but the alternative would be having the girls spend the period doing nothing in the detention room, putting them even farther behind in class.

"We can be tardy, you know," said Megan with a laugh. "Nobody gonna bother my homegirl 'cause she's in that Special Ed. class and the hall monitors are all afraid to mess with her in case she goes off on them." Megan seemed completely unaware of how crass she sounded.

Reyna appeared not to care that her friend might be delivering a put down, and argued, "No, it's because they pretend they don't even see me, just like my parents used to do. The one around here who's really crazy is Sandi."

Carol considered that remark as she herded the girls through the west entrance and up a flight of stairs. She'd been involved with both girls' placement into foster care and tried to stay current about their circumstances. "Reyna, don't say that. How are you getting along with her at the Home?"

"I got yelled at for faking when my knee got hurt bad at gym," whined Reyna, "but she cries and gets to go to the doctor every time she pops a zit."

Carol knew Sandi was still trying to deal with her father's sudden death and the subsequent events including the rough, and illegal passage to America. Sandi also refused to accept that her mother had found a new love and had moved in with the man. Although he seemed to have Sandi's best interests at heart, Sandi had run away repeatedly. Carol would have expected Sandi, or any teenage girl, to be thrilled to live in such a luxurious home, but it hadn't worked out that way.

45

Mickey Hoffman

Megan chimed in, breaking Carol's train of thought. "Sandi's step daddy, he likes her a whole lot, don't he?"

"Shut up, Megan, don't spread smack like that," said Reyna, giving her friend a shove.

"So, who's that guy you were talking to?" asked Carol, deciding the conversation couldn't possible get any more out of control.

Megan shrugged and exchanged a look with Reyna that told Carol she wasn't going to get a reply. At any rate, they'd reached the art room now, where the girls had their next class. Carol put her hand on the doorknob to stop them for a moment and said, "Reyna, I'll send someone in to your sixth period PE class with a pass. Come to my office and we'll talk." The only answer was a noncommittal grunt.

Fighting a burgeoning headache, Carol returned to the privacy of her cubbyhole, set in a corner of the counseling office. As she dug in her purse for a pill bottle, she wondered if Reyna would really show up, and if she'd tell the truth if she did. Carol wasn't even sure if she wanted to know what the girls had been up to. Working with these kids, these families, she gathered a lot of information, much of it unsavory, and she wasn't protected like a doctor, a lawyer or a priest. School counselors were required to report all suspicious or illegal activity. Contrary to what seemed right on the surface, filing a report sometimes only made a bad situation worse.

Suddenly, she placed the man who'd been at the back fence, and where she'd been when she saw him. She winced as a shaft of pain stabbed behind her eyes. The pill bottle almost slid from her shaking hands as she fumbled with the cap. Don't overreact. No one knows. This was, in fact, a useful wake-up call. She picked the spilled tablets from her lap, resisting the urge to cram the entire handful into her mouth.

What if Megan was telling the truth about Sandi's stepfather? She feared her own judgment may have been clouded by Roger's expensive gifts and hours of very hot sex. Clearly, she needed to reevaluate her take on Roger. If she'd been manipulated, she'd do whatever it took to protect herself. The more she thought about it, the more certain she became. She'd seen the guy at the fence today a few days ago, driving away as she arrived at Roger's house. Now that

46

she'd seen the guy in action, she wondered what business he could possibly have with the attorney. A lawyer-client relationship? She was going to find out. She gulped two pills down with the cold remains of her morning tea and felt herself slowly relax.

Chapter 11

The exuberant, Star Trek Next Generation theme song rang out from Kendra's cell phone, spoiling the dramatic denouement of the audio book she was listening to. She stabbed at the STOP button on the boom box with such force it almost slid off the shelf. Ready to transfer her irritation to the caller she snatched up her phone. "Yes?"

"This is the A.S.S. Institute—Advanced Study of Self-pity, should you not be familiar with our esteemed organization," said Maretta with a spot-on imitation of an upper class, British accent. "Would you care to participate in a survey?"

"Is this paid research?" said Kendra, smothering a laugh.

"That's better. Now you're sounding almost sane. You had me worried for a second. What put you in such a good mood, anyway?

"Don't ask. Your call has already cheered me up. I didn't expect to hear from you today. I thought the great Mrs. Edwards, peace-giver to all wayward students, had a meeting after school at the Cap Home, to be followed by a much needed session at the hair salon."

The Cap Home—short for the Capitol Street Home for Children—housed school aged children rejected for placement with foster families or temporarily caught in some sort of legal limbo. Maretta, like Kendra, taught Special Ed. at Standard High and they always had one or two students who lived at the Home on their class lists. They attended staff meetings there when asked, although their input was seldom taken seriously.

"Very funny, and yes, I'm done with both. Actually, at the moment, I'm parked three doors down from your house. Can I come in?"

"Of course."

Kendra patted down the winkles on her clothes and, after a quick look to make sure Bobbins wasn't near the front door, opened it to admit her friend. Maretta twirled once to show off her freshly permed hair, which barely grazed the collar of one of the shirred and pleated dresses she favored. The shorter, curlier cut did

48

Deadly Traffic

little to soften the angles of her body, but seemed to mitigate the sharp tilt of her narrow nose and the determined lines around her mouth.

"So, to what do I owe the honor of your visit?" asked Kendra.

"Mostly, I felt the need to vent. Nothing more exciting, I'm afraid."

"Would you like a drink of something?"

"No, I'm good, thanks."

Kendra showed her into the living room, but quickly commandeered the recliner before her friend could throw herself into it. Maretta laughed at their familiar skirmish and took a seat on the leather couch instead, dropping her ever-present carryall on the floor to one side. After slipping off her shoes and propping her feet on the coffee table, she pointed at a large photo album that lay open beside her left foot.

"Is that corner one a new photo of your brother? It doesn't look familiar."

"No, he hasn't sent me photos or anything else. Look again, I know you've seen it. See, he's leaning on his Mustang."

"Which he signed over to you before he left town. Admit it. You love the car so much I think you secretly don't want him to return because he'll want it back."

"You know that's not true." Kendra looked down at the photos and sighed.

"So, you've been wallowing in the past again," said Maretta reprovingly.

"Not exactly the past. I got a text message from him last week. He said he's in town and he'd call me, but he hasn't. I'm worried."

"Maybe he's busy."

"What if something happened to him?"

"You're being melodramatic."

"All right, all right. But I'm tired of waiting and worrying about him. I'm going to try to find him."

"How, by using your psychic powers and channeling him through photographs?"

"Seriously, I got them out 'cause I can't remember the name of his childhood sweetheart. I thought if I saw her picture, maybe it would come back to me."

Maretta reached over, grabbed a cushion, removed a clump of

49

cat fur, and squished the cushion behind her for back support. "Next time I will get that chair of yours. So, why do you want to know his girlfriend's name?"

"They used to keep in touch. I could look her up, see if he's called her."

"Why would he call her and not you?"

"He might like her better. I really blew it. The last time we spoke was last Christmas, and most of our conversation was me pouring out my guts about the troubles in my life. I must have freaked him out."

"How so?"

"I got myself all worked up telling him about how the cops had questioned me at school, all that stuff. I hardly gave him a chance to talk or tell me how he was doing. After I hung up, I felt bad and called him back, but when I dialed the number he'd called from, I got the manager of a business center in a hotel in St. Louis."

Maretta's eyebrows shot up. "I take it they didn't locate him for you."

"No, privacy issues and all that. I left a message, but he never called back, never got in back touch until he sent the text message last week. Then nothing. Probably regretted sending it."

"What's with your family, anyway? Never forgive or forget."

"In this case, it's my fault, the way I reacted to his arrest. You know how I got bitter, disillusioned—okay, paranoid if you want to call it that—about the police and the court system. I hate to say it, but...I wouldn't even go to his trial to give him support. Then, I had a teenage hissy fit and blamed him for our parents' divorce."

"But you were a teenager. You're both adults now."

"Well, for whatever reason, I think Linc regrets he messaged me and he's gone back to avoid mode." Kendra closed the album and, folding her arms across her chest, sank back into the plush upholstery of her recliner. In response, Maretta pulled the cushion from the small of her back and threw it at her.

"Hey, now!"

"How about I take Ms. Kendra shopping for a new couch? The least you could do is not sit there looking so comfortable. The only one who ever gets that recliner besides you is the cat. You know, the day I see a man sitting in it, I'll know you've found true love."

50

Deadly Traffic

Kendra deliberately stretched out in an even more comfortable pose.

"Rub it in, fine. Hey, your leg is bruised." Maretta leaned forward for a closer look.

Kendra gazed at the purple-brown blotches. "You should have seen this three days ago. A dog I was walking went bonkers and pulled me down an alley. At least, for once in my life there wasn't anyone around to watch me trip over my own feet."

"And you think teaching is dangerous? Speaking of that, at the meeting today one of the Cap Home staff asked me to contact you. She has a problem that's right up your animal loving alley."

Kendra gave an involuntary laugh. "Thanks for the alley reference. You're wearing out your welcome, girl. And really, I don't think I want to hear any more. Issues at the Home tend to be chronic."

"Well, too bad, I'm telling you anyway. The situation is a few of the kids over there have been capturing frogs and lizards and bringing them home. Some counselors have let them keep the things, or buy a goldfish or two as a replacement, but only if the kids promise to do the pet care themselves."

Kendra groaned and buried her face in her hands.

"Yes, you can imagine how it goes from there. Little Johnnie brings in a frog, begs to keep it and the overworked staff member doesn't want to argue about it, lets the kid keep it in a jar or something. It should be obvious the kids don't have a clue, but the counselors there didn't things through, at least not until one of them caught a 14-year-old taking a bath with her goldfish."

Kendra interrupted. "Please don't tell me any more. You know I can't stand mistreatment of animals."

"Does it make it any better to know the cruelty's unintentional? The girl believed she was giving her fishy a nice treat. Okay, okay, I won't give you any more details, but now that you're a pet professional, so to speak, I sort of volunteered you to go over and do a presentation on the correct way to take care of animals."

Kendra was silent as she let the request sink in. She didn't know if she was ready to stand up in front of a group of kids yet. This gig might be okay, though. It wasn't like she'd be responsible for the follow-through, and it might do her good to keep her hand in. She couldn't afford to lose her high school teacher demeanor, not after that essential skill had been forged in the trenches of Standard High.

"All right, Maretta, I'll do it as a favor to you. But mostly to protect the poor little animals."

"Great, I knew you would. Can you drive there, or will you take a bus? Are your eyes any better?"

"A little better, but I don't want to drive yet. The doctor says everything's going fine and the eye drops seem to be helping."

"After this is over, you'll be glad you had the Lasik surgery."

"Leave it to me to have complications. Why did I have to be in the one percent of patients who get an autoimmune reaction?"

"Well, at least you don't have a condition that won't heal. There's always a risk with a makeover, as you should know from the time you tried that ultra hair straightener and nearly went bald," said Maretta.

"I wish I could have worn contacts." Kendra disliked the very word makeover, especially since all of hers had ended in disaster. She believed people took her less seriously because of her curly hair—a scientific study backed that up—and the thick eyeglasses she'd been teased about from early childhood.

"Look at the bright side. You already were on a leave of absence. Imagine how it would have been otherwise, trying to teach a bunch of adolescents hell bent on your demise when you can't see what they're doing with their sneaky, sweaty hands."

"Oh, the gods be shaken. Hear what Mizz Role-Model Teacher is saying," said Kendra, laying a hand over her heart in a mock display of shock.

"Don't be hard on me, Kendra. I had a terrible day. Maybe I should quit and join you walking dogs."

"Well, I'm loving the way the pets accept me. Animals really seem to know who has their best interests at heart. Yeah, they're much better at judging character than I am."

"I know where you're going with that. You're too hard on yourself. Neither your looks nor your judgment had anything to do with Brian's lies. Put him out of your mind, it's been what, ten months now?"

"Yeah, and four months since I moved here to avoid him. You know, I still hear from the grapevine he thinks we're going to get back together."

"He really never did understand you, but he's not alone in that. Half the teachers at school still think you're a pushover."

"I'm no door mat, but I am a real pro at screwing up my life."

"I think you've learned your lesson, how your habit of over-thinking everything can take you places you don't wish to go."

"The place I don't want to go is back to Standard High. That reminds me, I haven't shown you the leaflet."

Kendra went to her shoulder bag, extracted the flyer she'd received at Doggie Day. "I know you how shocked you were when I called about Imelda. Seeing this is even worse. You're sure you want to see it?" Kendra waited, and after receiving an affirmative nod, placed the leaflet into her friend's outstretched hand.

Maretta glanced at the flyer and closed her eyes for a few moments to marshal her emotions before reading the text. "This is too horrible. I can't let this happen to any more students."

"I wish we could stop it, but we can only do so much." Kendra went over and put a comforting hand on Maretta's shoulder. "Maybe you really should join me, take a break from Hell Hole High. We could be partners, especially since I'd prefer to take care of cats only. You could do the dogs."

"I'll pass on the opportunity, but you should enjoy it while it lasts. When you come back to teaching next semester, you can fortify yourself with memories of all the pet love you're getting these days."

"Let's not talk about school."

"So I guess you're not interested in hearing the latest about the newly recruited, Filipino kindergarten teacher who's been hired to teach Computer Lab and what she said to one of my students today?"

"On the contrary, I'm all ears," said Kendra.

Chapter 12

Inside Roger's home office, an opulent display of Chinese porcelains and lacquered trays glowed in their specially made, halogen lit glass cases. Asian artifacts and weapons including hunting bows and small knives hung from pegs on an adjacent wall. Otherwise, the room was dark, except for the pool of light around Roger's desk, where he was hard at work.

The open balcony doors admitted a refreshing fall breeze, which rustled branches of nearby poplar trees and skittered newly fallen leaves on the patio below. The only other sound came from the click of the wireless mouse in Roger's hand.

He'd been on line, researching a particularly obscure point of law, and had just located the elusive citation when a knock at the door broke his concentration causing the mouse in his hand to jerk. The electronic document began to scroll uninhibitedly down the screen, as if it had been waiting an eon for the chance to run free. He frantically hit a succession of keys in a futile attempt to stop it from rocketing all the way to the end, but it had acquired a will of its own. Since he hadn't bookmarked the location, he would have to begin searching all over again from the top.

In a pique, Roger clenched his fists and launched himself out of his executive chair. "I told you not to disturb me," he roared at the closed door.

From the hallway, Thida said, "Sorry, Mr. Rhus, but a man is here and says he has to see you. I know you are busy, but he won't leave."

Roger opened the door to find Thida nervously standing there with Elias looming mere inches behind her. The look on Elias's fleshy face was a mixture of belligerence and mirth.

Why did that damn woman let him in? She knew he screened visitors, keeping a careful eye toward the day when he ran for District Attorney and his private life would come under scrutiny.

"All right, Thida, I'll take it from here." Roger nodded a dismissal.

Elias lingered in the hall, ogling Thida as she hurried down the stairs. "When you get tired of her, I could use some of that," said Elias, making a vulgar gesture. Without waiting for an invite, he walked past Roger into the study.

Deadly Traffic

Roger imagined his fist crashing into the man's smirking mouth, but years of practicing law had inured him to the bravado of the criminal classes. He went to adjust the room lights to buy himself a moment to think, then turned back to his visitor and asked, "So, what brings you here? I thought we agreed you wouldn't come here again without an appointment unless it was an emergency, and I don't see how there could be one since we've hardly got anything running yet."

"Nothing running? You can say that again. What did you do to my business?"

Rhus slowly took a seat on one of the chairs in front of a compact entertainment center and calmly waited for Elias to join him, motioning toward an ice bucket and tray of assorted liquors. The invitation seemed to catch Elias off guard and the angry look on his face dissipated somewhat. After considering the drinks for a moment, he sat down empty-handed on a low couch across from the attorney.

"What business would that be?" asked Roger. He knew, of course, and had been expecting this confrontation. Just not this evening and not at home.

"Don't play dumb. You shut it down. I got nothing left."

"I merely told Win to stop collecting protection money from your former, undocumented clients."

"Where do you get off? You know how much money I lost?"

"If you'd prefer to return to prison, I can arrange it."

Elias opened his mouth, then closed it and stared at his feet, struggling to regain his composure. "Look, Roger, we made a deal, but you don't own me. If I want to do my own business on the side, what's it to you?"

"Actually, it is my concern, both because I acted as your attorney and because now we have a partnership. I'm not going to import or harbor undocumented workers."

"Yeah, you're too high class, right? It's always schmucks like me who get told they can't do this and can't do that, while rich crooks do whatever they want—for twice the money. But those guys are rich enough to manage to keep their hands clean."

"I see you learned only part of the lesson from what happened to you at West Ridge," said Roger. "You get the part about who goes to jail, but not the reason."

"Sure I do, it's not the crime, it's about who breaks the law. I went to jail but the West Ridge CEO didn't."

"That's an oversimplification and you know it."

"Yeah? Look at how Immigration always goes after the easy pickin's, not big business or the real threats. They should worry about terrorists bringing nukes into the country instead of hounding little guys like me and the poor migrant workers." He gave a smile of triumph like he'd delivered an unassailable justification for all his deeds.

Roger watched with horror as Elias reached over and gave a twirl to a finely crafted, Chinese porcelain bowl that sat on the table at his side. He tore his eyes from the spinning treasure only after it came to a complete stop. Channeling his displeasure into sarcasm, he said, "Unfortunately, Mr. Carmona, the Feds don't share your compassion for the downtrodden. Instead of storming over here ready to pick a fight, you should be thanking me for keeping the bulk of your misdeeds from coming out at your trial."

Elias turkeyed his chin in indignation. "Misdeeds? Who'd I hurt? Those ungrateful jerks. I hired and trained them, protected them from the syndicates that smuggled them in. I even found them extra part-time work so they could make money faster to pay off what they still owed those blood-suckers."

"I see. So your drug dealing was a non-corporate benefit plan?" He knew he'd hit the mark when he saw Elias's eyes widen as he took in the breadth of Roger's knowledge. "Your way of helping them out of their financial problems was to have them sell drugs for you under the threat of being deported."

"Maybe I took risks and got caught. Still don't give you the right to tell me what to do."

"And I don't have to cover for you."

Elias blinked, then looked away. Roger waited him out.

"Tell you what, Mr. Rhus, I don't want to ruin a good thing. How about we forget we had this talk?"

Roger rose to his feet and made for the door to let Elias out, but Elias caught Roger's forearm in one of his huge, calloused hands.

"I was wondering, maybe, if Win is the one who told you about the sales, like, maybe he talks too much? I can shut his trap—"

"No worries there," said Roger. "I found out all on my own, and, in fact, Win denied everything at first. Like I said, he's loyal."

Chapter 13

Thursday, October 14

The West Ridge kitchens occupied most of the ground floor of the Center's main building, the remainder being used for storage, the employee locker and break rooms and two small offices. Win knew that Elias didn't have an office any more. That change certainly wouldn't improve Elias's temper. The bright side was that Elias wanted to meet him here at work. If Elias intended to do something to him, he'd show up at Win's house or hunt him down on a dark street instead.

The kitchen was noisy, and today, smelled like overcooked beef—what was the stuff some of the old women residents talked about, biscuit? No, brisket, that was it, he recalled with a shudder. Maybe they liked it because they didn't have any teeth. He pushed the thought from his mind. It was good to be working fewer hours at the old folk's home. From the time Mr. Rhus hired him on as a helper, he had been able to pare down his kitchen hours to one or two shifts a week. The rest of the time he only had to come here to ferry paperwork back and forth between Mr. Rhus and the offices upstairs. The folder in his hand gave him a legitimate reason for being here today.

Through the double doors, he easily spotted Elias at one of the stoves, a mountain of white with his huge chest straining the fabric of a kitchen apron, his shining head topped with an undersized, poufy hair covering. Win saw the makings of a perfect viral video before him. He turned on his phone cam, but he'd missed his moment. Elias had seen him and beckoned him over.

"Hey kid, long as you're here, grab a spoon and stir this hot water while I pour in the Jell-O powder. Or are you too good these days for this kind of work?" Elias pointed at a tray of oversized utensils stored under the stainless steel counter. Win reluctantly shrugged out of his denim jacket and brought the spoon over.

"Stop looking at me like that, kid. You surprised I don't look as pretty as you wearing an apron? You're thinking Pillsbury

Doughboy, right? I wouldn't go there if you know what's good for you. And good for me Mr. Rhus convinced them to hire me back, even if I look stupid and I'm not the manager. At least I get to keep my hand in, as they say."

"Right now, it's covered with orange powder," laughed Win, carelessly leaning in too close to the cauldron. He felt a giant tickle in his nostrils and gasped. Elias gave him a shove, but it was too late. Win discharged a hearty sneeze directly into the dissolving mixture. Undeterred, Elias kept pouring in a steady stream of powder.

"Sorry, Mr. Carmona. Let me pour this out and help you start up a new batch."

Elias barked a laugh. "Nah, it's okay. Boil it for a few and all the germs get killed off. With your sensitive nose, you probably shouldn't even work around food. If you can call Jell-O food. You gonna keep stirring or what?"

In spite of Elias's reassurance, Win hesitated and looked around, but the woman at the nearest table appeared not to have noticed a thing. She faced away from them, busy doling out mashed potatoes into tiny serving cups. At the next work stations, separated by a bank of open shelving, several other women bent over slicing machines, filling trays, then slinging the sliced meat into the warming ovens. Even an elephant sneeze would be lost in the clamor of their activity. Win resumed stirring, trying not to stare at the new skull tattoo on Elias's thick forearm.

Elias shut down the burner. "Okay, kid, you're done here, get lost. Go get some air." He glanced meaningfully at the wall clock.

Break time in five minutes. Elias wanted to meet him outside in his car like they used to. Although Win always felt safer talking to him when there were other people around, he was glad to leave the oppressive smells of the kitchen. He stopped to buy a drink at a machine in the corridor. On his way to the employee lot, he worked his way through four pieces of Kleenex. His allergies always got worse when his nerves kicked up.

Elias was already waiting at the pickup truck. They got inside and Elias lit up a cigarette, making like he intended to blow the smoke at him before turning away with a grin. He tapped the console between them with his free hand. Win set down a small envelope containing the take from drug sales, continuing unabated in spite of Roger Rhus's orders.

Elias slid it into his pants pocket without bothering to count the cash. Both of them knew what would happen to Win if the amount wasn't right.

"Look, do we need to keep selling? Rhus said to knock it off and he's going to find out."

"If you don't tell him, he won't." Elias glared at Win.

"Why take the risk when we'll have plenty money coming in soon. By the end of next week, we'll have our cut from the five foreign workers starting here, and one more at the Live Oak Country Club."

"When I see that money, I'll believe it. Meantime, we stick to what we know. What's the matter, you in trouble? You haven't been boinking the peddlers again, have you? Is it the ladies or the guys this time? Whatever, with your looks, you should collect extra for your services, and I'll take a cut of that, too." He laughed, grabbed the soda out of Win's hand without asking and finished it off in one long swallow. "Hits the spot. So, kid, anything else to tell me?"

Win did have something. He wondered if this was the right time—if there ever was such a thing with Elias. He put out a feeler.

"Look, I might be tied up for a few days, my sister ran away again. I know you need money bad right now, but she comes first." He both hoped and feared for a reaction that might tell him something.

"Look kid, she ran away lots of times before, right? She always comes back. She's probably out partying or shacked up with some guy."

Win dug his fist into the seat cushion to keep it from flattening those big, fleshy lips. After the buzz in his ears subsided, he realized what Elias said sounded plausible. The guy needed his help; what would be his motive for messing with Sandi and losing his best lieutenant? They had an agreement, after all. Sandi was supposed to be hands off.

He got out of the truck to put some distance between himself and Elias. "Well, if you hear anything on the streets, let me know," said Win.

"She's probably having the time of her life, but if I hear anything, I'll call you."

Evasive, or innocent, wondered Win. Maybe he should just

risk asking Elias straight out, but even a veiled accusation might get him in a world of trouble. "I should be going. Mr. Rhus wants this taken up to the offices."

"Hold up." Elias came around and put a heavy hand on Win's shoulder, towering over him. "I have a question for you, speaking of the streets. Where are my girls? They seem to have run off while I was inside."

"You always took care of that stuff. I didn't really know—I don't have your talents."

"You? No talent with ladies? I think maybe you got ideas about walking away. You try it and my conscience just may force me to tell the cops you raped that old woman last winter."

"Hey, you know she made that up. I caught her stealing food from the storeroom, so she lied and told you I tried to rape her. You know I never touched her, that's why you shut her up."

"Not really. You were undocumented at the time and it wasn't convenient for either of us for the cops to zone in on you. But now you got your precious visa, I don't have to worry on that score. I bet the old lady's fuzzy on the timeline. For all she remembers, it could have happened yesterday." Elias lit another cigarette and looked contemplatively at the residential wing of the senior center.

Win said quickly, "There's no need to bring that old stuff up. I'm still with you, man. I did my best, but some of the regulars just disappeared while you were inside." He felt a trickle of sweat run down between his shoulder blades. "Honest, I don't have your…"

"I told you who to go to for help." Elias was leaning toward him now.

'I never got that information. There's something you don't know yet. The letter you sent from prison, I didn't get it."

"What do you mean? If you didn't get my letter, how do you even know I wrote back?"

"The woman next door to me, the one with the mailbox we decided to use? The mail came crazy early one day and before I could get to it, she came out to pick it up. I did everything I could. I did something to distract her but—"

"Hold up. You better start from the beginning."

"I, er, saw the mail carrier coming and I knew the chick was at home, so I ran over to grab her mail before she did, but I banged the mailbox lid by accident and it made a loud noise. I figured she heard and might come out to get her mail, so I did something to distract her, to make her run out back while I checked to see if there was a letter from you. But she came running out the front door instead. I saw the jail envelope but—"

"Elias held up a palm to cut off Win's explanation. "Never mind. I get the idea. The point is, what did she do with the letter?"

"Probably nothing, it didn't have her name on it, just her address."

"We never should have used her place for a mail drop. How do you know she didn't open it? You got a camera inside her house? She could screw us over big."

"Hey, we didn't want any jail mail coming to my place, and you said it would look funny to the warden if you were writing to a P.O. Box. The system went fine 'til the mail got delivered at noon all of a sudden. At least I was home and noticed…."

Elias ground his cigarette stub under a heavy work boot. "Anything else I need to know? Like maybe she's always wanted a pen pal in jail and gets it into her head to go visit the nonexistent inmate who sent her that pathetic letter?"

"All right, I can't prove she didn't open it, but look, if she didn't toss it, she probably just sent it back."

"Then the Warden won't see nothing but the usual inmate letter filled with a guy longing for female companionship. But we can't take the chance. You need to get with that woman, do whatever it takes to find out what she knows. She young? You can charm her. All the ladies think you're hot. Do what you need to. Just find out what she did with the letter. I don't like loose ends."

Win considered the idea. The neighbor lady was kind of cute in a frizzy haired way, and he'd heard from friends that older women could teach you a lot in bed. He didn't feel right about using someone like that, but how he could refuse? Like Elias said, if he was out, he'd be all the way out…

Before Elias read his thoughts, Win said, "Okay, no problem."

"You really cocked up the whole thing, didn't you? I'll forget your mistakes for now, but you're replaceable. Clear?"

"Sure, Mr. Carmona."

Elias laughed at the deference. "Before you go, fill me in a bit on the new kitchen boss, Mose. How much does he know about me—about what happened in the past? He didn't seem too happy

61

when I showed up for work."

"From what I've seen you don't have to worry. Mose doesn't notice anything unless it's printed on one of the menu plans he gets from upstairs."

"Okay, I get the picture. But he might get to wondering why I got hired back, or why all his new workers are from CrapHoleSisStan."

"From what I hear, he doesn't seem to care. In fact, he seems pleased about it. I wouldn't worry about Mose."

"I got to get back to work. I'll call you later with suggestions for some new recruits so you can make up some of my losses. And I know you won't make me wait." He forcefully stomped the empty soda can under his heavy work boot, kicked it in Win's direction and walked off toward the employee entrance.

Win picked up the flattened piece of metal. He felt battered as well. He'd hoped that the partnership between Mr. Rhus and Elias would mean the end of Elias's sex business. Maybe Mr. Rhus could stop it, unless he knew and didn't care. Surely, Mr. Rhus was too educated, too refined to get involved with anything like prostitution? And if he found out, he'd have Elias sent back to jail for a long, long time. No, that was stupid thinking. Morality didn't count where money was concerned. Mr. Rhus had ordered Elias's drug business shut down, true. But Win guessed it had more to do with catching Elias off guard and putting him in his place than anything else. Mr. Rhus was smart enough to know what Elias might try to pull. It really depended how much risk Mr. Rhus was willing to take. He'd probably overlook Elias's sex business as long as it didn't affect him directly. Maybe, Rhus would even ask for a cut one of these days.

And if Mr. Rhus didn't know about the sex trade? Win still couldn't ask him for help. If the attorney proved to be revolted by the sex trade and decided to send Elias off to prison, Win's involvement would also come out. He was caught. He wanted out, but no way would Elias let him walk. He'd make him pay one way or another. Maybe he already had. Maybe he really was behind Sandi's disappearance.

He'd have to play along and leave things as they were, or he'd be targeted as a traitor by both of those powerful men. He only hoped his sister didn't have to pay the price.

Chapter 14

Friday, October 15

Kendra set down the stuffed animal she'd been using to demonstrate the proper way to pick up a cat and surveyed her restive audience, only kept there in semi-acquiescence after being promised individual bags of Halloween candy.

"Any more questions? Okay, then. Remember, your pets depend on you."

A few unenthusiastic handclaps followed, but most of the children got up, grabbed their rewards and rushed over to the lumpy, stained couches in front of the TV where they noisily vied for seats. An argument immediately broke out over what show to watch. An elderly staff member tried in vain to break them away to go do their homework. Kendra suspected this was a daily battle and one the kids usually won. In her experience, children who lived at the Cap Home seldom turned in homework on time.

A young staff member tried in vain to get one of the kids to help him put the folding chairs away. The day manager plowed through the maze of overturned chairs and gave Kendra a weary smile. "Thanks for coming, Ms. Desola."

"You're welcome, Mrs. Nasiri."

Before the woman could say more, a tall, pimple faced boy and a much younger one began to push and shove each other only a few feet away. Mrs. Nasiri turned away to separate them before their argument came to blows.

In this environment, not even a stuffed cat could survive in one piece, thought Kendra, hurriedly gathering up the materials she'd been using. She was two steps from the hallway and a clean escape when a teenage girl bounded up to her and squealed, "Ms. Desola. I heard you were here, but the counselor wouldn't let me come, she says 'cause I don't have a pet."

Kendra hadn't seen Reyna in months and had mixed feelings about seeing her now. The girl's nervous aura and spicy perfume combined to accentuate her volatility, a character trait she stubbornly maintained was part of her heritage and not a symptom of mental instability. She claimed her father had been a bullfighter in Mexico and her mother came from El Salvador, but in the eighteen months Kendra had known Reyna, she'd only met a series of foster parents who tossed the teenager from one home to the next like the proverbial hot potato, until she finally landed at the Cap Home. The girl was incredibly needy, with mercurial mood swings: one second cooperative and affectionate, the next unaccountably aggressive. Like many teens, she refused to take medication prescribed for her attention deficit and bipolar disorders. On one occasion, she'd threatened to hit Kendra with a broom and was only stopped from doing it by the timely intervention of another teacher. Still, Reyna had a creative mind and a lively sense of humor. Kendra couldn't completely dislike her.

"Nice to see you, Reyna," said Kendra, thinking the opposite.

"Please come see my room, Ms. D. Please?"

"Um, I really don't know if I'm allowed to." Kendra looked around, hoping for a reprieve, but Mrs. Nasiri had moved farther away, drawn into the TV dispute. Well, perhaps it would be enlightening to see one of the bedrooms without being on a guided tour. Kendra was sure the kids' rooms were set up like Potemkin villages during the yearly open house for educators and social service agencies.

Reyna led the way through a hall that passed a cluttered office and two bathrooms and down a short flight of stairs that exited to a walled-in yard featuring patchy grass and the remnants of a volleyball court that had probably last seen a net before Kendra was born. Three faux brick, dorm buildings ringed the yard. Reyna's room was located in the smallest of these so-called Houses, the one reserved for older females with "issues," ostensibly segregated to give them some breathing room.

Kendra believed the isolated placement actually worsened the girls' coping skills, which might have improved with an opportunity to mix with a more stable group of their peers. Kendra knew girls like Reyna were difficult to manage, that the staff implemented this separation more for the House managers' convenience than for the welfare of their charges.

They entered the nearest House and climbed a wooden

staircase with worn treads to the second floor. One of the upper floor residents had either been experimenting with perfume or the housekeeping staff used cleaning products scented with "Tangy Rose." Reyna's twelve-by-twelve room held a bunk bed, two wooden desks and a pair of three-drawer chests. The door to a small closet had been removed and a pair of shoes and the edge of a suitcase poked out from behind a gauzy curtain. Posters of pop stars covered the walls and stuffed animals, knick-knacks, cosmetics, and discarded clothes speckled the room like the acne the girls tried so hard to eradicate. A backpack lay under a desk on a pile of candy wrappers.

"How do you like it?" asked Reyna excitedly. "Come up and see what I did to my bed."

Kendra found herself being pulled toward a ladder leading up to the upper bunk. From below, Kendra saw it had been draped with an iridescent blue material bordered with tassels and silk flowers.

"I really can't go up, I hurt my knee at the gym yesterday," lied Kendra. To change the subject, she pointed at a tidy desk with a stack of textbooks on it. "I see you've been using your desk for homework. Good for you."

"No, that's my roommate's desk, or was, I guess," said Reyna without a shred of embarrassment. "She—my roommate—ran away, so I have the room to myself right now. I wish they'd let me at least borrow her clothes and stuff, but Mrs. Nasiri won't let me. It's not fair. Why just let them lie here and go to waste? Wait, lemme show you."

Reyna went to the dresser, opened a drawer and fiddled with something. She came back to Kendra with her arm outstretched to show off a studded leather wristband. A matching belt hung from her other hand. She obviously hoped Kendra would also be enamored with the accessories and support her way of thinking.

"Very pretty, Reyna, but these look expensive. If you lose or damage one of these, can you afford to replace it?"

"She's got more anyway, but she still won't let me borrow any 'cause she says they're only for club members and I haven't been voted in yet."

"Then you'll only cause trouble for yourself if you wear them," Kendra said without hope that logic would hold sway.

65

"Just at school maybe. I don't care. Anyway, I don't think she's coming back. If no one from her family claims her stuff, they might give me some of it anyhow."

Kendra knew that kids routinely ran from the Home and that most of them were found and brought back within hours. She wondered if she knew Reyna's roommate. Because of the Home's location, almost all the teenagers went to Standard High. Many girls from this House were enrolled in Special Education due to their disruptive behavior, whether or not they really should have qualified for Special Ed. These girls were especially open to exploitation, and with the police bulletin still fresh in her mind, Kendra wanted to caution Reyna without scaring her.

"You don't sound worried about your roommate. You should be. The streets are dangerous, especially for young women. I know you might not love it here, but at least you're safe."

"Oh, don't worry, Ms. D. I can take care of myself."

Judging from the look of the room, not so much, thought Kendra. These kids believed they were street-wise and invulnerable. Perhaps she should talk to Mrs. Nasiri about having an organization like Bridges come and work with the girls. She couldn't say more to Reyna without overreaching her authority. Instead she asked, "Do I know your roommate?"

"No, she was at another school before, just got in my class this fall. But you were gone," said the girl with a pout to indicate she disapproved of Kendra's absence. "Here's a picture of her. She's from some other country." Reyna stuck a small, framed photo directly under Kendra's nose. A sense of personal space was something Reyna completely lacked, but perhaps that trait came in handy if one had to live in such tight quarters.

Kendra took the photo over to the open window as much to get some fresh air as for the better lighting. Instead of a current photo, she found herself looking at an old Polaroid of a family of four posed in front of a rounded, squat pagoda. The backdrop was the sort of dense foliage common in places with heavy rainfall. A strikingly beautiful woman cuddled a girl who couldn't have been more than five years old. The man at her side had one hand resting on the shoulder of a boy, likely the older brother. No one in the photo smiled except the boy, who playfully held up his fingers in a two-fingered peace sign. The curve of his lips invited her to be his friend, almost made her feel like they shared a secret.

"Skinny, ain't she?" remarked Reyna, without the realization that the photo might not be the best representation of her assumably sixteen-year-old roommate.

As she passed the photo back to Reyna, her gaze landed on the wristband. The style looked familiar. She'd probably seen other students wearing the same kind since they all tended to shop at the same stores.

"She's pretty, if she still looks like that," replied Kendra tactfully.

"Yeah, she does, I guess, but she ain't pretty. If she was, wouldn't do her no good. She's kind of nuts, you know? Makes trouble all the time, she's always mad. She's gonna get all her privileges took away if she comes back. They do that when you run."

The last thing Kendra wished to discuss with Renya were the psychological problems of her roommate. Fortunately, Reyna had lost interest and was rooting around in the mound of clothing on the lower bunk. She pulled out a dress and draped it across her body.

"Look how many dresses she's got. If she's not coming back, I'm taking this one. It's really cool, don't you think?"

Kendra sighed inwardly and steeled herself for a fashion show.

Chapter 15

Saturday, October 16

Feet dragging, head pounding, Kendra counted down the blocks until she reached home. The walk home from the bus stop took her over mostly flat ground, but at the moment it felt like an uphill stroll in San Francisco without the charm. First a row of newly built, unsold town houses, then a block of 1960s courtyard apartments, followed by a muddle of eloquently labeled "mixed use" buildings. One block more to go.

Dog care had its down side. This morning, an uncooperative German Shepherd had almost pulled her arm out of the socket during their walk at the park, then knocked her to her knees in his haste to push past her into his house. The experience was capped by a miserable bus ride back downtown with a bunch of adolescents who thought they were auditioning for Rap Star Idol.

She was two houses from home when she noticed the bundle of clothes lying on her porch. Her afternoon plans did not include having to clean up a mess left by some homeless person. After a few more steps, she revised her observation and decided she was looking at a mess of third class mail and newspapers blown there by the wind. By the time she reached the bottom step, the image resolved itself into a patchwork of tissue paper wrapped around a ceramic vase full of flowers. A plastic rod held a florist's envelope in its prongs.

This couldn't be for her. Her birthday was in March. Today wasn't a holiday, either. The delivery person must have missed his mark. She plucked the card out and held it to her eyes, expecting to see someone else's name on it, but the tiny envelope was addressed to her. The handwriting was unmistakable. Brian had found her.

She whipped her head around. No one in sight. Was he lurking somewhere up the street, watching for her reaction? In case he was, she held the unopened card out and ripped it to shreds. Fisting the pieces into a ball, she flung it over the side of the porch. She was raising a foot to kick the vase down the stairs when a voice came out of nowhere.

"Hey, how's it going?"

Kendra jumped. Her shoulder bag slid off her shoulder, doing to the vase what her foot hadn't had the chance to. With a dull thunk, the vase and its fancy wrappings rolled off the porch and landed in the marigolds below, leaving a rivulet of water in its wake.

"Sorry."

She glared with a mixture of relief and irritation at the not Brian guy standing on the top step. His broad smile didn't make him look sorry. She thought she saw the gleam of a gold tooth. In her present mood, it made him seem predatory. What's he doing here?

"I didn't mean to scare you. You remember me, I live next door—Win?" He pointed at the vase. "Do you want me to pick that up for you?"

"No, I'll take care of it," she said. I'll wait until dark and see how far I can throw it. Turning away, she grabbed her house key and reached a hand toward the lock with the hope he'd take the cue and go.

He didn't. "Did you get your door fixed?"

She forced herself to be polite. "The landlord decided to replace it, but you know how landlords are. He dumped the new one in the back yard and said he'd get around to it when he could. The bright side is he didn't ask me to pay for it. So, no, it's not really fixed."

Kendra wondered why the guy cared about her door. Was he looking for work? In this part of town, strange men often rang the bell and asked if they could do odd jobs. They usually just wanted a hand-out to make them go away. Win didn't look like a panhandler or a handyman, but she understood what it was like to be unemployed. So she didn't want to be rude or dismissive. What she really wanted was to go inside, but he stood there looking like he wanted to say something. She wondered if she would have to slam the door in his face. When she stepped inside he spoke up.

"Hey, if you want, I'd be glad to hang it for you, no charge. Let me go get my tools and I can get right on it."

Kendra questioned why an almost total stranger would do that

69

for her, but her innate compulsivity overcame her reluctance to accept his help. She hated having unfinished projects even more than she hated having unanswered questions. Every time she saw the new door marooned against the back of the house, it gave her brain an itch she couldn't scratch. "Really, you wouldn't mind?"

"No, I like to fix things."

"I'll be glad to pay you something for your trouble." Kendra hoped she didn't sound calculating.

"Nah, really, you don't have to pay me. I'll be back in a minute." He leapt off the steps and headed for the house next door.

"Meet you in the yard in a few minutes, okay?" she called out at his retreating back.

By the time she'd showered, dressed, and given Bobbins the attention he demanded, she heard the whine of an electric screwdriver. Apparently Win had gone ahead with the task on his own. When she joined him in the back yard, he'd already finished hanging the door and was attaching the mechanism that kept it from slamming.

"All done, give it a try." He squatted down to put his tools back into a metal case. His fluid motion accentuated lithe muscles his form fitting T-shirt did little to hide. He had the type of body that attracted her the most, defined but not pumped. She'd sworn off men for the time being, but when she looked at him she felt her determination slipping. She must be losing her mind. For one thing, this guy had to be too young for her. And even if he wasn't, he looked like his interests couldn't possibly go deeper than partying. Couldn't hurt her to look, though, could it?

When he turned to face her, she could see beads of sweat on his brow. His dark eyes were guileless and intelligent. She faulted herself for judging him without really knowing him while simultaneously taking advantage of his free labor.

"Would you like a beer?" She assured herself the offer was to assuage her guilt and not a means to extend their contact.

"That would be great." He smiled and said, "Actually, I brought home a pizza, was going to have it for dinner. We could share if you haven't eaten yet and don't mind double cheese and mushrooms."

It sounded perfect. She usually thought twice about visiting a man's apartment, but he lived right next door and seemed sane enough. Wouldn't it be impolite to refuse? "I'll grab the beer and lock up," she said.

She followed him next door, admiring him from the rear while trying to guess his age, deciding on twenty-three, tops. Too young—not scandalously young, but out of her acceptable range. The way he carried himself sort of reminded her of her brother back in his college days. She almost missed the offhand remark he threw over his shoulder as they reached his apartment.

"Nice building, but not too friendly." He bent to take a piece of mail off his stoop. "Our mail gets mixed up all the time and some of the other tenants don't even bother to bring it to the right person, or like this here, they just throw it around. Had to pay a late fee on my phone once 'cause the chick in the front apartment took two weeks to bring over my bill. I don't know what's up with our local post office. You get the wrong mail much?"

"I haven't had any real problems yet."

Win held the door open and waved her toward the living room while he went to heat up the pizza.

His apartment occupied the back end of a Victorian mansion recently converted into four rental units. The front door opened directly on the kitchen and main living area, a rectangular room with a length of about twenty feet. Many of the original architectural features remained, like the high ceiling, elaborate molding and tall windows that looked out toward her yard. The space had been awkwardly bisected with a fixed wooden table meant to provide counter space and divide the sitting area from the kitchen. On the far wall were two closed doors she assumed led to a bathroom and bedroom.

Kendra carried the beers to the coffee table, but found the sofa so lumpy she got up to try a wooden armchair instead. A shirt had been left on the chair and when she picked it up, she found a kick boxing magazine underneath. Somehow, knowing this was how he shaped his body made her feel even more out of her element. And the last thing she needed to think about was his superb physique.

"I like your purple shoes," she said to break the silence and to bring her mind around to the mundane and away from his toned body.

"The shoes aren't purple," he replied. "They're clear Converse, the purple is my socks."

71

He's wearing transparent shoes? Are they plastic? Kendra flushed with embarrassment for not knowing what, clearly, every hip person knew. Must be true what they say, when you stop teaching you lose touch. For lack of anything else to say, she offered, "I guess that saves money because you don't have to buy different color shoes."

"Sure does," he agreed with a laugh.

So much for making things better. She was an idiot. What would he think of her? But, then, why did she care?

"Hey, can I have that beer now?" he asked.

"Sure, sorry, I should have given it to you." She walked it over and handed him a bottle. Apparently, he'd chosen to heat the entire pizza before serving any of it. Given the size of his microwave, which only held two slices at time, dinner wouldn't be any time soon. Not only was she starving, the longer it took him, the longer she'd be in his company.

"Good beer," he said. "Never had Becks before."

Should she chat about German beer? What else could they discuss? They were strangers. What was she thinking when she accepted his invitation? She retreated to her chair and gazed around for something half way intelligent to say to start a conversation.

A wrinkled poster of Degas ballerinas in pastel colors hung to the left of the two closed doors, a portrait of Madonna in her Frozen phase hung between and, incongruously, a large, laminated photograph of the 1927 New York Yankees flanked the perpendicular wall. Kendra deduced the mismatched décor came from a succession of transients who'd added their own decorative touches without bothering to remove what former tenants had already done. She wondered if any of the wall decorations belonged to Win. Surely not the Degas. In any case, taking the place holistically, she believed he wasn't into art or design, ruling out one of her favorite areas of conversation.

Win seemed perfectly content not to talk, but Kendra thought she'd better say something or he'd think she was just sitting there staring at him, which she was, to a certain extent. On the big table, she spotted a small, framed photo resting among a litter of coffee mugs and newspapers. Although she couldn't see it that well from where she sat, she took another stab at discourse.

Deadly Traffic

"Is that a picture of your family?"

"Yeah, good looking aren't we?"

"I'll take your word for it, I can't really see the details," she admitted.

"Oh, you wear glasses?"

"I had some eye surgery a while ago and everything's still a bit blurry." She instantly regretted mentioning her problem, but something about him made her expect he wouldn't feel obligated to give her all the awkward, unwanted sympathy of a stranger. Her take on him proved to be correct.

"Better for me you can't see it," he said, "because it's an old picture, and I look silly. Dad used to cut my hair when I was a kid, and he did a pretty bad job. My hair stuck out all around my ears and I got teased about being an elephant—not the Disney one, a real one—we had those around where I grew up."

"Where's that?" she asked.

"Myanmar." He opened the microwave and exchanged slices. "You probably call it Burma," he explained as an afterthought.

So, that was where he came from. Kendra knew he must be of Asian descent, and had guessed from his accent he'd been foreign born. She knew little about his home country except Myanmar was run by a dictatorship that fueled its economy by selling precious gems mined under brutal conditions. She'd never met anyone from there and didn't think the citizens were allowed to emigrate, but balked at asking him how he'd managed to get to America. She settled on a less intrusive question. "Is your whole family here?"

"My father died when I was little—in the tsunami in Thailand. After that, my mother brought me and my sister over here."

Win pulled the last of the pizza slices from the microwave. The mouth-watering smell and her empty stomach were enough to temporarily kill her curiosity. He brought over a roll of paper towels and a square dinner plate piled haphazardly with pizza slices. The slices had stuck together and he laughed as she struggled to get one free.

"Let me do it, it's my fault they're glued like this," he said.

When he handed her the piece, their fingers touched and Kendra felt her skin tingle. She took the slice and slid back in the chair to put more distance between them.

"That must have been hard   the tsunami I mean," she asked

73

after swallowing a mouthful.

"Well, time moves on. We're in America and my mother has a new husband now."

She reached for the paper towels, but he quickly ripped one off and carefully set it on her knees. Did he leave his hand there too long? Not allowing her mind to dwell there, she said, "I'm glad she found happiness. Your mother must be a strong person, going through such an ordeal and raising two kids by herself."

"Yeah, she's very strong." He looked older suddenly, as if what he'd experienced added greatly to his years.

"The tsunami was big news here, but I haven't met anyone that actually went through it. But maybe you'd rather not talk about it?"

"I think it's good to talk about it, especially to let people know what it's like in other places where they don't have all the, what is it, inter- structure? You had Katrina in New Orleans, but there's no comparison when something like that hits in a poor country."

"Yes, infrastructure is very important." She pronounced the big word slowly, to correct his vocabulary without being too obvious, and instantly hated herself for being unable to stop being a teacher.

If he was offended, he didn't show it. "This is such a different world," he said wistfully.

She was about to change the subject when he continued.

"The big tsunami waves were only the start of the disaster, but you probably saw plenty of it on the news. My family, we had nothing left at all, and the officials were stealing the food and medical supplies that were supposed to be going to people like us. The police were the worst. Instead of helping, they kept threatening us because we couldn't show them any identification. What a joke. We didn't even have a change of clothes. We knew what they really wanted. If we didn't give them money, they'd take us to a camp and we'd be deported. The other authorities were almost as bad, only out to see what they could get. The disaster became a big, money making experience for them."

"I didn't know Thailand was like that."

"Everywhere is like that, no? The people who have the most take more." He finished his bottle of beer and peeled at the edges of the label.

74

Kendra shrugged. He had a point.

"Anyway, my mom, she's smart, she found a friend of my dad's who helped us, somehow she got us on a plane—"

He broke off, evidently realizing he'd said more than he wanted, but Kendra was more interested in his earlier remarks; they resonated with her on a personal level. "I know what you mean about corrupt police. My brother was accused of drug dealing, set up by some cop who probably wanted a promotion, and spent two years in prison before a lawyer was able to get the conviction overturned."

"At least he got out. In my country, if you go to jail, you stay in forever."

"That's what I've heard."

"He ever write you letters from jail?" Win seemed to sense her quizzical reaction and immediately added, "I'm just asking because I always hear prisoners in this country have all kinds of rights, too many even."

"He wrote a few. I'm sure prison conditions here are much better than they are in other countries, but the idea of being locked up makes my skin crawl."

"Me too." He shook his head and then said apologetically, "Sorry about the depressing talk. And for the overdone pizza."

"No worries," she said. "My brother always jokes that my cooking comes straight from the Roadkill Cookbook."

"I was going to serve that for dessert," he quipped.

Kendra laughed. He's pretty quick, she thought. Not at all what she had expected.

He offered her the pizza plate again with a grin. "Your turn. Is your family here in town?"

"No, my parents split up and moved to the east coast, and my brother has been working in another state."

Instantly, Kendra wanted to slap herself. She never volunteered information about family, especially her brother, and now Win knew more about her than many of the people she'd been working with for years. There wasn't really any problem saying her parents were divorced, but details about her brother weren't for public consumption. There was enough gossip about her at school without adding an ex-con relative.

"How's your brother doing now, then?" he asked.

"Okay I guess," she said stiffly.

Kendra didn't like thinking how Lincoln had changed after his prison experience, let alone the collapse of their relationship. Instead of the teasing older brother she'd always loved, he'd turned inward and had shut her out of his life before she'd been able to make amends for her earlier, selfish behavior.

Either Win read her tone of voice or was bored with family talk, because he gestured toward her house and asked, "Have you been living there long?"

"A few months."

"I moved in here a few months ago. I like it, but I guess this neighborhood's not the safest. Is that why you don't put your dog in the yard?"

Kendra supposed he'd seen her carrying leashes. Did he spend a lot of time looking over at her house? She warned herself that perhaps he wasn't as harmless as he seemed. "I don't have a dog. I'm walking dogs for a living right now."

"Ah, okay. I saw a leash lying on your front porch one day, I thought. . . Anyhow, if I had a dog, in this neighborhood I think I'd keep it inside even if I had a yard. Has anything else happened on the block besides your broken door?"

"Not since I moved in, but you know what it's like downtown. There's a lot of property crime."

They each took another piece of pizza and he seemed to be turning over something in his mind while he chewed. "What's dog walking like? Can you make enough money doing that?"

She shrugged. "It's kind of fun really, but it's only temporary for me. Actually, I'm a teacher, Special Ed. I just took this semester off."

"No kidding. Where do you teach?"

"Standard High. You know it?"

He wiped his mouth and stood up, offering her the last slice of pizza. When she refused it, he took the plate to the kitchen and put it in the sink. She strained to hear his reply over the running water.

"Standard High? Sure, that place makes the news all the time. Must be lousy working there with all the fights and stuff."

"Most of the kids are okay and deserve good teachers no matter what neighborhood the school's in," Kendra said defensively. "The media makes it sound worse than it is. Well, okay, maybe not...."

"I'm just glad I didn't go there," he said.

Kendra thought he couldn't have been out of high school very long. She hadn't asked him if he went to college or any of the other usual things people discussed when they first met. Maybe next time, if there is one.

"I need to get going, I have more dog walks to do. Thanks for working on my door and for the dinner."

"My pleasure," said Win, leaning on the counter and flashing a megawatt of white teeth. "I enjoyed our dinner. If you ever need help with anything, let me know, okay?"

Chapter 16

Roger walked to the wet bar, picked up the half empty wine bottle and waved it. "How about a refill? We can take it with us into the bedroom." He looked toward the stairs that led up to his palatial master suite.

Carol pretended to have a problem setting her glass on the marble coffee table, hoping he'd think she was tipsy. To give him a better view of her full breasts, she sat forward, elbows on her knees. She wanted him to feel in control, sure of his hold on her so he'd be unaware of her real motive in setting up the impromptu, afternoon tryst.

"No thanks, I've had plenty. Work has been so stressful lately I've been drinking too much as it is."

"I know what you need. Doctor Rhus has the cure. It has to be a quickie, though. I have work to catch up on today."

Does he think he's my stud service? What a jerk. She resolved to conclude her business quickly and leave before she shoved the wine bottle someplace where he'd need to have it surgically removed. She wasn't about to repeat the behavior that had gotten her into this relationship in the first place. Apparently, men who were too good-looking were also too much trouble.

"It would really help me to talk something out. I could use your opinion."

Roger gave her a tight-lipped smile. She knew she had to spring her carefully concocted story on him before his innate sense of caution overcame his egomania.

When he returned to the sofa, she slid over and nestled against him. "There's a rumor going around school that I'm having an affair with a rich man."

She felt his body tense but his expression only showed puzzlement. "Why is it anyone's business?"

"I'm a school psychologist. Part of my job is to counsel kids about the dangers of sex. Anything except abstinence is politically charged. And how do I have any credibility if they think I'm a slut with a sugar daddy? Many staff members also frown on sex outside of marriage."

"What do you care what they think? You're divorced." He stroked her thigh. "Anyway, you know how rumors are, they blow over after a while."

"I'm worried about now. The principal's secretary left a message saying the principal wants to see me. She can't really do anything to me, but the rumors could hurt my career in the long run. I'd like to know how it all started."

"A student with a grudge?"

"I heard different. I heard it came from a man, one who doesn't even work at the school. I don't know who could be talking. I haven't told anyone I'm seeing you."

"Same here."

"We only went out to dinner a few times, but someone who knows me must have seen us together." She'd purposely kept her voice bland. Roger seemed almost bored now. It was time.

"Who was the big guy I saw pulling out of your driveway in the pickup truck a few nights ago? He could have seen me coming in."

The wineglass froze against Roger's lips for a moment. He took a slow sip and put the glass down with a solid clink. "Do I look like someone whose friends drive pickup trucks?"

Carol hid her amazement. Was he for real? And he talked about wanting to run for office? On what ticket, the Planet Neptune Blue Party? He probably thought Burger King was Henry the Eighth's German uncle. She pushed him further. "Who was he, your gardener, a delivery man?"

"Who comes and goes around my house is none of your business. If I wanted a woman to interrogate me, I'd have a wife."

"I know your tastes, Roger. What you really want is a harem, keep them out of sight, out of mind, when you're not in the mood."

"You're big on fantasies today. So, is this an interrogation? If it will make you happy, I didn't have a visitor driving a truck or a flying carpet either, but I don't have to give you a list of people who visit my house."

"I'm trying to find out who's ruining my reputation, and why, before I'm run out of my job by slander and innuendo, and instead of helping you're treating it like it's a joke. I think you know more than you're telling me."

"Are you accusing me?"

"Maybe it wasn't an acquaintance. Maybe you started the rumor."

"And why would I do that?"

"I don't know, but if I find out it was you—"

"Enough! I think you'd better leave."

Carol stood up. "Thanks for the wine and the so-called romance. I won't be coming back for more of either."

"Yes you will. You're hot for me. You won't be able to stay away."

"You're so hot for yourself it amazes me you'd even notice."

"What I do notice is I'm sick of you." He picked up her handbag and thrust it at her.

Carol walked out with no regrets about the end of this relationship. The problem was, moving forward, what would she do about what she'd learned?

Chapter 17

Sunday, October 17

The limestone ground cover crunched under Kendra's feet as she followed the high stucco wall to its end point at Mr. Rhus's garage. She'd been treading the circuitous garden paths for several minutes, looking beneath and behind every sizeable shrub and ornamental rock formation, but the only creature she'd found was a very large mosquito that had been dive bombing her with great persistence. Wherever the dog had gone, he wasn't responding to her calls. He must be inside the house playing a version of hide and seek. At a loss for what to do next, Kendra went past the garage to the back entrance and got on hands and knees to peek through the doggie door. The only thing visible was a blank wall.

"Jackson, auntie Kendra's here, want to go walkies?"

No response. She whistled and called Jackson's name again, this time waving a dog treat through the opening, but nothing happened. In desperation, she swapped the dog treat for the remains of her afternoon snack, a blueberry muffin, and tried again. The first time she'd come to walk him, he'd almost ripped her shorts trying to stick his nose into a pocket holding an empty packet of Fig Newtons. Once she'd managed to coax him out of his doghouse, that is. She knew the owner would frown on such an unhealthy dietary supplement, but she'd run out of ideas.

"Here boy," she called again.

Even for Jackson, this was the height of hard-to-get. She would have already dismissed the Lab from her client list had he not been obedient and friendly as soon as she attached the leash to his collar. Jackson showed every sign of having a touch of canine oppositional disorder, rather than a shy disposition. Or maybe the dog's behavior reflected his environment. The house emanated a spiked, unstable energy that clashed with its meticulous, showcase-like appearance.

She thought back to her initial visit, when she came here to have Mr. Rhus sign the contract for her services. He let her in the front door, but immediately escorted her through the house as fast as he could to the back patio where they conducted their business at a beautiful teak wood table. And afterward, he'd let her out by the back gate, making her feel like a package that had to be delivered to the rear. Yeah, he definitely didn't want her to see the interior of his house—odd considering the amount of money he'd obviously spent decorating. The brief look she got while passing by the living and dining room told her Mr. Rhus had hired an interior designer, probably an exclusive one. The living room could have come straight from a photo spread in Architectural Digest. The accessories and wall paintings were tasteful, but unexpectedly generic and adhered to a lifeless color scheme of gray, ivory and indigo. The overall look was awesome, but sterile, with nothing to give her a clue about Mr. Rhus's personality. It was as if he'd chosen to hide his real self from visitors. Perhaps he compartmentalized, put his stamp on the more private spaces of his house away from public view. He treated her with strict formality as well, never varying from his professional demeanor, the one he probably used in court.

He also stipulated that she collect the dog from the yard instead of the house, reinforcing Kendra's belief that either he was an extremely private person or he suspected she'd steal the silver if he gave her a key. Oh well, as long as he was willing to write big checks, why should she care what Mr. Rhus thought of her? Her ego could take it. After all, she'd never have been able to stand up in front of a class of high school students if she worried about what others thought about her.

She started to cough. Her throat was dry. She realized she'd finished off the muffin herself while squatting there like an idiot in front of the dog door. And she'd already used up nearly half the time allocated to walk the dog in the futile attempt to locate him. Her legs were cramping, so she stood up and did a calf stretch. Then she noticed for the first time that the side door to the garage was slightly ajar. Perhaps the dog had wandered in there.

"Jackson, are you hiding? Two more minutes, then I'm leaving and you won't get to go for your evening walk."

She took a step into the garage and paused to let her eyes adjust to the darkness. Along with the expected smells of motor oil and something that might have been paint thinner, the air carried traces of something fragrant like sandalwood incense. To her left was a workbench and beyond, a parked SUV. Was the dog laughing at her from behind it? Now she noticed a light switch in a square of light cast by a small window in the garage door.

Impatiently, Kendra rounded the SUV and flipped the light switch. No dog. The back wall held a rack of skiing equipment, a metal shelving unit, and a door that most likely gave access to the house. Sitting on the lowest shelf, below boxes of detergent and plastic storage tubs, a tiny Buddha statue held a raised palm mudra and gazed serenely at an equally small incense burner. The ceiling bulb illuminated nothing else of note except a partially opened carton that had a women's handbag poking out of it. Maybe that belonged to Mr. Rhus's wife, if he had one. Or he was a cross-dresser. At this point, she was ready to believe anything about the man and his neurotic pet.

Kendra looked at the closed access door and hesitated. Part of her wanted to just call it a day, but it wasn't fair to pin the owner's faults on to his pet. What if Jackson was shut inside the house, alone? He might end up urinating—or worse—on the man's couch if he hadn't done it already. Since she was willing to lose this client, she didn't care if she got the blame for a mess, but would the dog be punished? She couldn't deal with that on her conscience.

If she lost the account, so be it. Although Mr. Rhus had told her not to disturb the housekeeper, she went around to the front and rang the bell. Twice. She heard the bell sound. When no one responded, she got out her cell phone and dialed Rhus's home number. After three rings, an answering machine picked up and she clicked off. Perhaps he was at his law office. He'd told her he'd been putting in long hours. But she didn't have the courage to call there and interrupt his work to tell him that his dog had outsmarted her. She was sure he'd be annoyed at the disruption and say something like, "Jackson has never acted like this with anyone else," before firing her. Not that she cared. Lesson learned: never, ever take on a client who wouldn't give her a house key.

She should just leave. But the more she thought it over, the more certain she felt the Lab might in trouble inside and clearly, no one was home. She thought of a way to check on him.

She went back in the garage and turned the knob on the

83

connecting door. It wasn't locked. She hesitated now, faced with the reality of what she was doing. At best, entering his house was a flagrant breach of privacy. Maybe she could be arrested for trespassing. Surely, she was being overly anxious about Jackson's welfare. She'd take one step in, call out, and if he didn't come she'd leave, knowing she'd tried her best.

Kendra looked up and down the long, marble-tiled hallway. There was a glass-fronted cabinet in the room at the far end, the kitchen or perhaps a butler's pantry given the nature of the home. A few yards on, a staircase led to a higher floor. She called out softly, then louder, but heard nothing and was about to give up when an urgent, whining sound came from the floor above. She immediately discarded her decision not to enter the main area of the house. What if something really was wrong with the dog?

"Anyone home? Mr. Rhus? Jackson? This is your dog walker, Kendra Desola. Is anyone home?"

Now she heard a keening noise, a cry of doggie distress and took the stairs two at a time to the second floor hallway. Three doors were shut tight and the fourth, directly to her left, gave into a home gym with no place for a dog to hide. The dog cries seemed to be coming from the end of the hallway, so she went in that direction without bothering to check the closed rooms.

To her surprise, she found another staircase leading up. At the top was a large home office. The lights were off and she didn't see a light switch, but the setting sun shone through a pair of French doors at the far end of the room. She couldn't see Jackson but she could smell him now, and another, unfamiliar, putrid smell that made her stomach churn.

She walked around a high backed chair to get a better view of the room. Unlike the parts of the house she'd already seen, her client had put his personal stamp here. A built-in unit of deep mahogany hugged the facing wall. Overshadowing the flat screen TV and sound system was an impressive collection of bronze statues—Hindu or Buddhist deities, she thought—along with a set of red, gold and black lacquer ware. A huge porcelain vase occupied its own pedestal.

And finally, there was Jackson, crouching, ears low. When he saw her, he growled and backed away. What at first appeared to be a shadow turned out to be a soiled area near the wall where the dog had emptied his bowels on the dove gray carpet. Why hadn't the dog gone outside through his doggie door?

Now she noticed dark paw prints that led from Jackson's original position toward the other end of the room where the desk sat in front of the French doors. Mr. Rhus wasn't going to be pleased with the damage to his carpet, but surely, he'd care more about the dog's welfare.

"Jackson, you poor baby. It's okay, don't be afraid."

She bent down and started to coax him to her. As she moved forward, she noticed the floor near the desk to her right was strewn with papers, and the doors of an adjacent low cabinet hung wide, the shelves empty but for a 3-ring binder that hadn't joined the rest lying in the jumble. The desk lamp had been tipped over and the desk blotter cantilevered out over a corner. She took a few more steps and saw a scattering of multi-colored address books—were they passports?—lying near an upended box. In stark contrast to all this chaos, on the wall behind the highly polished desk, a small armory of ancient-looking weapons dangled undisturbed from pegs.

No dog could have taken the room apart like this. Maybe Jackson had a good reason to be scared. But if there had been a robbery, the thieves were either going for something besides antiques or they hadn't found what they were looking for—yet. What if she'd interrupted them?

She snapped her head around to make sure no one was coming up behind her. She held her breath and listened. Get a grip, don't be such a drama queen. No, she sensed the taint of violence. Either Mr. Rhus had really lost his temper or someone had come here searching for something. Whether this was the aftermath of a robbery or some kind of domestic dispute, or even the evidence that Mr. Rhus was stark, raving mad, her instincts said run. She needed to get out of there, now. Then she heard a snuffling and remembered the dog.

She went down into a low crouch to appear less threatening and awkwardly moved toward him. "You're safe now, everything's okay, Jackson."

Wholly focused on the dog, she stepped on a stray pen and her foot slid, landing her on her butt. It was then that she saw a shoe sticking out from behind the desk. She leaned to one side for a better look.

Things were not okay for Roger Rhus. He lay on his back with his arms at his side, one leg straight, one splayed under the well of the desk. The front of his shirt was slashed and stained with blood. She quickly looked away, but her eyes seemed to freeze on the gummy-looking, red mess on the carpet beneath him.

The dog's plaintive cry brought her back to sanity. Was Rhus dead? It looked that way, but she had to check. She crawled to his side. The stench from his soiled pants made her gag, and a wave of bile surged up her throat. With clumsy fingers that wouldn't obey she tried to find a pulse. She felt nothing.

She stood and skittered backwards, out to the landing, wishing not to see any more of this, especially the dead man's outstretched fingers, streaked with red, still wearing the gold ring that she'd noticed when he handed her the signed contract.

She flew down the stairs to the second floor and frantically opened doors until she found a bathroom. After heaving until her throat was raw, she moved to the sink and rinsed her mouth. She forced herself to take slow, deep breaths until the room stopped spinning around her. Then she realized she'd left Jackson. She had to get him out of there.

The ramifications of her situation sank in: alone with a murdered man and she wasn't even supposed to be inside his house. Or worse, she wasn't alone and the murderer was still on the premises. She felt the same panic she'd experienced on her tenth birthday when she almost drowned trying to swim out to a raft.

Back at the study door she whispered, "Jackson, come on, boy. Let's go outside. Everything's okay now, everything's okay." How could she convince him of that when she didn't believe it herself?

Yet the dog came toward her, belly to the rug, and let her grab his collar, perhaps sensing they were of the same mind to flee. She pulled a spare leash from her waist pack and, on shaking legs, led him swiftly down the stairs and out to the lawn. Suddenly, the ground tilted, and she fell to her knees and started to dry heave.

The next thing she felt was something tickling her face. She opened her eyes and saw Jackson standing over her. Then the image of the dead man floated in front of her and she bolted upright.

Had she fainted on the lawn? Surely, not. But she must have.

The sun had gone down already and the landscape lighting had come on. Otherwise, nothing seemed to have changed. She was still there alone with a dead man and his dog.

She had to call the police but what would she tell them? They might even think she'd done it. But running away wouldn't work either. It wasn't the right thing to do and anyway, her DNA was all over the place. Kendra dug in her fanny pack for her cell phone.

Chapter 18

The squad car skidded to a stop on the gravel driveway. Two uniformed police officers jumped out and approached Kendra, radios blaring. She tried to read their names off their chests and couldn't, yet had no desire to get close enough to see. She decided to call them Moustache and Porky.

Moustache asked, "You the party that made the 911 call about a body?"

"Yes, I found...there's a..." She swayed on her feet.

Porky took her arm and steered her to the portico. Kendra shook her head when he asked if she was injured. "Why don't you sit on this bench and tell me what you saw."

She felt nauseated. Coupled with the flashing lights from the squad car and the harsh squawks from their radios, she could barely focus on the officer's questions. Her mind kept trying to zone out. After she told them the house contained nothing more threatening than a dead man, Porky told Moustache to go inside and check while he stayed to take her through everything for the second time. When Moustache came back to report all clear, Porky gruffly ordered her to stay put. Before she could protest, the two officers walked toward the street to make calls.

Too wired to remain on the bench she paced the tiny porch. She'd been confined to what amounted to an outdoor holding cell. Why weren't they letting her go? At least they didn't ask her to show them the crime scene. She could still taste the rotten odor in Mr. Rhus's study, now mixed with her own vomit. Something hard struck her in the leg. Frightened, she looked down and saw the dog's leash swinging from her hand. The metal hasp had hit her in the knee. Where was Jackson? She must have let him loose. She couldn't remember. They let her keep the leash, which in a cop's eyes could be a weapon. That must mean she wasn't under arrest. Yet.

A second patrol car arrived. Two officers got out and after pushing back some curious neighbors drawn by the sirens, they split up to secure the area. Almost immediately, an unmarked sedan drove up behind the squad cars, partly blocking the street. Porky went to speak to the occupants. Maybe he'd hand her off to someone who would realize that keeping her there was pointless.

Her optimism lasted only until she recognized the new arrivals coming toward her from the unmarked car. Kendra waited for the one of the worst days of her life to hit rock bottom as she watched the approach of Detectives Howard and Tapia.

"Ms. Desola. What a nice surprise," exclaimed the stocky female detective, with a stare that meant the opposite. In the twilight, the colored flashes from the roof of a squad car cast a sickly hue on Howard's sallow skin.

Detective Tapia, her male partner, tilted his lion-like head to get a better look at Kendra in the spotty lighting. "You don't look too happy to see us, but then, finding a dead body does tend to make people irritable."

"We'll find out what she really did," put in Detective Howard with her usual helpfulness.

Kendra wanted to scream but couldn't summon the energy. She'd happily expected to live the rest of her life without seeing these two again, especially Detective Howard, who'd given Kendra a very hard time during the investigation of a suspicious death at Standard High the year before. Detective Tapia had redeeming qualities, but Kendra disliked his all too obvious attempts to manipulate her. His "earnest, older brother" routine rubbed her the wrong way. He knew just enough about her to try and play her, but she'd vowed to never trust anyone connected with law enforcement, not after her brother Linc's experience.

"Officer Hanson tells me that you're a pet sitter now?"

So, Porky must be Officer Hanson. "That's right."

"You get fired from your teaching job?" Tapia asked, dark eyes probing.

"No, I didn't get fired. Pet sitting is my choice and it's temporary," she said acidly.

"I see. Well, you sure turn up in unexpected places."

"I came here to walk a dog." If he thought he'd loosen her up with chit-chat, he'd done the opposite. All this was a waste of her time. "When can I go home?" she asked.

"When we've satisfied ourselves you're clean," said Howard. "Until then, you stick around."

Mickey Hoffman

"What are you talking about? You can't keep me here!"

"Your choice," said Howard. "Either wait here or we can get you a ride down to the station."

When Kendra didn't reply, the detective motioned to Officer Hanson and said, "Get her away from the house before she pokes around and pollutes the crime scene like she did last year." Hanson's eyebrows went up, but he didn't pursue the subject.

Kendra was about to protest Howard's uncalled-for remark when she realized the detectives were now giving their attention to Moustache, who took Tapia and Howard inside, leaving her with Officer Hanson. He took her down the driveway, past the area that was now taped off, opened the back of a squad car and told her she could sit inside. His tone was more of an order than a request. Then he went to stand where he could watch the action and keep an eye on her at the same time.

Kendra knew the difficult position she was in. The person who found a body was always a suspect. Would they believe that Mr. Rhus was already dead when she found him? Maybe they would, but she still would have to fudge the way she'd gotten into the house and hope they didn't ask her if she had a house key.

The air inside the vehicle was stale with despondence and years of take-out food. She could hardly breathe and her head felt leaden, like it would snap her neck. She called out to get Hanson's attention to ask if he'd mind if she waited somewhere else, but either he didn't hear her, or more likely, ignored her on purpose. His rigid posture told her he might react badly if she took it upon herself to leave the car. For all he knew, she was a hardened criminal wanting to wrangle some sort of advantage for herself. What would he do if she puked all over his car? But then, maybe that was something cops were used to. She wasn't.

She tried to relax by leaning back, but the vinyl car seat stuck unpleasantly to her bare arms. She quickly recoiled from the contact, and her skin came free with a popping suction that hit a visceral part of her brain, sending her into another brief attack of the dry heaves. Exhausted and drenched with clammy sweat, Kendra lost track of what was happening outside.

A loud thump brought her back to awareness and she saw the yard was now choked with vehicles. Crime scene personnel were setting up, carrying equipment and barking orders. Their

90

businesslike attitudes didn't calm her. They were used to this. She hoped the dark night would keep her from seeing the corpse if they brought it out.

Did anyone even remember she was there? Her throat hurt and she badly needed a drink—of anything. Didn't the cops on TV treat people who found dead bodies with consideration, give them bottled water or something? But then, she wasn't a big fan of cop shows, didn't have much basis for comparison. She called out again and banged on the window, but no one responded. She needed to get some air. She'd say she needed to pee. Surely, they couldn't refuse that. She had her hand on the door handle when the driver and sidekick doors swung open. Detectives Howard and Tapia slid into the front seats. Tapia looked at her through the heavy grating and said, "I'll get your story now."

Here we go again. Kendra leaned forward to suck in some of the fresh air that was blessedly coming into the car from the front. "He's dead like I thought, isn't he?"

"Yeah. What time did you find him?"

"I'm not sure, maybe 6:00? Can't you tell from the 911 call?"

"Did you have a look around before you made the call? If I remember correctly, you don't miss much." He paused a second for the remark to hit home.

"The study was already a mess when I first saw the room." Kendra knew he was not only alluding to Mr. Rhus's ransacked office, but to the events that had brought them together on campus last fall. Last year it was a tampered desk drawer, now—what was Tapia thinking, that she made a habit of snooping through other people's stuff?

"Did you touch anything?"

"I might have. I'm not sure exactly because I saw…he…you know." She felt a shiver come over her again.

"Okay, take it easy. I don't want you puking all over Officer Grayson's vehicle." He leaned out and yelled for someone to bring a bottle of water. Kendra's hands shook so much he had to open it for her. When she'd downed half the bottle, he picked up his pen again and resumed the interview. "Just tell me exactly what happened from the time you got here to when you made the call."

Kendra recounted her movements, including, when asked, a superficial explanation of her career switch. She didn't mention she was supposed to pick up the dog from the yard, hoping he wouldn't probe for details, like whether or not she had a house key. If he knew anything about pet sitting, he'd assume that she did, and would think she had a perfectly legitimate reason for being inside. But, once again, Kendra wasn't that lucky.

"Okay, let's take it again from the top. What time did you first get to the property?"

"5:30, maybe a little after."

Detective Howard jumped in. "You made the 911 call at 6:30. What were you doing for all that time then?"

Kendra didn't like the look Howard was giving her. She wanted to see how Tapia was reacting, but knew if she broke off eye contact with Howard, they might think she was cooking up a lie.

"The dog likes to play hide and seek, but this time he wasn't playing. He was scared and hiding. It took me a while to find him and then, uh, then when I saw the body...I mean, Mr. Rhus, I ran outside and threw up. And then, I guess I passed out."

Tapia took over again. "So, you were looking around for the dog for quite a while. You didn't see anyone else?"

"No."

"Did you hear anything, like sounds of an argument or a fight?"

"No, nothing. I didn't think anything was wrong until I got to the study and saw what happened."

"From the beginning, exactly where did you go? What did you touch?"

"When I saw the dog wasn't waiting for me in the yard, I saw the open garage door and went in to check. I put the light on. Jackson, that's the dog, he wasn't there either. I rang the doorbell but nobody answered. Then I called the house, but no one answered the phone."

"You didn't call or text Mr. Rhus's cell?" asked Howard suspiciously.

"He said if no one answered the home phone it would ring through to his cell, but it didn't."

"You don't have his cell number, but the victim gave you carte blanche to go through his house, all the way up to the top floor? Sounds like you were a regular house guest."

Great. Howard's decided Mr. Rhus was my lover and we were texting love messages all day. Fortunately, she hadn't brought up the fact that Mr. Rhus had given her his office number. Why should she volunteer information when doing so would only fire up Howard's suspicions?

Detective Tapia brought the interview back to his original line of questioning. "What did you next?"

"I told you, I was trying to find the dog. I thought he might be shut inside. I went in to find him. As soon as I got into the house, I heard dog noises and followed them upstairs. I didn't realize anything was wrong until I saw the mess in the study. Do you think it was a robbery?"

"What makes you think so? Was anything missing?" Tapia looked at Kendra with interest.

"I can't say because that was the first time I was ever upstairs." She aimed a glance toward Howard, whose pouchy eyes narrowed with disbelief. "The office looked like someone might have ransacked it, but for all I know, Mr. Rhus was just a big slob."

"What did you touch upstairs? Have a look around?"

Here we go again. Kendra forced herself not to take the bait. "I don't think anything in the study, but I needed to use a bathroom after...and I used one in the hall."

"Except for the study, the house is neat as a pin," said Tapia. "I'm thinking a man as wealthy as Mr. Rhus would have servants to clean up after him. You ever meet any of them?"

She shrugged. "I heard him yell out to someone the first time I visited the house, but I've never seen anyone else around."

"How about his family?" asked Tapia, pen poised above a fresh note page.

"I don't even know if he's got a family. Look, he only hired me to walk his dog a few days ago and he didn't talk about himself, except to mention he was a lawyer when he first contacted me about dog walking."

"When's the last time you saw him alive?" asked Howard.

"About a week ago."

"You say no one let you in. But you had access? You got a key?" asked Tapia.

Kendra forced herself to breathe normally. "Well no, but I

didn't break in, honest. When Jackson wasn't in the yard, I got worried. Like I told you before, the connecting door from inside the garage was open. I heard the dog whining and I went in to check on him." She waited for Tapia to ask her to define "open" but this time, her luck held.

"Your love of animals at work again." Tapia's lips twitched. He flipped back through his notes and scribbled something. "All right, Ms. Desola, that will be all for now. Put your contact information down and you can go. Come to the station tomorrow to make a formal statement, and if you think of anything else you haven't told me," he gave her a searching look, "call this number." He handed her a card.

Kendra bolted out of the car and ran. She didn't stop until she reached the end of the block. The noise and lights from the crime scene were muted here. As she waited for her heart rate to slow, she realized there was no way she was taking the bus home after this. She scrolled her cell for the taxi company's phone number and had her finger on the send button when she remembered the poor, orphaned dog. Reluctantly, she headed back to the scene of the crime.

After explaining what she wanted to three different officers, she received permission to wait for Jackson. Another hour passed before the techs finally released him. So tired she could hardly stand, Kendra finally got into the oasis of a yellow cab, this time with a heartbroken Jackson at her side.

Chapter 19

Carol stopped for a red light and checked again to make sure the car doors were locked. Being alone in this part of town made her nervous. Normally, she only ventured into this neighborhood during the day when the Asian specialty stores and supermarkets were open. She'd asked several friends to ride with her, but none were willing or able to come along.

She craned her neck to read the inconveniently placed dashboard clock. Five past midnight. She'd been driving around since 10 p.m. Perhaps it was time to give up the search that had been inspired by Sandi Ni's truancy and some unreliable, but frightening rumors going around school.

During the course of a long day spent mining the student grapevine, she'd heard over and over about an older man who'd been coming around to flirt with female students. Of course, to the kids, 'older' probably meant twenty-five or thirty, which meant this guy might be the same man, the one she thought she'd seen at Roger's house and at the school fence chatting with Megan and Reyna. Carol had asked Reyna about him, seeking a name to go with his face, but the girl would only say he was "some guy who liked to flirt."

Because students often didn't confine themselves to the truth, as a school psychologist once euphemistically put it, Carol had a policy that she had to hear the very same story from at least three adolescent sources before she believed a word. If the stories about Sandi were true, she was hooked on drugs or under the spell of a pimp who operated in the neighborhood near Jefferson Blvd., an area of town of great renown in the gangsta mythology upheld by a certain group of kids. For kids enchanted by this wrong-headed ideology, Sandi's situation merited only a shrug or the appellation, "messed up." Even Reyna, who knew Sandi well, was either unwilling or unable to give Carol any useful information.

From the Cap Home Carol had received even less: guarded accounts of when the girl had vanished, bland reassurances that every avenue would be looked into, and conflicting reports about

Sandi's state of mind. One woman went as far as to put the blame on Carol for leveraging Sandi's placement at the Home, saying she had covered up Sandi's uncontrollable temperament and was therefore responsible for any problems they had with the girl. The accusation was unjust, but had just enough truth in it to bring Carol out here late at night. No, she wasn't responsible for the girl's behavior, but she'd been too willing to overlook discrepancies between the actual psych reports and what she'd been told by Sandi's mother and Roger Rhus, acting as her attorney.

Could it be true that Roger had forced himself on Sandi on numerous occasions until the girl became so distraught she began a pattern of running away from home? The same Roger who'd contacted the school and pleaded with Carol on behalf of Sandi's mother, a mother unable to cope with her daughter's emotional needs. The same man who provided the documentation to have Sandi labeled emotionally disturbed because of her out-of-control, aggressive behavior toward her own family. Behavior brought on, perhaps, by Roger. If this was true, Roger had acted in his own self-interest. After a designation of mental illness, who'd believe any accusations the girl made? The mother had petitioned to have Sandi placed in a suitable and secure residential environment where she could receive treatment. Roger put up resistance at to the foster placement at first, but in the end he'd acquiesced—to avoid Social Services becoming suspicious at his contradictory behavior?

Carol knew no one she could ask to corroborate what Reyna had said about Sandi's home life, not without raising a lot of eyebrows and bringing her own actions into question. And without proof, Carol didn't dare make accusations, especially after advocating on behalf of the very same people who might have abused the girl.

Carol had to consider the possibility Roger might have set out to use her in her capacity as a counselor, relying on his prominent social status to gain her trust, then, his sexual attractiveness to seduce her until she readily accepted what he told her about the girl and her troubled history. In her own self-defense, however, she'd believed the girl's psychological test reports were inconclusive. Since everyone knew those tests weren't foolproof,

Deadly Traffic

Carol could justify going along with Roger's suggestion to slant the test results to leverage Sandi's placement into Special Ed. and then, foster care. Now, she felt remorseful. But even if the placements weren't entirely appropriate, well, Sandi had been removed from Roger's house. If the terrible allegations were true, Sandi really was safer in foster care. Until she had chosen to run off.

Carol came out of her reverie as a likely prospect came walking out of an alley halfway down the block. This one was much like the others, dressed in a crotch length skirt and a bra top, gaudy earrings dangling six inches below her earlobes. For the umpteenth time that night she drove toward her target, pulling to the curb to attract attention. This woman was the oldest she'd seen thus far, and in spite of her revulsion for the lifestyle, Carol felt a twinge of pity.

Before she even brought the car to a stop, the woman had gamely approached and after peering into the car announced, "Ten extra for homo stuff."

"I'm looking for someone," said Carol.

"Oh sure, I heard that before. Ten extra."

"I'm not here for sex, really."

"You a cop, then? A gay cop, twenty extra." She cackled showing several missing teeth.

"No, I'm a high school counselor."

The whore laughed. "I don't think I ever done one of them. So, tell you what, I give you my teacher discount, only five extra for the gay."

Carol held up a twenty dollar bill. "I only want information about an Asian girl, name of Sandi, but she might be calling herself something else. Here's her picture." Carol brought out a photocopy of Sandi's school ID card.

The woman rubbed her fingers making the universal sign for "pay me" and Carol handed over the twenty along with the photo. Glancing around to make sure no one was watching, the woman tucked the money under the waistband of her skirt and moved away to stand directly under a street light, where she pulled a cigarette seemingly out of nowhere and lit it with a throw away lighter. The minutes dragged by as she leaned against the lamppost, puffing away while she contemplated the little photo.

97

Carol's patience ran out. Making the distasteful decision to get out of the car and retrieve the photo, she had one foot planted on the street when she saw the woman returning.

"Well?" asked Carol.

"Yeah, I seen her. Fifty bucks'll get you where."

That was the most expensive request in a night of dead ends. It would be the last deal Carol would make. This whole effort had certainly been a learning experience. One she vowed never to repeat.

"Thirty. I'm trying to help a runaway girl."

The woman thought for a second, then took the money with a sigh. "Okay, lady, only 'cause I believe you got good intentions. I seen her a few hours ago. See, what happened, me and my homegirl, we gonna run off this strange Asian chick 'cause she come to work our territory, but she be so sorry looking we just moved her over where she won't get the shit beat out of her." The woman described the location.

Carol thanked her and followed the directions to a rundown block occupied on one side by a self-storage warehouse, and opposite by used car dealer, a liquor mart with barred windows and a vacant lot clotted with trash and waist high weeds. She parked near the corner and took up watch.

Ten minutes. She took a sip of tepid bottled water and watched a drunken, probably homeless man stagger by. Ten more minutes. The liquor mart sold several six-packs to a carload of kids who looked too young to legally buy alcohol. A slender young woman came shuffling around the corner holding what looked like a cereal carton in one hand and a pair of flat shoes in the other. As she passed the car, the reason for her shuffle became apparent; her feet were clad in plastic bags. Carol drank more water and stared bleakly down the block.

No young women in sight, no Sandi.

A low-rider sedan cruised by with rap music blaring. The bass notes rattled Carol's teeth as well as her nerves. The car slowed as it passed, and a window rolled down. She trembled as three pairs of eyes examined her while the young man in the passenger seat laughingly suggested a few unspeakable things she could do for him. She held her breath until the car turned the corner. The aftermath of the drive-by confrontation and the vibrations from

Deadly Traffic

their car stereo left her needing to pee. As if she wasn't already uncomfortable enough, with sweat running down the back of her neck and pooling under her breasts in spite of the air conditioning. She drank again, realized it only made things worse. But even without a bursting bladder, she would have to leave in the next few minutes or else risk sleeping right through the alarm clock tomorrow morning.

As Carol started the engine to make one final circuit of the block, she heard the screech of tires, then a car accelerating hard. She looked over her shoulder in time to see a car making a rapid turn, tail lights fast receding into the darkness. Carol was about to shrug it off when she saw two women standing where the speeding car had made its turn. Carol quickly made a U-turn, rounded the corner and seeing what was going on in front of her, jammed on the brakes.

Curbside, a longhaired, bony woman wearing a halter top and shorts squatted on six-inch heels while the second woman, a short blonde clothed in half as much fabric tugged at her companion's shoulder, urging her to run. Long hair ignored her and continued to lean over the gutter. When she stood up she was holding what looked like a wallet. Her blonde friend started to wave her arms in agitation, motioning for her to hide it.

Carol leapt out of her car and raced toward the commotion. The two women quickly backed off, the longhaired one palming the wallet against her side. In the gutter, shadowed by the high curb, a female form lay motionless, her face turned away. Carol stepped forward to get a closer look at the recumbent face. With horror, she realized she'd found Sandi.

She bent to check for vital signs, but heard harsh whispers behind her and looked up to see the wallet thief pointing a witchlike finger at her. "You killed her!"

The blonde whore's heavily circled eyes narrowed and she chimed in, "We seen you do it, seen you run her down!"

Before Carol could open her mouth to protest, the two women scurried away, their stiletto heels popping like exclamation points on the pavement. She bent over the body, and tried to find a pulse, but she couldn't discern a thing. She tried to remember something of the CPR training she'd taken many years before. Only one coherent thought came to her, call 911. But she couldn't do that

99

from here, now that two women had accused her of murder. She didn't want her name in tomorrow's paper in connection with two hookers and a dead body. Something like that could sink her career as a school counselor. Let alone trying to explain why she'd felt the need to come down here by herself in the middle of the night instead of reporting her assumptions to Sandi's guardians. What had she been thinking when she decided to come here?

She ran back to her car and drove to the nearest freeway entrance. Using the throwaway cell phone she kept in the glove compartment for emergencies she made the 911 call, then tossed the phone out the window as she merged into traffic. In her rearview mirror, she saw the phone shatter under the tires of the car behind her.

Chapter 20

Monday, October 18

The stench of overcooked beef lingered even after Elias slammed the locker shut on his work uniform. He went into the washroom and stuck his head under the tap. His hair was starting to grow out, but the downside was that it seemed to absorb all the food odors. What would the old geezers here think if they knew some of their meals were no better than prison food? Probably scream about it, for all the good it would do them. Higher management didn't give a rat's ass what the final meals tasted like as long as they furnished a balanced diet.

The door squeaked and he turned his head to look, banging it on the faucet. He pulled away and gave the intruder a murderous look.

"Mr. Elias, I need to talk to you." The young man spoke in accented English that reflected his Nigerian birth.

Elias ran his fingers through his bristling hair and flicked his hands toward the young man who flinched and wiped the water from his pudgy cheeks. "I'm going off shift. Make it quick, Sam."

"I want my papers back." Samuel cocked his head pugnaciously.

"I don't have them. Ask Mr. Rhus." Elias crumbled a paper towel between his hands and wondered if it would bounce if he threw it at the man's round stomach. "But I can tell you one thing, you ain't gettin' your passport or visa back until you pay us back for bringing you over here. And you got a long way to go."

"I'm getting paid so low, how will I ever earn enough? I was promised a higher salary!"

"That's between you and Mr. Rhus. I think maybe you should have read your contract better. All I know is I'm offering you a way to make extra money."

"I am not selling drugs for you!"

"Then don't. I don't care what you do as long as you make your payments twice a month."

Mickey Hoffman

"I'm already working double shifts here and it's not enough."

"You got a problem then. Maybe you need to cut back on your expenses."

"I'm already visiting the food bank. I don't know what else I can do."

"Your wife came here with you, right? She can help work off the loan—on her back."

"We go home before I let that happen!" The double chin shook with indignation. "This is a free country, you can't force me to do these things."

"No one's forcing you. If you don't like working here, you can quit this job any time, but your legal status goes bye-bye. Maybe you can find someone to smuggle you out of the country before immigration locks you up. Without papers you ain't flyin' home on British Airways."

"I am an educated man. I refuse to be treated like a common criminal."

"No, you're just a man with some, shall we say, legal difficulties in Nigeria? Ones we erased on your visa application, if I recall correctly."

"I demand to speak to Mr. Rhus!"

"I'll let him know. I'm gonna clock out now. See you at the drop off spot on Saturday evening."

As the door swung shut he heard Samuel shout, "I won't be there."

Elias shrugged. Then bye-bye U.S.A., hello Nigerian jail.

Chapter 21

Win coasted his bike in a wide arc to avoid a reeking puddle of vomit and pulled in alongside a battered old pickup fitted with a camper shell. The bumper sported a variety of faded stickers about eating spotted owls and being married to guns. Were they jokes? Maybe he'd look up the owls on the internet. Hopefully, the inside of the tavern was more upscale than the cars in the parking lot, but the building's graffiti covered exterior and dented metal entrance door didn't provide much reassurance.

Bending to lock his bike, he heard a muffled knock. He quickly turned but saw no one. Quietly fastening the cable, he stood and looked around. Another knock. He stepped around to see past the camper shell. As Win ran his eyes over the lot he thought he saw a flash of something white in his peripheral vision. An old silver Toyota, a white minivan covered with mud and Elias's truck were lined up across from a dumpster at the side of the tavern. Then he saw it again, and heard the noise, coming from the cab of Elias's truck. No! He took a step, then stopped. He knew what he should do, but if he got caught?

Before his better judgment took over, Win ran to the truck and looked inside. A teenage girl lay across the seat, her eyes half closed, her heavily glossed lips parted in a drugged smile. He banged on the window and she sat up, and nonsensically waved a shoe. The other one, he saw, rested on her lap. She wore a red dress with a plunging neckline. A pair of studded leather bracelets and matching choker set off her dark skin. The window was open a few inches but not enough for him to reach in. "Open the door."

"He tol' me not to," she said, waggling a finger at him. "Waz your name?"

Win put his mouth closer to the window. "I'm Win, Sandi's brother."

She nodded like a bobblehead doll. "I'm Brittany. You're even cuter than she said." Her words were slurred and she had to put a hand on the dashboard to keep from sliding off the seat. "Wanna go out? Elias promised to go to a private club, but this here is borrring."

Private, as in you won't be leaving.

"Brittany, hi. Do you know where Sandi is?"

"Nope. Lez go dancin', I dance real good." Brittany banged the heel of her shoe on the dash to mimic a drumbeat.

Win thought quickly. "How about I meet you later at Harkey's? I'll call a cab for you and meet you there."

She appeared confused. "I dunno, tell Elias first?"

"I'll let him know. It'll be fine." When she opened the door, he stepped away and called a cabbie he knew, instructing Jake to take the girl home, and make sure she got all the way inside. He'd draw out his business longer than the ten minutes Jake told him he would need to drive over. Then he propped Brittany up against the back of the tavern and went in to find Elias.

Although the place appeared to be struggling to rise from the last century, Win kind of liked the ambience. The steel rimmed, glass slab bar looked new, in contrast to the wall behind it paneled in smoke-darkened 1950's knotty pine festooned with plastic beer signs, the kind that lit up. The turquoise vinyl flooring screamed 1970. He let himself relax. Nothing here was intimidating except the man he'd come to see.

Elias sat on a barstool, chatting with the bartender and a bearded man who held a shot glass with the reverence of a Geisha in a tea ceremony. The only other patrons, a middle aged couple and an old man, were at small tables below a flat screen TV tuned to a sports channel playing highlights from the day's MLB playoff games.

Win noticed that the barkeep hadn't asked him what he wanted to drink when he entered, which gave him the uncomfortable feeling he'd been expected and the stranger knew something about him. Could this be the place Elias used to call his "office away from his office"?

Elias stood and motioned for Win to follow him through a door near the short leg of the L-shaped bar. Inside the small office an oscillating electric fan sat on a metal table, puffing a feeble breeze in an arc between a free-standing safe and a pair of folding chairs. A faded, framed portrait of the Hamm's beer bear hung over the safe.

Win stood awkwardly with the back of his legs against a chair. He didn't want to sit down in case he needed to run. Elias cleared himself a corner of the table, sat down and said, "You're late, as usual. Have trouble finding the place? I thought you knew every late night joint in town." He held out his hand. "Let's see it, and I'm counting every centavo this time."

Win handed over the thick envelope and watched his boss do the count. After the second go round, Elias grunted and said, "Here you go, kid, your cut from this week's take."

Win pocketed the money and said, "How about a drink?"

"We ain't done."

Win turned back. "Huh?"

"Just 'cause I done time don't mean I'm willing to live on this sorry wad of cash." He held up the envelope. "You know this ain't nothing compared to what we used to pull in."

"We got the two guys who still owe us five K from before, they'll be paying it down."

"No more excuses, they pay in full by the end of the month or their dear daughters will do it for them. The young ones gonna get the most out of living in America anyhow. Only fair they pay part of the tab." Elias's grin made Win's flesh crawl.

"By the way, kid, your mom ever pay back what I gave her snakehead to go away? If you don't mind, she can square it now. She must have plenty extra cash, living rent-free with Mr. Moneypots. If not, she can sell some of the expensive goodies he buys her. Tell her I might even be willing to let her get off light if she's nice to me."

Win felt his chest and shoulders tighten with the effort it took to remain silent. He should have expected this. The sound of breaking glass came from the other side of the thin wall. Would his skull crack like that if one of Elias's huge fists made contact?

"No offense, kid. Your mom is the last resort, you know that. But I'm really strapped for cash. I can't lay out for product without it. I need my lady business where I don't need cash up front. Something for nothing, just like they work it on Wall Street. I need everything up and running like it was before I got sent up. You find out where my pretty little mares went? No?" He frowned. "What about the fresh meat I told you about? Tell me who you got lined up and I'll slot them into the new stable." Elias's impatience contained a veiled threat.

Win pretended to search in his pocket. "I haven't found all of them, it's taking a while. I got some addresses and cell numbers, but, uh, sorry, I must have put the list in my other jacket."

Elias's face darkened. "I didn't think you'd be keeping it in your pants. Don't be diddling all those chicks—can't have you wearing out the merchandise before we sell it, boy. Okay, we do it like this. You help me round up those girls in the next forty-eight hours or I find another helper." He shook his head as if he was saddened by the thought of ending a long and deep friendship.

Win well understood that dismissal would be unfortunate for only one of them. Maybe life threatening.

"Speaking of your exciting sex life, kid, how you getting on with your neighbor lady? I hope you found out more about her than her panty size."

Win smiled because he thought Elias expected it. He had mixed feelings about Kendra. "We're cool. I found out she has a brother who did time. If your letter got her attention, I think she would have said something."

"Interesting, maybe she's not on the straight and narrow herself. That all you got on her? Losing your touch?"

"No, I got to go slow. She says she's a teacher, and she likes to ask questions. I don't want her to figure out what I'm after. But get this, she's not teaching this semester, she's walking dogs instead." Win shook his head. "Standard High is so bad, I guess the teachers would rather pick up dog sh⌐⌐⌐—"

"Standard High?"

"Yeah. The place is a real hole."

"You don't say. What's this teacher lady look like? Maybe I should check out the staff over there. The young ones might want to earn a few extra bucks, I hear teaching don't pay that well. Anyway, I see your point. Teachers have brains, so be careful."

"Maybe not her though, she teaches Special Ed. Those teachers don't really teach anything, do they?"

"Don't know, don't care. Use your head, kid, and any other body parts you need, but find out what she did with that letter and fast. If she says anything else about the school, let me know. I got interests there."

Win's stomach folded in on itself. Sandi went to Standard High. What had Elias done to his sister? Or worse, what had he done?

Chapter 22

Tuesday, October 19

Kendra stood in her yard, rinsing a bucket with water from a garden hose when she heard someone call her name. Who could possibly be visiting at this early hour? The last thing she wanted right now was company. After coming home from Rhus's, she'd spent the few remaining hours of Sunday huddled in bed with her cat, after which she'd gone through her busy Monday schedule in a little remembered daze. She'd hit the mattress early, hoping to wake up Tuesday feeling normal, but a second night of broken sleep had done nothing to fade the horrible experience from her mind, let alone assuage the paranoia brought on by the police interview.

"Hey, good morning."

Win came through the back gate, keeping to one side, where he wouldn't be sprayed by the hose. Watching him smile and finger back his long hair, the image of a fairytale Prince Charming came to mind. She bet Win practiced that smile in front of a mirror. Whatever his intentions, his effort was futile because her hormones had hit an all time low this morning, to say nothing of her irritation at his assumption it was okay to wander on to her property at will. She'd probably encouraged this by sharing pizza in his living room.

"You're out early," she said listlessly.

"Sorry to bother you, but I heard you out here, so I knew you were up and I wanted to ask, did you find my school ID in your yard by any chance? I think it might have fallen out of my pocket when I was working on the door."

"No, but if it turns up, I'll let you know." What school? Too tired to ask, she turned off the hose and set the bucket down on the patch of scraggly grass her landlord called a lawn.

"Hey, a dog," exclaimed Win, noticing Jackson for the first time.

The Lab had been moping under a small lemon tree in the

back corner of the yard ever since she'd brought him home. Kendra thought she might have to explain because she'd already said she didn't own a dog, but Win didn't seem to register the contradiction. She was surprised to see the Lab get up and walk right up to Win, who leaned down to rub his neck.

"You must have good dog karma, or else you smell like kibble," said Kendra. "The poor guy's hungry and all I have is cat food, and not enough of that for a large dog anyway." She held up an almost empty bag.

"Oh, you have a cat, too."

"Yeah, an indoor cat which is why the dog's outside."

Win looked confused, and she guessed he now remembered their earlier conversation. She tried to explain, "It's not my dog, his owner..." She dropped the bag and helplessly started to sob. The light touch of a hand on her arm only made her tears flow faster.

"What's the matter, did I say something?" he asked. He dropped his hand but remained close by.

Go away, she thought. No, don't go away....

"Is everything okay?" This time he sounded quite concerned.

She nodded and tried to smile, knowing she looked like an idiot. "I found a dead body," she said.

Everything played back in her head now, the dog's distress, the corpse, and maybe the worst, the awful smell. Even Win's Citramint aftershave couldn't overpower that memory.

He touched her arm again. "What did you say?"

The shock in his voice returned her to the present, with all its attendant problems. How odd that he turned out to be the first person she told. She hardly knew him, but he had a way about him that got her to open up. Now she'd have to tell him something, but didn't intend to answer a lot of questions.

"I went to walk Jackson Sunday night—this dog—and his owner was lying there, murdered."

"Wow. How—totally freaky!"

He didn't know the half of it yet he appeared more shocked than she would have expected, given his history. He'd probably seen plenty of dead bodies after the tsunami.

"Yes, it was. I'm still kind of upset. Sorry I overreacted, I'm short on sleep."

108

"Anyone would be upset after that. What time did it happen, anyway?"

Kendra wondered a bit about the question, but if that was where his interest lay, it suited her fine. She didn't want to go into any bloody details. "Around six, I guess. It was my last walk of the day."

She determined to play it down, so he'd drop the subject. She picked up a broom and started to sweep the flagstones to make it look like the topic no longer held her interest.

Sadly, he wanted more. "You weren't in any danger, I hope. I mean, how did he—or was it a woman—die?"

Jackson let out a whine as if he understood. Kendra's broom caught on the edge of a flagstone and popped out of her hands. Out of control, she thought, just like this conversation. She picked up the broom and leaned on it saying, "It was a man, but sorry, I'd rather not talk about the details. I had nothing to do with it, but I think the cops wanted to arrest me anyway. Well one of them did."

"Don't take that personal. They always suspect the one who finds a body. So, were you the only one there? What about the guy's family?"

"I didn't see anyone else, except for a million cops after I called 911."

"That must have been a major scene."

"Yeah, my own installment of CSI."

Win nodded as if he got the image. "But they let you go, and let you take the dog?"

"I couldn't just leave the poor thing. I guess they didn't need to keep him for evidence, although I think they might have vacuumed him or something before they handed him over." Kendra sighed. "I wish I would have thought to bring his food home. I'm not in shape for a shopping trip right now."

"Hey, I'll be glad to go get some for you—darn, no, I can't, my bike's acting up."

Kendra hesitated only for a second. "If you have a license, you can drive my car and I'll ride shotgun."

"Huh?"

"That means in the passenger seat, like when the gangsters rob a bank and someone protects the driver," she explained.

Win laughed. "Okay, now it makes sense, but you don't have

to come. I'll go myself, and I promise not to steal your car."

She was too tired to argue and went inside to get the keys.

Chapter 23

Kendra carefully maneuvered the Mustang into the one remaining vacancy in the student parking lot and cut the motor. She reached to pull her keys from the ignition and found that her fingers were locked like talons around the steering wheel. Although she'd made it to Standard High without incident in the light mid-morning traffic, she'd been tensely gripping the steering wheel with all her might. Although the eye surgeon had given permission, she wouldn't have driven on her own if she hadn't desperately needed to see a friendly face. There wasn't time to take the bus if she wanted to catch Maretta on her prep period when she'd be free.

Kendra checked the area for kids lurking around armed with spray paint or other tools of destruction, but saw no one. Perhaps the students hadn't fully woken up and didn't have enough energy for vandalism. She hated to leave the Mustang there, but only active faculty members got a parking sticker. Cars weren't much safer in the segregated lot anyway. Teachers often found their cars decorated with magic markers or scratches.

The first floor halls were empty except for a pair of overweight boys, sheepishly carrying hall passes cut from a bright pink, teddy bear pattern. The style had been deliberately chosen to discourage unnecessary requests to leave class. The boys bent their heads together as she passed them at the bottom of the stairs.

"I thought Ms. Desola got fired. I wonder, what's she doing here?" whispered the fatter of the two.

"Maybe she's trying to erase her fingerprints," said the other.

Kendra sped past them and up the stairs to Maretta's classroom where she found her friend alone at her desk. The window behind her was cranked open to dissipate the miasma of cheap perfume the students doused themselves with. She'd already cleaned up the debris the students always left behind at the end of a period. Tidiness distinguished Maretta's room, that and the collection of pull down maps on the back wall.

Maretta smiled a greeting, then bent her head back to her

work. "I see you're having fun," said Kendra, leaning over the desk. "Have I interrupted a critical moment in the District's cruelest form of torture, the Classroom Goal Matrix?"

"Just a sec. Okay. I had to fill in an auxiliary services provider code before I forgot it." She pushed her chair back and really looked at Kendra for the first time. "No offense, but you don't look so hot. Are you feeling okay? Did you have breakfast? I've got granola bars." She opened a drawer and handed one to Kendra. In common with most Special Ed. teachers, she kept a stock of energy bars, instant soup products and crackers in her classroom to feed students who had missed meals because of poverty or chaos at home.

"Thanks, but food won't help. I haven't slept the last two nights and coming on campus doesn't exactly lift my spirits."

"You really have to get past it. Next January you'll be back, you know. I actually think you should come around more to desensitize yourself."

"Well, I'm not starting today. I wish we could've met at the Bakery. They have real chairs and it's halfway between here and my house." Kendra slid into a plastic desk-chair and wiggled in a futile effort to get comfortable.

"I'm too busy today to run out on my prep and you said you didn't want to talk on the phone—"

"I found a body."

Maretta's mouth froze half open. A blink later she managed, "Tell me you don't mean a dead human."

"I do. I went to walk a dog and the owner was lying there in a pool of blood." Kendra's voice cracked.

"You found the attorney who was murdered? The story was on the news. Lucky your name wasn't mentioned, that's all you need. Wait. You weren't there at the same time as the murder, were you?"

"Whoever did it wasn't there anymore. I guess I lucked out."

"For you, yeah, that constitutes luck." Maretta sighed deeply. "How did it happen?"

"I'm not sure, I think someone stabbed him."

"No, I mean, tell me everything from the beginning."

"The guy's dog is usually in the yard waiting for me, but he didn't come when I called him, so I went looking and found the body lying there. I totally freaked."

"You called the cops, right?" Maretta's tone conveyed doubt, given Kendra's determination to avoid all contact with police.

"I called 911 right away. Well, as soon as I was done throwing up and passing out."

"Good girl. They took care of everything after that, right?"

"I had to stick around for hours. Are you ready for this? Guess who showed up? Howard and Tapia, the same detectives who were here last year."

"No way. Forget what I said about luck. Were they hard on you?"

Kendra frowned. "You know Howard. I think she still suspects I lied back then. Tapia wasn't as bad, but he kept asking me to repeat myself over and over, like he wanted me to slip up and admit I killed the guy. You know cops, they always want to pin the crime on the first one they see."

"Never mind your police phobia, finish the story. Tell me about the dead guy, who was he?"

"Mr. Rhus was a lawyer—a very rich one, from the look of things. I can't tell you anything else about him. I just walked his dog, and only did that for about a week."

"Maybe he handled dangerous clients, you know, like the mafia."

"You get points for imagination, but it's more likely he interrupted a burglary. His study was a mess." Kendra thought for a moment. "Now that I think about it, a lot of expensive stuff hadn't been touched. But all the file drawers were emptied out, papers lying everywhere. Maybe the murderer wanted private information, not valuables."

"In any case, knowing how you seem to get yourself into, shall we say, interesting situations, you should be more careful who you do pet sitting for. Especially since you're not trying to make a career of it."

Kendra was used to Maretta's lectures and had to admit they usually had a basis well grounded in history.

"Careful? Why would I expect trouble from a lawyer who lived in such an affluent neighborhood? It's not like I took a job walking a Pit Bull across gang turf. How was I supposed to know I'd find him murdered? You know, it's odd there wasn't an alarm system working because Mr. Rhus seemed to be extremely cautious. I'm sure he didn't open his door to just anyone. He was so protective of his house he didn't trust me enough to give me a house key, made me pick up the dog from outside."

"Wait, then you found the body in the yard? I'm confused."

"Um, well, no, it was in the study upstairs...."

Maretta gave Kendra the same look she gave her students when they were avoiding the truth. "Kendra, Kendra. Do I want to know how you got into a house you don't have a key for, a house with a dead body inside?"

"I told you, I was looking for the dog. I was worried because he wasn't in the yard, and the door was open. I didn't break in. I'd never do that," Kendra protested.

"All right, but still, don't you think it would have been smarter to decide the dog didn't want your company and call it a day?"

Muffled laugher came through the wall from an adjacent classroom, signifying either an interesting science experiment or a minor brawl. Major fights usually didn't happen until lunchtime. Kendra turned her attention back to her own self-defense.

"That would have been irresponsible. I called first, but when no one answered the phone I thought I should check. Mr. Rhus hired me because he wasn't home much and I was afraid the dog might have been locked in a room without food or water, or maybe something worse had happened. The door wasn't locked, so I went in." All that had spilled out so fast, Kendra wasn't really sure what she had just said.

"Which is it? Now the door wasn't locked? First you said it was open. Kendra, really."

"You working for the cops now? My clothes from yesterday are still in the laundry basket at home if you want to check for bloodstains."

Maretta picked up her car keys like she took the idea seriously, then laughed. "Don't be so sensitive."

"Okay, sorry, but don't jump on my every word just because I wasn't being precise. No matter what I said, I didn't break in and it's a good thing I went inside because the poor dog was totally traumatized, crouched there watching over the corpse of his owner. At least he's safe in my yard now."

"You took the dog home? Do the police know?"

"Yeah, I got permission."

"Hard to believe a few days back you were complaining about being bored."

"As soon as the terror wears off, I'll be bored again, and I look forward to it." Kendra suddenly felt hungry. She peeled back the wrapper and took a huge bite from the granola bar. She hadn't eaten since yesterday afternoon, hadn't been hungry. The oatmeal and brown sugar hit the spot. Lost in the sensation, her mind went suddenly, blissfully blank. She started working her way through the treat.

From a distance, a bell sounded to mark the dressing period for the Phys Ed. classes. Kendra shot out of her chair. "I'd better go before the dismissal bell. Thanks for listening. I feel much better." Kendra pocketed the rest of the oatmeal bar.

"Will you be home around 4:30 or are you dog walking? I could come by and take you out for coffee, or whatever."

"You don't have to check up on me, but I'd like that. See you later."

Chapter 24

Kendra unfolded a paper napkin and spread it out on the park bench, weighing a corner down with Maretta's cell phone. Kendra had left hers at home. She wouldn't have answered it anyway because she'd gotten a call earlier from Detective Tapia reminding her to visit the police station. His next call probably wouldn't be as polite. She'd go there first thing tomorrow. Sure she would.

Although the maple trees still held most of their leaves, autumn made its presence known by an infinitesimal sting in the air that brought with it the promise of cooler nights. In a field across from where they sat, a man began a game of Frisbee with his dog, scattering a flock of crows. Kendra broke off a piece of her sesame coffee cake and looked up into the thick lattice of the oak tree branches overhead. She felt calm for the first time in days. "Thanks for bringing me here, I feel saner already."

"No, thank you, I love driving the Mustang." Maretta carefully pried the lid off her takeout coffee. "Hey, look over there, what a cute face."

"I can't make it out. What breed is it?"

"I was talking about the man, so that would be homo sapiens."

"Well, Mrs. Edwards, I'm telling Mr. Edwards," teased Kendra.

"Just kidding, it's a spaniel of some sort, I think. That reminds me, how did your pet care presentation go at the Cap Home?"

"Fine, at first. Miraculously none of the kids talked back, but Reyna showed up afterward and insisted I go see her room." Kendra rolled her eyes. "I didn't want to, but couldn't think of an excuse fast enough and she's so…needy, I guess is a good term for it."

"Well, now she's missing." Maretta frowned.

"What do you mean, missing?"

"She ran away from the Home, apparently."

"Oh yeah? I bet something weird's going on there. Reyna had a room to herself, told me her roommate had run off. Maybe there's a connection."

"I bet there is. When I called about Reyna's truancy, I guess it was too much to expect the dorm supervisor to tell me Reyna's roommate took off, too. I would have liked to know. In spite of what the Home professes, they're not equipped to handle our Special Ed. kids, however good their intentions might be."

"Might be, I like that." Kendra believed most foster homes were in it purely for the money.

"Who's the roommate?"

"I didn't ask. Maybe I should have, but I've been trying to stay uninvolved with student stuff until I go back. If Reyna mentioned her name, it got lost in all of her other babble."

"Aren't you worried? Anything can happen to a girl out on the streets, like what happened to Imelda."

"Sure, I gave Reyna a mini-lecture about it. Now I feel awful I didn't say more. I wonder what's going on. Do you know if the police ever identified the other murdered girl?"

"I don't know. I haven't contacted Bridges again. I wanted to, but I've been so busy. I'll do it as soon as I get the chance. Finding Reyna comes first, before she winds up like Imelda." Maretta paused with a pained expression. "After she spends a night or two on her own maybe she'll realize foster care is a better alternative. Or maybe not. She doesn't have a good sense of what's good for her, even when it concerns everyday things. Her attendance was already borderline and I told her over and over what would happen, that the days add up. But she'll flip out anyway when she finds out that by missing these last few days of class she'll have to repeat the entire semester."

Kendra sighed. "No matter how many times we tell the kids they're not earning credits for graduation when they're absent, the message doesn't sink in. The parents are just as bad, keeping their kids home to baby sit while they go off to work. And some kids do a scary job with childcare. Last semester I had a freshman girl tell me how cute it was when her baby nephew ran around drinking from open beer cans."

A woman with a runner's body jogged by pushing a stroller. Maretta pulled in her feet just in time to avoid the wheels. She cast a dark look down the path and said, "Hey, you think a family member took Reyna in so she would help out? One of my students left her foster home last year and turned up living at a relative's house doing all the childcare while the mother went to work."

Kendra thought for a moment. "It's possible. Doesn't Reyna have a cousin in King Park? She might have gone there."

Maretta nodded. "Thing is, the entire situation is sensitive, because as far as I know the entire family's here illegally. I don't want to give the truancy officer the address or the whole family might bolt, which won't help Reyna one bit. I planned on going over there myself, but seeing as how they're undocumented they might not be receptive."

"You want me to try? I have time and my Spanish is better than yours."

"No kidding. My nephew's hamster speaks better Spanish than I do," said Maretta. "I'd tell you to go for it, but I don't know the family and I'd hate to send you into an uncomfortable situation."

"It's just a home visit. We do them all the time. I'm prepared for the worst."

"Okay, you talked me into it. I'll text you the address later."

"I'll get right on it."

"Hope it goes well. We should write a Home Visits for Dummies book. Remember the girl who lived in the brand new, three-bedroom house? We rang the bell thinking what an easy visit it was going to be and the mother invites us in, and—"

"There was a kilo of marijuana sitting on the kitchen table," finished Kendra. "Another reason you can't completely judge people by outward appearances or the look of their houses."

"Okay, you made your point," Maretta grumbled.

"Actually, I had a weird thing happen at my own house last week. I never told you because after practically tripping over a corpse, a rock is no big deal."

Maretta gave one of her signature looks up to the heavens. "Okay, I'll bite. What rock?"

"I was at home playing with the cat and all of a sudden came this loud BAM. I felt the floor shake like something hit the back of the house, but you know how hard it is to tell with sound. So I checked and found out someone threw a big river rock right through my storm door." Kendra held her hands several inches apart to designate the size.

"You're kidding."

"Wish I was. It broke the glass, even chipped a bit of trim off the inner door, but luckily it didn't break through into my kitchen."

"Living where you do, you need one of those metal security doors."

"The landlord won't pay for it and I'm not about to buy him an expensive present."

"Did he at least fix the storm door?"

"He sent over a new one, and a neighbor put it up for me."

"Nice neighbor. Male or female?"

"Male." Kendra felt her face burning. "Before you ask, yes, he's very good-looking, in a metrosexual sort of way. Not exactly my type, and too young for me anyway. He can't be more than twenty-three, tops, and you know my philosophy: males don't achieve their peak mental maturity of twelve until they've reached the physical age of twenty-five."

"You're only twenty-seven. Don't try to bluff, I can tell you're tempted." Maretta hid her smile behind her coffee cup.

"Only because it's been a while since I've gotten positive male attention."

"Enjoy it while you can, but don't fall into anything you'll regret—unless you already have?"

Nope. I've kept him at a distance." She ate the last morsel of cake, then folded the empty bag thoughtfully. "You know, I think I might have a use for him."

"Did I hear right? A use for him? That sounds cold, not like the Kendra I know."

"Well, the old Kendra is dead where men are concerned, thanks to Brian. That's my other home related news. Somehow he found out where I'm living and left a vase of flowers on my porch."

"Oh crap. Did you see him?"

"No, he's probably waiting for me to have a change of heart and call. I'm running out things I can do to prove to him I've moved on in more ways than changing my address."

"You could tell him you're into women now, it would probably make him give up."

Kendra smiled. "Might work, but I have a better idea. Listen to this. I saw a flyer from Brian's basketball league. They're going to have a fundraising dinner and auction Friday night. Suppose I ask the guy who installed my door to go with me posing as my new boyfriend? Win looks so amazing I think Brian will feel totally outclassed and give up trying to get me back."

Maretta almost spit coffee over them both. "Where do you get these ideas? Even if this Win of yours agrees to such a crazy scheme, it won't work. I don't agree with your overall philosophy about men. They evaluate their competition by more than looks. Men care about professional and social status too."

"Same thing, all show and no heart. Look, I know my idea sounds like the plot of a chick flick, but honestly, Brian's been acting like the lovesick nerd who supplies all the laugh lines. Except I'm not laughing. I just want him to leave me alone." She got up and deposited her trash into a nearby can.

Maretta rose and shook the crumbs off her skirt. "My advice is to scrap your plan. Brian plays basketball. He's competitive. How do you know dangling Win in front of him won't just egg him on? How about trying to get a restraining order instead?"

"I don't think I have grounds for legal action and you know how much I love lawyers. Anyway, Brian's not a physical threat, he just wants my attention."

"Are you sure? What if he's the one who threw the rock?"

"I thought about it, but he's not a violent person."

"He wasn't, but maybe he is now."

"Thanks for cheering me up. Look, if it makes you feel better, I'll think it over."

Maretta looked at her doubtfully. "Once you get rolling with an idea it's hard to stop you."

In the distance, a car alarm sounded. Maretta got up and looked. "Not the Mustang, I hope"

"No," said Kendra. "I didn't set the alarm. I never do.

"How did I know that?"

Chapter 25

Win stole another peek at the time display on his TiVo. Eleven minutes since Detective Howard had taken a seat in his living room. The way she kept jumping from topic to topic he couldn't tell what she was really after. Routine questioning, she told him when she arrived. He tried to submerge the memory from his childhood when his father had gone to collect the body of a relative at a police station, all that was left after a week of routine questioning. Win could smell his own fear. "Mind if I open a window?"

The cop gave an infinitesimal nod and continued to assess him with heavy lidded eyes, like a somnolent iguana who wasn't quite sure if the prey in front of her was worth the bother.

"So, you haven't seen your mother in days, but the man she works for—lives with—gets murdered and she doesn't even call you. That's your story?"

"I told you, we're not close."

"And you didn't know Roger Rhus was murdered until you heard about it at work."

"Right."

"When did you find out, and who told you?"

"I heard some of the women at the West Ridge Center talking about it on Monday. Some of them knew Mr. Rhus because he took care of their immigration papers."

"Like this?" Howard handed him a sheet of paper.

Win did his best to keep his face expressionless. This copy of his visa could have come from West Ridge, but he suspected the cops had his real one now, much worse for him than Mr. Rhus holding it. What could they do to him now?

The detective confirmed his supposition by saying, "This is just a copy, of course. We've got the originals for your mother and your sister as well, all found in the victim's house. Maybe you can tell me why you weren't holding your own visa?"

Win realized the strongest reason for a homicide cop to ask that question was if she thought he'd killed to get it back. "Mr.

Rhus said he needed it to put through a renewal. I didn't understand, but I gave it to him. He's the lawyer. Was, I mean."

"The date on it appears to be good," Howard said.

"Um, I wanted to change jobs and he had to fix it, for me." Win hoped the explanation sounded feasible. He counted on the detective knowing even less about visa rules than he did himself.

She wrote in her note pad again and then gave him a smile that would make even a used car salesman shudder. "The people closest to the victim are often very helpful in solving a crime. Your sister and mother must have known Mr. Rhus quite well, living with him. Did they notice anything out of the ordinary going on?"

"Why don't you ask them?" Win instantly regretted the outburst. Where he came from, he would have been beaten to a pulp for a rejoinder like that and he wasn't entirely sure cops were different here. He had some fighting skills, but Detective Howard had a gun and a fifty-pound weight advantage.

"I'd love to, and was hoping you would help me do that. I haven't been able to find either of them."

He wanted to pretend he didn't know what Howard was talking about, but she wouldn't believe him. What could it hurt to admit he didn't know where they were either? After all, he'd told her already he hadn't spoken to his mother. He felt a sting on his finger and looked down. He'd been rolling the photocopy in his hands and given himself a paper cut. The paper was smeared with blood. Howard reached over and took it from him, sliding it into an envelope. So much for trying to play it cool. She had his fingerprints and DNA now.

"Like I told you, I haven't talked to my mother and I don't have much to do with Sandi either these days."

"Then you can't say where they were at the time of the murder?"

"I don't know where they were."

"When's the last time you saw or spoke to them?" asked Howard.

"I haven't seen Sandi since last Saturday. I saw my mother on Monday. She had a day off and we went for a drive." Win wasn't sure how much the cops knew, but they obviously didn't know where Sandi was and he wasn't going to ask for police help to find her. The cops would just accuse him of killing her and dumping her body somewhere. Not that they'd really care. Rhus's murder made the news, but he hadn't seen anything in the news that would help him find Sandi. Maybe that meant she was okay, but maybe she just wasn't important enough to make headlines.

Howard looked up from her notes. "You must also have spent time at Mr. Rhus's house?"

"Some, yeah."

"How were the three of them getting along?"

"My mom and sister loved it there and Mr. Rhus treated them real good." So, Detective Howard didn't know Sandi wasn't living with her mother in Mr. Rhus's house. What would she think if she heard about Sandi's crazy temperament and the foster home? With information like that, the cops would try to pin the murder on Sandi because she couldn't fight back. Win couldn't let them do that to his sister.

Howard went on. "The man who provided for your mother and sister was murdered, but you don't seem very worried about them. Why is that?"

He didn't think Detective Howard was really concerned about the well being of his family. "I guess I don't show my feelings. You know, I'm Asian." Win smiled deprecatingly but the comment didn't prompt the usual laugh.

"They may have useful information."

Win would also have liked to find out what his mother knew. She'd been acting strange lately, for sure. He had to find his mother before Detective Howard could. In his most accommodating tone, he said, "If I get a hold of them, I'll call you right away."

Howard peered out the window at the house next door. "How well do you know Kendra Desola?"

The abrupt shift surprised him. "Kendra...you mean my neighbor? We talk sometimes, like neighbors do. Why?"

"Then maybe she told you she was the one who found the body. A pretty wild coincidence, don't you think?"

"What is?"

"Your neighbor finding the body of your mother's employer."

"Actually, I was gonna say something to you," said Win.

"Really? But, you told me you found out Mr. Rhus had been

murdered from a coworker. Do you want to change your story?"
Howard tapped her teeth with her pen, creating a noise that shot
like pins through Win's skull.

"Uh, no. I ran into Kendra later and she told me her story, and
I found out she knew Mr. Rhus. I thought it was a crazy
coincidence, too. She told me he hired her to walk his dog."

"How long was she working for him?"

"I don't know, but I think maybe she knew him better than she
says because she brought his dog home to live with her."

Howard began to write energetically. He'd meant to redirect
the cop's attention toward Kendra, but hadn't expected the tactic
to work this well.

"Anything else you know about the relationship between her
and Mr. Rhus?" she queried.

"Well, I saw her in her yard, crying, after he died. She kind of
seems like she wants to hide the fact she's keeping his dog." Win
actually did wonder if there really had been a relationship besides
the dog walking. For all he knew, this wasn't the first time Kendra
had kept the dog at home with her either. After all, she'd been
quite huffy when he'd mentioned seeing a leash on her front porch.
He knew Rhus well enough to know the guy could get any woman
he wanted, but would he have wanted Kendra?

Finally, Howard collected her things and got to her feet. Win's
fist clenched in rhythm with her march to the door.

"I'm sure we'll be talking again soon. When you hear from
your mother or sister, we'd like to know right away."

"I'm going to do my best to find them," said Win, finally
telling the complete truth.

Chapter 26

Rick Tapia put down the powdered creamer, carried the cup of coffee to the drinking fountain and poured the coffee down the drain.

"You calling the plumber, Rick, or should I? The last person did that, the fountain was out of order for a month."

Tapia smiled at his partner who had suddenly appeared at his side. "Better the pipes and a plumber than calling a paramedic to save me. Want to run out for something non-lethal?"

"Why don't you grab a Coke from the machine like you usually do?"

"I just felt like having coffee for a change." He pulled a bill from his wallet. "Can I buy you a drink? Mountain Dew, right?"

"Maybe later. I got us some leads in the case, including Rhus's financial records, going back five years." She waved a thick folder. On the wall, a faded department notice flapped in response.

They headed back toward their desks at one end of a large, open room with a row of windows shielded by an external metal grating added after 9/11. Tapia envied the officers on the higher floors who were able to see over the barrier to the street beyond.

"You could stack my lifetime transactions and have less than what you got there."

"Me too, but we're peons compared to him."

"Is that bitterness or envy I detect?"

"Neither. I've got a jackhammer of a headache from reading this stuff. Now I see why rich people hire accountants."

"That's why I keep you around, to do the fun stuff." Tapia exchanged a grin with his partner. He'd found Alicia Howard to be a shrewd, hard-working detective although he believed her kamikaze interview style could use some tempering.

"Check out the bottom line." She pulled her chair over to join him at his desk, opened the folder in front of them, and pointed to a highlighted row.

"Green, nice touch, Allie. Yeah, he sure had pots of money, but I expected it from an attorney."

125

"Yeah, but compare the difference between his income from the law firm and his bank balance." She reached over and pulled out another sheet and set it down so he could see them side-by-side. "Guy's been socking thousands in cash into his account and there's no direct way to paper trail where it came from."

"Looks like someone's paying him in cash for something."

"Yeah, for legal services that aren't legal."

"We don't know that yet." Tapia's chair squeaked as he leaned back. He drummed his fingers on the armrest as he thought out loud. "We didn't find a lot of cash, but the box of passports and visas was definitely fishy, even for a lawyer who specializes in immigration. I've got a feeling at least some of the passports and visas in his possession were doctored. I put a call in to Immigration and Customs Enforcement and got the sense the Feds were already on to him, but they weren't ready to share. I'm waiting for a call back from someone higher up. Looks like we might have a joint operation soon." Tapia frowned. "Just what we need, another layer of bureaucrats to slow us down."

"And to take credit later." Howard made a motion like she was polishing a badge on her chest.

"We need ICE's expertise if there's an illegal immigration angle. We could have a bunch of new suspects if Rhus was into human smuggling."

Howard took the folder out of his hands. "Actually, I don't think we need to go far a field on this case."

"What makes you say that?"

"I just talked to one of our computer techs. He retrieved Rhus's deleted files, including his emails." She paused for a moment like a magician about to open the magic box. "Guess who was on his email list?"

"You tell me, Allie. I don't want to ruin your fun by guessing right."

"Yeah, like you would. I got a better idea, smartass, let me read you something."

She turned and grabbed a clipped sheaf of printouts from her untidy desk. Tapia saw with amusement she'd already marked the one she wanted with a big orange exclamation mark. She read, "Ms. Desola, after going over your references, I am pleased to offer you employment. Please call me at the earliest convenience."

Howard looked up. "Signed off with Rhus's name, office and home phone numbers."

"We already know she walked his dog. What's the big deal?"

"Here's another one, from his inbox. Listen: "Dear Mr. Rhus, The meet and greet session with Jackson went great. He's my buddy now. Thanks for helping me get to know him. I can't wait for our first walk. Signed by Ms. Desola.""

"How's this germane to the homicide?"

"I interviewed one of the people whose visa we found in Rhus's office. Win Ni. Turns out he's Desola's neighbor, how's that for interesting, and there's more. He thinks she knew Rhus better than she admits. I don't believe she never went into his house until the night she found his body. And why lie about it if she's innocent?"

"People lie for all sorts of reasons. You really think she's involved?"

"I know she is. According to his records, he paid her 40 bucks a visit. I checked with a bunch of pet sitting companies and the average rate is less than twenty. So what was the extra twenty for? Maybe she really wasn't walking the dog and they just called it dog walking in their correspondence."

"We can certainly ask her, but I don't think there's anything here worth pursuing. What about Rhus's phone records, she on there?"

"Just one call, the one she said she made the night of the murder. Doesn't matter. Desola's not the innocent little lady you think she is. She's lying to us again, just like last year at Standard High. She got away with it then, and thinks she can get away with it now."

"We cleared her. She went sniffing around and got herself into trouble. That's all."

"She obstructed our investigation, broke into a desk and somehow wound up with the property of a dead man."

"Let's not rehash that, Allie. If I didn't know you better I'd think you're letting a personality conflict affect your judgment."

"What about you? If I didn't know you better, I'd think you're attracted to her. Maybe I should tell her you're known around here as Rick the Dick."

"And maybe I should tell her—"

The corner office opened and a gray haired man called out, "Rick, Allie, I got the Feds on conference call. You need to hear this."

Chapter 27

Wednesday, October 20

Kendra coiled up the water hose accompanied by a frenetic soundtrack of dog slurps. Apparently, Jackson thought filling his water bowl was a competitive sport. If he got points for soaking his opponent, he'd won big this time. Now that the fun had ended, the Lab showed no interest in the water bowl, preferring to drink from the puddle he'd created on the patio. Kendra felt an irrational need to get back at him, but short of picking up his water bowl and making a big deal about giving it to Bobbins, she couldn't think of anything.

She kicked off her clogs and sat on the stoop to peel off her wool socks, which looked and felt like swamp creature fins. She hung the water and dog drool drenched socks over the back of a lawn chair and went inside to put on dry clothes, all the while compiling a mental list of people who might take Jackson off her hands. The sooner the better, before the dog bonded to her. Fortunately for the Lab, the doorbell interrupted her plans.

Kendra went to the front and opened the door, expecting to see a contingent of evangelists or someone selling newspaper subscriptions. Instead, she looked into the piercing eyes of Detective Howard, who appeared to be in a very foul mood. Her hair apparently was having a bad day as well, with a dark wing sticking out behind each ear.

"Ms. Desola, I need to ask you a few questions. Can I come in?"

Kendra didn't bother to answer the question that wasn't really a question. Short of shutting the door in Howard's face—satisfying but ultimately counterproductive—she had no way to postpone the encounter. She led the detective in as far as the entrance to the living room, but didn't offer a seat. To her relief, Howard didn't ask for one, seeming content to lean against the credenza while she flipped the pages of her notebook. In that pose she looked like a treant from World of Warcraft dressed in a polyester suit.

"Tell me again what time you found the body."

Kendra suppressed the urge to snatch the notebook and see if Howard really hadn't written that very fact down the other five times she'd asked the same question. "Around six, like I told you."

"Were the kitchen cabinets open or closed?"

"I didn't go into the kitchen." Either Howard was trying to trick her or they'd found something in the kitchen. Like a missing knife?

The detective clicked her ballpoint pen with a flourish like she was expecting to write something momentous and asked, "Tell me about your relationship with Roger Rhus."

Whoa, where did this come from? "I didn't have a relationship. I only walked his dog a few times."

"But you brought his dog home and now it's yours."

She's suspicious about dog custody? Howard was out to get her. No, that was paranoid. The detective must have a better reason for this interrogation.

Kendra forced a smile. "Actually, I'm looking for a home for Jackson. Would you be interested in adopting him?" She stopped short of adding, "They say owning a dog can do wonders for a foul disposition."

"You signed a statement saying you first met the victim last week. Do you have some proof of that?"

"I have a copy of the contract he signed. The other copy should be at his house."

"Let me see it."

Kendra went to her desk, found it and brought it back to Howard, who quickly scanned the one-page service agreement.

"Forty bucks a visit is very pricey just to walk a dog. What else were you doing for him?"

"Nothing. I charged him high because I had to take a taxi to his place."

The detective pointed toward the street. "You have a car, why not drive there?"

"I had Lasik surgery two months ago and had a bad reaction to it. I still have trouble focusing, so I only drive when I have to."

Howard held the contract in the air like she'd been watching reruns of Perry Mason. "So you're saying this was the sum total of your relationship with Roger Rhus?"

"How many times do I have to tell you that before you believe me?"

"Until you convince me. We interviewed another party who told me your relationship was personal as well as professional."

"Who said that?"

"We're not at liberty to say. And how do you explain the emails? Looks like you guys were developing a quite a friendship."

"You've read my email?"

"No, his. So, Ms. Desola did you or did you not have a personal relationship with Roger Rhus?"

Kendra took a deep breath and let it out slowly to keep herself from shouting her reply. "I did not. He hired me to walk his dog. Nothing more."

"How do you explain bringing his dog home with you then?"

"I felt sorry for it.

"Maybe the dog's not the only thing you took from Mr. Rhus's house," said Howard.

Kendra's teeth chattered with stress. She rubbed her jaw so Howard wouldn't notice. Was Howard threatening her with a search warrant? She fought down memories of her family house being searched after her brother's narcotics arrest. The aftermath was with her right now, a fearful insecurity that her privacy could be violated at any moment by forces she couldn't control.

"Are you accusing me of stealing?"

"Maybe you picked up something by accident, like you did last year," continued Howard acidly. "At the very least, you're keeping something back."

"I made my statement already. I think you should leave."

"We'll talk again, Ms. Desola."

Should I get a lawyer? Kendra wondered as she watched Howard march to her car.

Chapter 28

The frame ranch house stood out from its neighbors, the only one on the block that didn't have at least one window covered with plywood. The remains of a wood fence marked the boundary between the dead grass inside and the bare ground along the sidewalk. A sudden, chill wind blew up, and Kendra blinked to keep dirt from flying into her eyes. She drew her long cardigan closer to her body but still felt exposed, like she didn't belong here and everyone on the block knew it. It would have been smarter to drive here so she could make a quick getaway if she had to, but driving was a last resort and the Mustang would attract attention to her presence.

Kendra double checked the address, then took the three sagging wooden stairs with caution. The floorboards of the porch wobbled under her feet. Of the two unmarked mailboxes tenuously fastened to the peeling wood siding, only one appeared to be in use. The other was stuffed with torn and faded third class mailers and a discarded plastic bag. A black and brown mottled cat lay on an old rug, surrounded by terra cotta planters evidently used to grow cigarette butts. Kendra hoped the cat wouldn't develop lung disease.

She looked for a doorbell and finding none, knocked on the door closest to the empty mailbox. Almost immediately, the door cracked open and a diminutive man peered out. He drew his heavy, white eyebrows together while he examined her. The hand on the doorjamb was wrinkled and frail.

"¿Qué quieres?" After giving her a hard look, he repeated in heavily accented English, "What you want?"

Kendra heard the hostility in his voice. Who does he think I am, she wondered, a social worker, a poll-taker, a salesperson? Not immigration, because he didn't slam the door. "Habla Ingles?" she asked, hoping that he did.

"English, yes," he said, still guarding the door.

"My name is Kendra Desola. I'm a teacher at Standard High School. I'm looking for the family of Reyna Soriano."

The man examined the area behind her, as if he expected someone else to come rushing from out of the hedges next door. When nothing happened, he grunted and stepped back, allowing her to enter.

He shut the door behind her and showed her into a small living room, where he pointed to a plastic covered armchair and left her to wait. Drapes were drawn tightly across the front windows, making the room look unused and gloomy. She knew drive-by shootings were common in this part of town; several residents had been killed inside their homes by stray bullets, but did it help to close the drapes? Kendra wondered if it would be rude to turn on one of the lamps, but decided not to take a chance at offending the family before even speaking to them, especially given the warm welcome she'd received.

She ignored the chair and stood as close to the front door as possible without making it look too odd. She followed the sound of little man's retreating footsteps and heard his voice coming from the rear of the house, speaking in rapid Spanish. Her curiosity overcame her instincts to leave. She made out the words teacher and girl, after which a deeper, angry male voice responded. A chair scraped against the floor.

The old man returned alongside an enormous younger man with tattooed arms and a menacing expression on his broad face. He blatantly appraised her breasts and apparently finding them acceptable, moved his eyes to meet hers with a bald proposition that turned her spine to ice. Kendra was glad she'd remembered to put a can of pepper spray in an easy-to-reach pocket and her cell phone in another.

She stammered an apology for intruding on their day, and backed away. The beefy man beat her to the door and said in heavily accented English, "Stop. You work school? Why you come?"

There can't be any harm in telling him that much, she decided, repeating her name and occupation. "Does the cousin of Reyna Soriano live here? I'm one of Reyna's teachers and I wanted to talk to Arturo Soriano," said Kendra, fudging the truth a little. These two didn't look like they were very concerned with the truth anyway.

"Arturo " The big man repeated the name thoughtfully.

133

Grandpa started to scold her interrogator who responded with equal displeasure.

They obviously believe I speak no Spanish at all, thought Kendra, and it's best not to clue them in. Concentrating hard, she caught the general drift of their exchange, boiling down to: You told me there wasn't going to be any trouble and You're the one who let her in.

"Arturo doesn't live here," declared Mr. Tattoo, suddenly speaking perfect, unaccented English.

Kendra took the abrupt change in the Hulk's linguistic repertoire as a strong signal she should go before she found out more than she wished to know about what game he was playing. But she really hated being treated like a fool, and Maretta was counting on her. Also, since the creep obviously didn't take her seriously, maybe he wouldn't care if she asked a few more questions.

"Would you happen to know where Arturo moved?"

"Maybe if you tell me what you want him for, I can help," he said, leaning on the door, effectively blocking her exit.

"I'm just making a routine teacher visit, but I guess the attendance office gave me the wrong address." She sighed, playing the tried, overworked teacher role while simultaneously feeling in her pocket for the pepper spray.

The old man had had enough, apparently, and began to yell at his younger companion. Before Kendra could do the mental switch back to Spanish, her cell phone trilled the designated Urgent Message chime.

While the two men continued to argue, she read the brief text. It was from Maretta: "Reyna dead. Dangerous. Call me."

Kendra heard Mr. Tattoo say her name and looked over to see that he'd moved away from the door, and had taken hold of the old man's arm, whether to support or restrain him, Kendra couldn't say. Both men were watching her curiously. She realized she'd been staring at the tiny screen, probably with her mouth hanging open.

"Sorry to have bothered you," she said.

The men exchanged a look of complicity. She didn't wait to find out what the two of them agreed on. What if the big man had managed to read the text message over her shoulder? She shot forward and tore the door open, saying, "Thank you for your time."

She sensed a huge presence moving up behind her, but he didn't move to stop her from leaving. It took all her willpower to control her shaky legs and get off the porch without falling. Both of the men were lying. What if one of them killed Reyna? She tried to recall the exact words of their Spanish conversation, but her fright had erased everything.

As she fled down the sidewalk, she heard Mr. Tattoo call out, "Hey, teacher-lady, come back soon and I'll let you give me some private lessons."

Chapter 29

Mose was on the phone when Win entered the Food Service Manager's office. Win couldn't help but stare. It was the first time he'd seen Mose without a uniform or the maroon beanie he wore for a hair cover in lieu of the caps the Center provided for the food service employees. With his brown hair exposed and a preppy outfit of jeans and a pinstriped shirt, he seemed older, and somehow more competent. Win cautioned himself to watch what he said.

The small office looked different than it had during Elias's tenure. A neat stack of business magazines sat on the top of the file cabinet and the wall calendar showed Yosemite Falls instead of beach volleyball babes.

The manager stopped dictating his purchase order for a second and invited him to take a seat on the visitor's chair. Win moved a carton of Styrofoam cups to make enough room for his legs. Elias used to sell "surplus" or "damaged" items to the employees, but it looked like now the office was being used to hold the overflow from the storeroom.

Mose circled something on the list in front of him and slotted the handset into the cradle, turning his attention to Win. "What's up? You're not scheduled to work today, although I was thinking of asking you to work an extra shift in food prep. I hope you're not here to tell me you're quitting. There's been a spate of that in the last few days."

"Spade?" Win didn't understand and wanted to, in case people were being forced to quit or something.

"S-p-a -t-e. It means a lot of stuff happening all of a sudden. Like in this case, a lot people have quit in a short time."

Win had just wasted half a day on a fruitless search for Elias. Perhaps he quit too, and left town. "No, Mr. Grant, I ain't quitting. I wanted to ask you, like, now that Mr. Rhus is gone, if you could help me with something."

"Let's hear it."

"Um, you mind if I shut the door?"

136

A look of mild surprise. "Go ahead."

The room seemed to shrink in size with the door closed. Win cast off his anxiety and met Mose's eyes with a look of practiced innocence. "Rhus was in charge of the visas and took mine to update it, and now that he's dead, I don't know how to get it back. Could you maybe get it for me?"

"You heard about the murder, I see. Word got around here fast when the cops showed up to interview the staff. Half my kitchen help took off in fright. The way they acted, you'd think they'd seen a murder happen right in front of their eyes." Mose cocked his head. "What's this about Mr. Rhus having your visa?"

Win had anticipated the question. "Mr. Rhus wanted to hire me to work for him full time, said he needed the visa for a day or two. Now, after what happened, I don't know how I'll get it back."

"So, you were going to quit. Just not today. Never mind, it's a free country. Relax, I'm not trying to give you a hard time." Mose thought for a minute. "I don't know how I can help. The visa ain't here."

"I think he maybe had it in his home office."

"Doesn't your mother work there? Maybe she can get it for you?"

What else does he know about my family? He must have talked to that big-mouth cook who used to be tight with my mom. "Rhus's house is a crime scene. My mother can't get in, and she's too freaked out to go back there anyway." Win believed both of those conditions might be true, but it might complicate things if he let Mose know his mother, like his sister, had vanished. "Mr. Grant, if you can't get the visa, is there at least a copy in my records I could have? I don't feel safe without it. My mother was out shopping the other day and a cop stopped her and asked her for proof of citizenship. She was lucky she had her visa with her."

"Yet you gave Mr. Rhus your visa without making a copy?"

Win cursed himself for extemporizing about his mother. "I know it was stupid, I didn't think about it until afterward."

"Guess you learned your lesson." Mose nodded and Win felt more hopeful until Mose asked, "Have you called his law office?"

"I did. Talked to a woman who said they were going through his stuff, to call again in a few days."

"There you go then."

"Even if they find it, in the meantime I'm without papers."

"I see. There might be a copy on file upstairs in Human Resources, but I can't just go up there and ask for it. I'm not authorized take out personnel files." Mose leaned back in his swivel chair and chewed at a fingernail.

"I guess I can't ask you to get into trouble," said Win, preparing to leave.

"Wait a sec, tell you what, I'm willing to stick my neck out for you if you'll help me. I want to get a better feel for how this place operates."

"I make sandwiches. What do I know?"

"But you've been here a while and also worked with Mr. Rhus. How'd that happen, anyway, you working for him?"

Win didn't know where Mose was going with this, but was relieved to hear he wasn't asking about his predecessor, Elias.

"He, uh, met my mother, and hired her to be his housekeeper, so we got to know each other. He said he was starting up a business and he wanted to give me a chance to get out of the kitchens. I lucked out, I guess."

"His new business importing foreign workers?"

Win's heart missed a beat. "I'm not sure exactly what all he was doing, I just started and was really just an errand boy."

"Can you tell me when the hiring here started being outsourced to Mr. Rhus? First I heard he was a lawyer for West Ridge, but then I learned I wouldn't get to do any of the hiring because he would take care of it."

"I don't know that stuff. All I can tell you is Mr. Rhus told me West Ridge has trouble hiring American workers and wanted an expert like him to find foreign ones." To his discomfort, Win noticed a quickening in Mose's eyes.

"Did Mr. Rhus provide services for the foreign workers after they got hired? Like maybe renew or update their visas like he was doing for you?"

"I have no idea. I don't think I can tell you anything you don't already know." Win doubted he'd said enough to trade for his visa and Mose already seemed a bit suspicious.

"Well, thanks for the information. Let's keep this conversation between you and me. Back to your situation, Win. I know you only work here part-time, but if you are still planning to quit, I would like advance warning."

"Sure."

At least Mose didn't seem to know about any of Elias's criminal activities. Before Win could bring up his visa again, the phone buzzed.

"I have to take this call. Before you go, give me your cell number. I can't promise, but if I can get my hands on the document you want, I'll call you."

Chapter 30

Kendra started the engine, leaned back in the car seat, and turned on her MP3 player, but no sound came out of the ear buds. Their time had come. She coiled them up and stuffed them in the little trash bag she kept behind the passenger seat. For lack of anything else to do while she idled the engine, she opened the Mustang's glove box and looked for a map to read before she remembered the print was too small for her to make out in this light. Defeated, she rested her head against the seat. What could be more boring than sitting in a car while the battery charged?

Something must be draining the battery because it seemed to run out of juice awfully fast if the car wasn't driven every day. Until she took the car in for a checkup, she was taking the precaution of idling the engine on a regular basis, especially since the car had been mostly sitting since her eye surgery. Her brother certainly didn't want to see her, so why rush to spend money to repair his precious car?

She sat back and surveyed the neighborhood around her. The FOR SALE sign was still on the lawn of the house across the street. Several buildings on this block were eyesores built in the 1960s, but many carefully restored, 19th century homes remained. Mature trees lined the street, their red leaves forming a lacy arch high overhead. A young man on a skateboard suddenly appeared, then zoomed quickly into an alley. His destination was where kids congregated before launching themselves downhill toward the street, unconcerned they might be hit by a passing car. Not that there was any traffic, motor or pedestrian, at this hour. Her neighbors who were not at work were probably walking around the lagoon in the park or having coffee at the lunch counter near Ninth Street.

The monotony broke at last when the house two doors down emitted an elderly man and an overweight younger woman dressed in a short dress and low heels. A little boy followed, wobbling unsteadily on an orange plastic tricycle. The man bent stiffly to kiss the toddler, got into a parked car and drove away, while the woman and child came down the sidewalk in Kendra's direction.

They'd just passed the Mustang when the toddler's tricycle veered left into the sloping driveway just behind Kendra's car, picked up speed and rolled out of control toward the street. His mother ran to catch him and managed to corral him just before he hit the Mustang's rear bumper.

The woman retrieved the tricycle and scolded the boy. Instead of heeding her, he babbled and pointed at something on the ground under the Mustang. His mother cocked her head and bent down. Kendra couldn't see what they were looking at. She hoped it wasn't a dead bird. The woman rearranged her skirt, which had hiked up from her exertions, and clomped over to Kendra.

Kendra lowered the window. "Is something wrong?"

"Do you know your car is leaking?" asked the woman in an accusatory tone, as if Kendra had deliberately tried to drown her son in poison. Then, without waiting for Kendra's reaction, she hefted her son to one hip, grabbed up the tricycle and stormed away.

"I didn't know and thanks for telling me," mouthed Kendra under her breath. Just her luck, she might have to get the Mustang fixed now. She killed the motor and got out. Hopefully, a neighbor had been watering the lawn or hosing their own car off. The water or suds, or whatever, would have drained to the lower lying end of the street, like where her car was parked.

She saw nothing odd until she got down on all fours and inspected the area between the rear wheels. She couldn't see a leak, only a small puddle of toxic looking liquid. That couldn't be good.

The Auto Club truck arrived after twenty nervous minutes. A copper-haired young man came toward her with a clipboard under his arm. He looked all of eighteen years old and had several visible body piercings, but greeted her in a cheerful businesslike way, as if her car trouble wasn't anything to worry about. Unexpectedly, his attitude did make her feel better.

"Something's leaking from the car," she said, after thanking him for coming.

He peered under the car. "I see that. You got gas in the tank?"

"At least half a tank. I checked the gauge. I was running the engine to charge up the battery when I noticed the problem."

He examined the pool of liquid again. "Isn't coolant or brake fluid." He dabbed a finger in the liquid, brought it to his nose and sniffed. "Yep, it's gas. Guess you got a leak in the tank or fuel line."

"Is it safe to drive?"

"Let me have another look." He lay down and eased his head under the car. A moment later he slid back out and stood. "It's a slow leak, but with gas, I wouldn't take the chance."

"What do think I should I do?"

"Get it to a garage."

What else could she do? "Okay, can you please tow it to the dealer, but can I ride along with you?"

"Sure, lady." He took down the dealer's address. "Can I have your credit card?"

"I have to go in the house and get my purse. I'll be right back."

Then it hit her that the dealership was at least a mile from the bus line back home and ten from the dog she had to walk this evening. Maybe Maretta could pick her up? No, darn it, Maretta had gone to a professional growth workshop in the Bay Area and wouldn't be back in time. Perfect. One thing after another. The fun never seemed to end. But on the plus side, how could things get any worse from here?

Chapter 31

Kendra took a final gulp and set the beer can precariously close to the edge of the table. The kitchen was spinning around her but she didn't care. As she reached for a fresh can, Maretta swooped up the remainder of the six-pack.

"Hey, I want another one," Kendra whined.

Maretta stowed the three remaining cans in the fridge and came back to the table with a box of Cheez-Its, Kendra's favorite comfort food, as a replacement. "I hope you haven't been like this all day," she said reprovingly.

"Not all day, just the moments when I think about my life." Kendra shoved a fistful of crackers into her mouth.

"I wasn't asking if you've been acting insane—it doesn't even need asking. What I meant was, have you been drinking all day?"

"Just since I capped off my fabulous day with a two hour bus trip and a dog walk with the Rottweiler from hell."

"I'm sorry I was out of touch. My cell phone battery ran down. I didn't know you'd been calling me until I got home and charged it."

"Beer!" Kendra demanded with petulance.

"No way. You had enough. Six minus three is—"

"Three. See? I can do arithmetic. I'm sober."

"Stop acting like a brat. You're making me regret I came over. I was already in my PJ's when I saw your message and who knows when I'll get back into them tonight."

"Is it that late? Sorry."

"Late enough. Past eleven. Look, you can't explain what put you in this mood if you keep on drinking. Finish your story, and then maybe we'll both kick back with a beer."

"What did I tell you already? I forget."

Maretta groaned and took a chair at the table. "Apart from asking me three times if I want a beer, all you said was that you had your car towed and the mechanic found duct tape on the gas tank. That's a joke, right?"

"No, no joke. Someone duct taped two firecrackers to my gas

tank. One was still there because it didn't go off."

"Back up a sec. Firecrackers?"

"Yeah, the mechanic said they were M1000s." Kendra spread her thumb and forefinger. "About this size, see?"

"Aren't they illegal?"

"Does it matter?" Kendra stood up.

Maretta put out an arm to block her. "No more beer."

"I'm getting water, okay? The crackers are wedged in my teeth."

"Go for it, but in your condition, maybe you should use a plastic glass," Maretta said with mock concern. Turning serious, she continued, "Someone put real thought into doing that, almost like it's not just random vandalism."

"Can you blame me for getting drunk? And lucky me, I get the only car mechanic in the county who also happens to be a volunteer fireman, and knows enough about incendiary devices to totally freak me out."

"I'm feeling a bit of that right now," said Maretta.

"It's not that bad. The mechanic told me the way cars are made these days they don't explode into balls of fire except in the movies."

"Let me get this straight. He tried to reassure you by telling you the bomb someone taped to your car wouldn't actually have exploded in a ball of flames?"

"I think he wanted me to know it wouldn't have killed me. But he did insist on calling the cops to make a report."

"I would hope so. Still, it does make a difference. Maybe the intention wasn't actually to hurt you. Also, only one firecracker went off, so we can assume the jerk who did it isn't a pro at bomb making."

Kendra gave her a sour look. "I knew I could count on you to cheer me up."

"I'm trying, but it's the best I can do at the moment. By the way, how much is the repair bill?"

"Couple hundred bucks with labor. The damage wasn't more extensive because only one firecracker went off, leading to a slow leak from a tiny rupture in the gas tank. I hope my insurance doesn't have a hidden clause like: 'not responsible when some lowlife bombs your car.'"

"Or a teacher exclusion clause. Nothing would really surprise me."

"I feel jinxed, like I've been attracting that random negativity"—she made air quotes—"the talk show gurus are always talking about." She took a sip of water and made a face. "Come on, one more beer, Maretta, please? I deserve it after a dead client, a rock through my door and a bomb under my car."

"So you're thinking they're all related?"

"Oh. I wasn't really. But now you mention it...." Kendra attempted to stack crackers into a tower while she considered her friend's words. Maretta loved to tell her to stay away from wild speculation, but now was doing it herself. Still, what she said was feasible. "Okay, you got me started. But if we suppose the two vandalisms are connected, the timeline still makes it hard to connect them with the murder. If someone thinks I'm a threat because I was at the murder scene, where does the rock come in?"

"Tell me again. What happened first, the rock or Rhus getting murdered?"

"The rock, then me finding his body, then the bombs on the gas tank. It's hard to see what one has to do with the other. Even if the order of events was different, this isn't a movie, you know, where the killer is trying to eliminate a witness. I didn't see anything, and I don't know anything about Rhus or his life. How could I be a threat?"

"The killer only has to think you saw something and doesn't want you telling the police."

"I think I'm sorry I called you...."

"Chalk it up as payback for how lousy I'm going to feel all day tomorrow—whoops, that's all day today. And as long as I'm on a roll, here's another thought. What if someone heard you talking to the Bridges guy about the flyer? Both Imelda and Reyna were strangled and dumped on the street. There definitely could be a connection. Remember, you went looking for Reyna. Suppose what's been happening to you is connected to the dead girls, not with you finding Rhus's body?"

"Wow, that's possible. But there's still a tie-in to Mr. Rhus. I first met him at the dog fair, right after I got the flyer and he got one too. I saw him throw his away like he thought he'd catch a disease from it."

"Maybe he has, if you get my meaning."

"I don't see someone like Roger Rhus picking up whores on Jefferson Boulevard. Men like him don't have to pay for sex."

"Don't be naïve, Kendra."

"Okay, you're right. He could have heard me say I knew Imelda and maybe he knew her too, in the way you're saying. But he's dead, so he wasn't the one trying to blow up my car."

"No, but he might have been part of an organization and someone there wants you out of the way."

"In that case, the same person might have killed him, and the girls, and thinks I know something about it." She gave a momentary shiver.

"Crazy as it sounds, that theory ties everything together. Except the rock, which really might just be coincidence."

"Well, thanks for all the new ideas, for totally freaking me out again. I don't know who's worse, you or the cop who responded to the mechanic's call."

"I didn't ask, what did the police say? Did they already know about you being at a murder scene? What are they doing about the car?"

Kendra sat up and puffed out her chest to mimic the officer who'd come to the auto repair shop. "He said, 'Ma'am, do you know anyone who wants to kill you?'"

"You're kidding. He asked you that?"

"Yeah, he did."

"I give up." Maretta went to the fridge and came back with two beers. She handed one to Kendra and popped the top of her own. "Your story has reached the point that requires a stiff reinforcement. Go on, what happened next?"

"Nothing much. They just asked questions. From the way they talked, I assumed they already knew something about Rhus, but they didn't ask me and I didn't bring it up."

"They gonna look for fingerprints on the car?"

Kendra wanted to tell it her own way. She waved her hand in a "down girl" motion. "One of the cops asked me where the car's been parked recently—easy enough for me to recall, because I haven't been driving much. The car dealer's outside the city limits, in a different jurisdiction, so the case will be transferred over." She took a sip of beer and peered into little hole in the top, staring at the liquid inside. "I swear, they're selling these cans half full."

Maretta snatched the beer out of Kendra's hand. "Will you get to the point already?"

"Sorry. Here's the kicker. After I told him I had left the car parked for an hour in the lot at school, he immediately lost interest. Dismissed the whole thing as another sorry episode in the long-running drama of Standard High."

"Did you tell him you're a teacher?"

"Yeah, but it made things worse. He told me to take it up with the administration, like it's a paperwork issue to be settled between them and me. He didn't even bat an eye when I suggested a student could be stalking me. Give me my beer back now, okay?"

"Unbelievable." Maretta reluctantly returned Kendra's beer. "As infuriating as the Standard High theory is, maybe there's truth in it. Perhaps you weren't singled out. When you parked in the student lot, your car automatically became a contestant in the Bomb of the Month contest."

"I thought of that. A kid could have done it easy while I was parked at school, and none of the other students would have ratted him out. A firecracker going off would have been mistaken for a car backfiring or maybe the morning's first shooting. Just another normal day at Standard High."

Maretta nodded. "Taping a firecracker on a gas tank is just the kind of thing a student might try after watching too many Bruce Willis movies, or whoever the action-adventure movie king of the moment is, I don't keep up. Remember that tenth grade boy who blew off two fingers playing with fireworks?"

"The officer sure acted like the whole incident was a waste of his time. Really, you would have loved the way the tone of his investigation changed from CSI to South Park as soon as I said Standard High."

"That tells me he didn't know you just found a murdered man, and you didn't tell him either, did you, Kendra." The remark came out as a statement rather than a question.

"I didn't want to complicate things." She drained the last of her drink and smothered a burp. "Look, let's not let my beer brain and your fatigue blow things out of proportion. In the past, I made simple things complicated, and jumped into situations I should

147

have ignored. No more, I learned my lesson."

"About time. Just don't go too far in the other direction and close your eyes to what's happening around you." Maretta stole a Cheez-It from Kendra's leaning tower, which collapsed immediately, sending crackers everywhere. Bobbins heard the clickity-tap-tap-tap, galloped into the kitchen, and leapt on the table before Kendra could stop him.

"Bad kitty." She dumped the cat on the floor, but not before he'd eaten several crackers and knocked the box over in his haste to capture the rest. Kendra looked with dismay at the mess while Bobbins retreated in a huff to wash his paws. Maretta laughed at them both.

"Where were we, before we were so rudely interrupted?" Kendra cast a sour look at her cat.

"Not repeating past mistakes," answered Maretta.

"Ah yes. Mistakes. I need clean break with the past, so I decided to go ahead with it."

"Go ahead with what? Your cat is making more sense than you are."

"I'm going to ask my neighbor to be my pretend date at Brian's fundraiser. Brian will see us together, see I replaced him with a guy any woman would be thrilled to have. Even if it doesn't work, I need an ego boost and going there will be a way to prove to myself I can dish out as much as I can take." Kendra put the cracker box away and returned with another beer.

"You've had enough." Maretta snatched it away before Kendra could open it. "You're talking total nonsense, begging for trouble. Going on your fake date won't prove anything to anyone, especially not Brian, and if you were sober, you'd see that. I'm going to put you to bed before you think of any more crazy ideas."

Chapter 32

Thursday, October 21

When Kendra waylaid him before he'd even reached his apartment, Win knew she'd been watching for him to come home. She stammered, "I hope you don't mind me coming up on you like this. I've been wanting to talk to you."

He gave her a wicked grin. "Are you stalking me?" He cradled his helmet in one arm and unlocked his door. "Then this is your lucky day, because usually there's a line out here."

She returned his smile with one of her own. "There was a line, but I took care of your ardent followers. I told them you gave me an STD."

Win found himself speechless at the comeback. He'd misjudged her, pegged her as an introverted intellectual, although packaged nice enough to make him wonder what she'd be like if she let her hair down. Finding her here was an interesting development. How long had she been on the lookout for him? For the last few days he'd been out day and night looking for his sister, chasing leads that had gone nowhere.

Kendra stood primly on his doorstep, as if she wanted a formal invitation to come in, but when he held the door for her, she took one step and hesitated on the threshold. He immediately saw the problem and went to the window. "Sorry about that." The drapes rattled as he opened them to admit the morning light. "I wasn't trying to pull an early Halloween on you. See? No coffins, no skeletons. Do you want something to drink? I have tap water, Pepsi and tequila."

"No thanks, I'm good."

"Well, if you don't mind I'll have a soda."

Win liked the way she propped her elbows on the big table to watch him while he got his drink and something to snack on. She was attracted, he could tell, but something made her hesitate. Maybe their age difference? She definitely had a reason for coming. Maybe to give him a chance to make a move? He cracked open his Pepsi and set a bag of potato chips on the counter between them. "So, what's up? I hope things are going better for you. What's that expression, All quiet on the western front?"

"You got the expression right, but unfortunately, the quiet part doesn't exactly apply. A student from Standard High just turned up dead."

A horrible, unthinkable image flashed through his mind: Sandi lifeless and cold on a morgue table, covered with a white sheet. He swallowed hard to force down the gorge rising in his throat. Somehow he managed to reply, "How awful. One of your students?"

"From last year, but I just saw her again the other day. Sorry, I shouldn't have even brought it up, but it hit me kind of hard."

Win exhaled. Not Sandi then. She just transferred to Standard High this fall. He felt weak with relief. He needed to know more, but how could he ask for the dead girl's name without it sounding odd? "You don't have to be sorry. How'd she die? An accident?"

"No, she was strangled. But she had so much heroin in her she'd have died of an overdose anyway." Kendra closed her eyes as if to clear away an image she couldn't handle. "I apologize for dumping this on you. I guess I'm the wrong person to ask 'what's up?' because I never seem to be able to just say 'not much' and leave it at that. I'll shut up before I go on about students being sucked into crime and drug use. Forget you even asked, okay?"

Elias had been on to something when he said to watch her. Kendra could be leading him on, mentioning the dead girl to sound him out. He opened a kitchen cabinet and pretended to search for something to buy time to think. He'd wait and see what he could find out about her motives later. "So, Kendra, why have you been looking for me?"

"I hate to admit it, but I came over to ask you for a favor."

"A favor? No problem, I already told you to ask if you need something." He popped a chip into his mouth and took a deep drink of soda.

"Well, this is a little different. Actually, it's kind of embarrassing.... I know it's short notice but I wanted to ask if you could pretend to be my date tomorrow, Friday night?"

Win stifled a laugh, swallowed the wrong way and began to cough. He waved off her concern. "It's nothing, a chip caught in my throat." He coughed again. "All better now."

She's into me, he thought, only she's come up with a little twist. How perfect. He wanted to gain her trust and find out what she knew, just wasn't expecting to find out so easy what she knew about sex, too.

"You want to pretend we're on a date? I'm not good enough for a real one? Usually chicks want the real thing." He raised his shirt to let her see his washboard abs, but stopped preening when he read the look on her face. She wants to back out now, thinks I'm laughing at her. Well, maybe I am, a little, but I'm going to enjoy every minute of our pretend date. "Sorry, Kendra, sometimes I don't know when to stop. Mind telling me why you want the date?"

"I shouldn't have been so blunt. I'm not saying you aren't good enough to date me, but I'm not up for real dating at the moment. I'm coming out of a bad relationship. That's where the favor comes in." She fished in the chip bag, avoiding Win's gaze.

"Go on."

"It's like this, my former boyfriend can't seem to get it into his head I'm totally done with him. I broke up with him almost a year ago, but Brian still won't let go. He called me until I changed my phone number. Then he started showing up at my door. Finally, to shake him off, I moved here. But he's found me again."

Win shook his head. "He sounds sort of creepy."

"Pathetic is more like it. He had his own business but it tanked with the economy being like it is. I think the experience really threw him. He wants a shoulder to cry on more than anything else. Without going into details, he doesn't deserve my friendship or support."

"Sounds to me like he wants you to support him all right, did he ask for money?"

"No."

"Well, do you want me to be at your place when he shows up? I can roll out a few of my boxing moves." He took a stance and threw a few easy punches.

"No, no violence."

"Don't worry. Actually, I sort of suck at martial arts. I just do it to keep in shape. So it wouldn't be much of a fight, but I bet I could scare him off."

"No, I don't want you to start a fight. The whole date idea is to make him give up on me when he sees I've moved on, hooked up with someone else. Then he'll move on."

"I've been told many times I rate as a ten, so he'll be positively crushed." Win laughed, although he wasn't sure if he was pleased or annoyed to be seen as a boy toy. "I'm flattered and I'll be glad to help." He aimed a dart of sexual energy at her, feeling a rush of anticipation when he saw the flush in her cheeks.

"Thanks. I know all this sounds odd."

"No, it sounds like fun. So, what's the plan?"

"Brian plays in an amateur basketball league and they're having a fundraiser at Pavano's Restaurant. I know he'll be there. I thought we could go there for dinner and get a table near the entrance to the private dining room, where he'll see us for sure. I know it's short notice but—"

Win's cell phone rang. He saw her eyes widen after hearing the first bars of Secret Garden. She'd probably had him pegged for heavy metal, not Bruce Springsteen. When he read the caller ID, he motioned for her to stay tight. As he moved to the bedroom for privacy, he decided he needed to change the ring tone. People either thought he was gay or a romantic nerd, and when he explained he just liked the lyrics they started to laugh. Must be a cultural thing.

"This is Win."

"I have what you asked for, but I don't want to give it to you at work."

"Wow. Thanks for helping. Want me to meet you somewhere?"

"Yeah, tomorrow evening good for you?"

"Sure, where?"

"You got a pen?"

Win took down the information and ended the call elated. His luck had turned. He came back to Kendra and apologized for the rudeness.

"Don't worry," she said. "At least you weren't texting while we were talking."

"Okay, you were saying tomorrow around dinner time?"

"Yes, I'd like to be over there by 7:30. Um, do you mind if I have that Pepsi now?"

He passed a can to her. "Works for me. I have to say I'm looking forward to it. I've never been on a fake date before."

"We don't have to stay too long, just until Brian sees us."

Win planned on that, on getting her out of there right after it happened, and bringing her back to his place. "So, where is this Pavano's we're going to?" he asked in a businesslike voice.

"If you have a computer I can show you on MapQuest."

"Yeah, let me get out my laptop."

As Win headed for his bedroom, he heard Kendra let out a deep sigh of relief. He felt the same way. She didn't know anything about him except what he'd told her or she'd never have asked him out. It couldn't have worked out better if he'd planned it. She'd never know she'd be helping him more than the other way around.

Chapter 33

Friday, October 22

Kendra leaned forward, chin almost touching Win's back, doing her best to enjoy the proximity and the motorcycle ride. Knowing she'd see Brian soon, she felt her courage slipping. She'd prepared for the event by rehearsing all possible scenarios again and again, and carefully choosing her outfit: a black mini dress and leggings paired with blood red, mid-heeled, ankle boots and a matching shoulder bag and leather jacket. To top it off, she'd deliberately put her hair up exactly the way Brian hated it. The jacket had been a godsend on the bike ride here. Kendra remembered October bike rides from her college days, but not the cold wind part.

Apparently, Win had decided to play his hot date role to the hilt. An ultra-tight cashmere sweater accentuated his muscular shoulders and flat stomach. And she'd had to tear her eyes away from his form-fitting black jeans. Good looks, check and mate. With his cocky air of assurance, Win would easily be taken for a young professional on a hot date. No one would think he was too young for her either.

As they were driving away from her house, Win asked Kendra if he could make a brief stop on route to Pavano's. Still intoxicated by his appearance, she'd agreed without even asking him why. She just leaned into his strong back and held on. By the time they hit the freeway she was deep in thought, planning what she'd say to Brian.

She came out of her rehearsals when she felt the Honda decelerate. Alarmed, she saw they were taking a freeway exit in the middle of nowhere. Nothing she could do but hold on and wait. The road narrowed to little more than one lane, and after several bends, petered out at a small, unpaved parking lot hemmed in by dense foliage. A wooden picnic table stood to one side as if it had lost its companions and no one cared to find it. The fast running American River peeked through a barricade of gnarled tree branches.

Win hopped off the bike and stretched. Removing his helmet, he looked around carefully, as if searching for something. This was the last place she'd expected Win to bring her when he mentioned having to run an errand. What if he just wanted to get her alone in an isolated spot? A lone car sat in the lot, but she didn't hear or see anyone. The greenery on all sides seemed to close in on her. Anything could happen here and no one would see or hear. She chucked off her helmet and marched toward the road.

"Where are you going?" called Win. He caught up with her in three strides and twirled her around to face him.

"I'd like to know what we're doing here," she said, taking a step back. She yanked her cell phone from her shoulder bag. "If I don't like the answer, I'm calling 911." Would her phone even work in this place?

"Take it easy. I'm meeting my boss. He picked this place, told me he was going to be doing some fishing. It wasn't my first choice. I got allergies." As if on cue, Win turned away and sneezed.

Kendra thought the sneeze was genuine, but not the rest. Fishing? She folded her arms across her chest. "Try again. What are you doing, Win, dealing drugs or something?"

"No," he said indignantly. He paused as if making a decision. "I should have told you. My sister ran away and my boss is helping me find her. She's kind of…wild. She hangs out with some bad people. The boss heard some talk, but didn't want to put his job in danger by talking about it at work, said to meet him here instead. He said he had a lead on where I might find her. Mose is a nice guy. He's the one who called when you were at my house."

"Why didn't he tell you over the phone?"

"No clue. Maybe he wasn't alone at the time and couldn't talk."

Kendra got a ninety-nine percent on her internal BS meter, but decided to probe a bit more before she panicked. "Is that his car?" She pointed at the white Honda.

"I guess. Look, you can wait right here if it makes you feel safer while I go see if he's down at the river fishing. Okay? It will only take a minute and then we'll go to the restaurant." Without waiting for her answer, he jogged down a narrow dirt path and quickly disappeared from view.

155

Kendra checked the time on her phone. Unwilling to take him at his word, she'd give him five minutes to do whatever he was doing. For all she knew, this "boss" didn't even exist. Why had she never asked Win exactly where he worked, what he did for a living? What had really brought him here? She resolved to see what he was really up to.

Kendra started down the same path he'd taken, relieved to see it did, at least, lead toward the river. A few hundred yards on, she heard two male voices and moved toward them through the underbrush. She closed the distance until she could hear them clearly, only stopping when she thought she might be discovered.

Win definitely was one of the speakers. If she leaned to one side she could see the two men through the foliage. Win faced her, talking to a man wearing a dark jacket and a baseball cap. The man's voice sounded oddly familiar, but even if he turned toward her, at this distance and in the fading light, she wouldn't be able to identify him.

Win took something from the man and put it into his pocket, saying, "Thanks, Mose. I guess I need to get a new lawyer now. That'll really cost me. Any way you could lend me a hundred bucks? I'll pay you back when I get my next check."

The man rubbed the back of his neck and adjusted his hat. "I might be able to swing that in exchange for a bit of confidential information about Elias Carmona."

Win's head jerked back when he heard the name Elias. Why such a big reaction, Kendra wondered.

"The old kitchen boss? Yeah, I know him from work, but I wouldn't say I really know him if you get what I mean. Why?"

"There's been gossip going around the kitchen. Remember, I told you how employees have been quitting all of a sudden? I think he might have something to do with it. I know he was manager right before me, but people in the front office didn't even want to mention his name. So I got curious about why he left West Ridge, and asked some of the old-timers about him, but they just gave me funny looks. A few days later, out of the blue, a guy calls from upstairs, says, 'Elias Carmona's been rehired, find a spot for him.' No explanation."

Win shrugged. "Yeah, I heard he's back."

"Soon as word got around, I had kitchen help quitting left and right, but nobody'd say why they were leaving. Then, his first day back, I overheard him on the phone talking to Mr. Rhus. But Elias is a U.S. citizen, right? I know Rhus helped you with your papers. Why would Elias need to talk to him?"

Kendra covered her mouth to keep from screaming. Win knows Mr. Rhus? Not only that, he hasn't mentioned his runaway sister. Does he even have a sister?

Win shuffled his feet, rearranging the pebbles with his expensive leather boots. "Beats me."

"Elias hasn't shown up at work since Rhus was murdered. Does he usually disappear without saying anything?"

Kendra furiously stormed out of the bushes, taking satisfaction over the way both men jumped at her unexpected appearance. Making a beeline for Win, she shouted, "Why didn't you tell me you knew Mr. Rhus? What kind of games are you playing? You think it's funny telling me a load of—"

"Kendra?"

She whirled around at the sound of her name. "Linc?"

No wonder the voice had seemed familiar. There was no mistaking him from up close, even though without his signature beard and his red hair dyed a mousy brown, he'd become a nondescript, thirty year-old man. Did he want to be able to vanish in a crowd? Her heart ached for him. Their eyes met, and for a split second she saw a flicker of something more than shock. Win looked from one to the other with his mouth flapping, completely at a loss for words.

Linc recovered first. "Nice to see you, little sister. But Mose Grant is the name now."

"Why...how..."

"Long story," said Linc, reaching to pick a twig out of her disarranged hair. He shook his head in the disapproving way she remembered from growing up. "I guess I owe you an explanation."

"You're darn right," said Kendra, blinking away the tears that began when she felt the light touch of his fingers on her cheek. "Why haven't you called me?"

"I'm working double shifts. I just haven't had the chance. I'm really sorry."

She detected an undertone, but nothing added up. Was he trying to tell her something? She was too confused to play along.

157

"What are you doing here?"

"The short explanation is," he continued, "I know Win from work and he asked me for some help."

"Really?" Kendra pointed an accusatory finger at Win. "You, with your missing sister. Did you make that whole thing up?"

"She's really missing. Honest, I—"

"Settle that later, if you don't mind," Linc snapped.

Kendra glared at her brother. "Okay. Tell me why you haven't called me. No. Skip that." She chopped her hand in the air. "Why you aren't using your real name?" She was whining like a dented saxophone but she didn't care. "And why are you—" The cautionary look on her brother's face stopped her. Now she'd really done it. If he's avoided getting in touch before, now he had good reason.

"I'm good." Win held up his hands, palms toward them. "I won't say a thing.

"Not if you're smart," warned Mose.

Kendra caught her breath at the implied threat. It transformed her brother into a total stranger. "What's with the name? You don't have a reason to hide, not unless you're—are you doing something illegal?"

"No way, sis. I'll tell you everything, I promise, but now isn't the time."

"What is this the time for?" demanded Kendra. She turned to Win. "Why are we really out here?"

Win spoke to Mose instead. "Look, you asked me about Elias. Are the cops looking for him?"

"Everyone working at West Ridge is a suspect in Rhus's murder, including Elias. If you know where he—wait a sec. How do you know Kendra?"

"He's my neighbor," she answered. "We were friends before I found out he's a liar."

Mose pursed his lips the way he used to when she was eight years old and wanted him to take her side in an argument with one of her little friends. "I'll let you two hash things out yourselves. I need to go. Kendra, give me your phone and I'll put in my number."

He's definitely keeping things back from me, she thought. What's he really involved with? Can I get Win to tell me?

158

"Maybe you can keep her out of trouble, Win, although judging from history, that might be impossible," said Mose grimly.

She stepped forward to keep him from going, but he gave her a quick, one-armed hug, and walked away. She flapped her arms against her sides in frustration. "He's not going fishing."

"Guess not," said Win. "Listen, I didn't mean to lie to you. I can explain, but it will take a while. Um, do you still want to go to the restaurant?"

"The date is cancelled," she replied. "For all time."

"I know you're mad, but things got away from me. My sister really is missing, and after what Mose told me, I think she might be in big trouble."

Kendra's legs ached. Her boots were wrong for this terrain. She turned and stomped up the path but Win caught hold of her arm.

"Where you going?"

Kendra jerked free and pointed toward the parking lot. "We need to have a long talk and I need to sit down."

Chapter 34

The powerful sound of the rushing river filled the silence between them. Win had come to an end of his story. As if he sensed the distance between them had grown, he reached across the derelict picnic table to take her hand, but Kendra pulled her fingers from his grip, pressing her palm against the table in rejection. His skin felt moist, even though the temperature had plunged with onset of night. She rocked back a bit, folding her arms across her chest while she weighed Win's words against his actual past behavior. His nervous sweat was another sign he still wasn't being completely honest in his explanations. Add in her mixed emotions and she wanted to bang her head on the table. She moved her head away before she actually tried it. Her hair responded by falling out of the elegant twist she'd worked so hard to fashion. Did it matter how she looked? She wouldn't be seeing Brian or anyone else she knew tonight. Just the guy across the table. Were all men liars, or just the ones she found herself attracted to?

"So you'll help me find Sandi, won't you?" he asked.

"We're not talking about that right now, or I'm not. You're supposed to be explaining yourself. You want me to believe you never met Mr. Rhus personally, only heard his name mentioned at work."

"Right, and you never gave a name when you told me you found a dead body. I didn't know it was him or I'd have said something."

Kendra decided to let that go for the moment. "If you came here because of your sister, what did my brother give you?"

"An address where Sandi might be."

"What did you mean about having to get a lawyer?"

"In case she's in jail."

"Why would my brother know anything about your sister in the first place?"

"People gossip at work, he listens."

"Tell me more about where you work, this West Ridge Retirement Center."

"Mose is the kitchen boss and he's your brother, how come you don't know anything?"

Kendra almost slapped him, but then realized it was a reasonable question. Win wasn't trying to provoke her. "Win, stick to the point. Why would people you work with be talking about your sister?"

"Not Sandi. Elias. Remember, Mose was talking about Elias."

Kendra gaped at Win. "You're taking in circles and I'm losing patience."

"Sorry. Sandi and Elias met a few years ago, at West Ridge. He was kitchen boss then and she used to come by sometimes during my shift to see me. Elias had a thing for her. I tried hard to discourage it. I stopped worrying about the two of them last summer when he went to prison, but he got out recently and came back to work."

"Prison? What for?"

"West Ridge has lots of foreign workers. Supposedly, Elias knew the ones he hired were illegal. I don't know if it's 'cause of that stuff or not, but the kitchen staff didn't like him showing up again. There's been a lot of whispering. According to Mose, one of the cooks mentioned she saw Elias out in the neighborhood with my sister a few days ago. She felt bad 'cause she was afraid to tell Elias to leave Sandi alone."

"How old is Sandi?"

"Sixteen."

Kendra frowned. "You think she's with Elias, right? She's underage. So why not contact social services or the police? They could send someone out to pick her up. Don't the cops want to talk to Elias anyway? Maybe they'll find them both together."

"Mose said the same thing, but see, I'm not sure. Maybe Sandi's gotten herself into some bad stuff. She might be doing something the cops wouldn't like. I guess you could say she's sort of out of her head, but she's, like…not really responsible for everything she does. She thinks everyone's out to get her, even tried to kill herself a few times. If the cops or some strangers show up, I'm afraid what she'll do."

"How did your sister get mixed up with Elias?"

"I don't know, he probably said he'd show her a good time, got her phone number and things went from there. Sandi's been

161

out of control for a while."

Kendra massaged her forehead where a tempest was forming. If there was such a thing as karma, hers had been calibrated to attract troubled adolescents. Their problems were wide ranging, the outcomes depressingly repetitive. A quarter of her Special Ed. students spent time in handcuffs before graduation. The majority of the petty crimes they committed resulted from a moment's poor judgment. One impulsive act could easily balloon into a week-long debacle. Afterward, the explanation they gave for their behavior was a bewildering muddle of irrational constructs. She wondered what Sandi's would turn out to be.

"Well, I'm really sorry she's missing." Kendra thought of another curiosity in Win's story. "Didn't your mother report it when Sandi didn't come home?"

"I did. I called her school counselor, asked if she knew anything, but the woman wouldn't talk to me. No one cares about my sister, especially the home where she lives."

"Hold up, your sister doesn't live with your mom?"

"She used to, but she kept running away. So she ended up getting sent to a foster home, that big Cap one." Not giving Kendra a chance to speak, he added, "She's always been kinda strange. None of this is my mother's fault."

"Do you know who her roommate is at the Home?" Kendra wondered if Sandi had been Reyna's missing roommate. In that case, Sandi might be in greater danger than Win thought.

"No, if she told me, I don't remember. What's it matter, anyway? I'm going to find Sandi, and I want you to help. She never listens to me, but you're a woman, and you work with kids like her, don't you?

"Yes, I do, but if finding her means finding Elias, it sounds like a bad idea to me. From what you're telling me, your sister really might be better off if the cops locate her."

Win spat back, "You sound just like the high and mighty teachers who made me cut class. Except you're in even less of a position to talk down to me, a dog-walking ex-teacher with an ex-con brother. Before you decide who's bad and who's dangerous, ask yourself about Mose. He knew Mr. Rhus, so he's a suspect, too. Maybe he's the one who killed him."

"You—" Kendra was too shocked at Win's sudden attack to

find the right words. She stood up and shouldered her bag. She wanted nothing more to do with him even if she had to hike ten miles to civilization. She headed for what she could see of the road, a faint ribbon that seemed to disappear at the top of a hill. The lights of the city were far away, separated by a darkness made more intimidating by the fog in her eyes.

Win came after her and blocked her path. "Stop. Take it easy. I'm sorry. I was out of line, but I'm a little sensitive about my sister—the same way you're sensitive about Mose."

Kendra recognized she might have gone too far implying Sandi would be better off in police custody, but now they were even. She wasn't going to apologize. "I get it. I wish you good luck finding your sister. Now, let me go."

"You got to help me," he said. "Please, before it's too late. Not for me, for Sandi." His voice broke as if he was close to tears.

She felt herself giving in. Sandi didn't deserve to suffer because Win was a jerk. "Exactly where would we be going?" she asked with resignation.

"A house in Station Circle."

Win still might still be skirting the truth, but she probably could help with Sandi. After all, she'd spent hours dealing with troubled teenagers. She fully understood why Win might not want to lead the police to his sister. Plus, she couldn't forget Win knew a lot about her now, and if she refused him he could retaliate by going over to Standard High and making her family secrets known.

She made her decision. "All right, I'll come."

Chapter 35

Win drove Kendra home from the riverside park, remaining outside while she went to change clothes. Surrounded by the familiarity of her own house, her own life and identity spoke to her, declaring all the good and sane reasons why she should skip Win's hunting expedition. Why get involved? Then she remembered Reyna. She couldn't let that happen to another girl. She quickly changed into a sweater, jeans and flat shoes. Grabbing a jacket, she stuffed a few necessities into the pockets and left the warmth and safety of her home.

When Win suggested they take her car instead of his motorcycle, Kendra objected until Win pointed out that if they found Sandi, his bike wouldn't carry all three of them. He took the keys from her and got behind the wheel. When her seatbelt snapped in place, the full sense of what they were about to do hit her. In profile, Win's tense jaw line mirrored her own apprehension. Neither of them spoke on the way to Station Circle.

The lights were on in Zazzi's Hair Palace, advertising its presence in a garish scribble of neon. The block also held a secondhand appliance store, a tiny burrito joint, a paycheck loan business, and an apartment house that looked like a cheap motel. A man wearing a bandana got up from the metal table outside the burrito place, threw his trash in the general vicinity of a garbage can and strolled away like he owned the street. Kendra wanted to tell him if he wanted it, he could have it.

At Kendra's insistence, they left the Mustang parked under a streetlight in front of the money store where the steady stream of customers might prevent it from being stolen. They walked until they were directly across the street from the two-story building that housed the hair salon. A CLOSED sign hung on the door.

"You sure this is the place?" Kendra asked. "What would Sandi be doing here? Does she want to be a hairdresser?"

"Not that I know of," said Win.

"Must be the wrong address. It doesn't look like anyone lives here." With luck, Win would see it her way and decide to leave.

"There's an apartment on the second floor, see? Elias could live upstairs."

A hefty and very permed blonde woman came into view behind the plate glass window. She was wielding a push broom, thrusting it like an assault on the floor. Her armpits were unshaved, and leg hairs poked out of the gaps in her fishnet stockings. Her upper arms, bared from a sleeveless top, were the size of Kendra's thighs. She had a hard look about her mouth, a look that said she'd earned it through years of low expectations coming to fruition. Kendra had seen the same expression on parents' faces during expulsion hearings.

"Wow, I wonder what she's wearing for Halloween?" said Win.

"Shh! You better talk to her, not me. Something tells me she'll be happier with attention from the opposite sex."

"You could be right," he said.

"You really think Sandi would stay with someone like her?"

"Probably not willingly. There's only one way to find out."

Kendra hunched into her jacket, only to realize the cold came from within her.

"Ready?" asked Win.

He tried the door, found it locked and tapped on the glass. The woman ignored the intrusion at first but when Win kept it up, she yelled, "We're closed!"

Kendra watched, half-admiring, half-disgusted as Win flashed a smile good enough to get him a star on the sidewalk in Hollywood. The woman gave Win a top to bottom look and invited them in. Amazing. At her age, didn't she know better than to open the door to a stranger on the basis of a sexy smile? But then, given the way she looked… Anyway, Ms. Zazzi appeared more than capable of defending herself if the necessity arose.

"Sorry to bother you. I'm looking for someone," Win said as the woman relocked the door. The click of the dead bolt made Kendra's breath catch. Escape route gone!

"I was hoping you were looking for me," said the woman with a suggestive bat of her false eyelashes. She fished a pack of cigarettes from a purse on the counter and offered them around, lighting up when there were no takers.

"I'm looking for Elias Carmona," said Win, holding the

woman's eyes with his own.

Kendra had to admit he really knew how to get what he wanted.

Zazzi examined the lipstick stained filter of her cigarette. The combined whammy of smoke and hair styling chemicals made Kendra's eyes burn. She found a Kleenex in her jacket pocket and dabbed at the flood of tears. "You a friend of his?" she asked.

"My name's Win. I work with him."

"Not anymore you don't. I'm your replacement." A faint smile played on her lips.

Kendra let out an audible gasp that went unnoticed.

Win shook off Zazzi's provocation. "Is Elias around or not? How about Danielle? I hear she hangs here sometimes."

Kendra stopped herself in time from blurting out, "Danielle? Who's Danielle?" Instead, she stood there nodding, like she knew what was going on. If she got out of this in one piece, she'd never believe another word that came out of Win's mouth.

Zazzi looked at Kendra with curiosity, saying, "Your tears won't help that skanky girl."

She thinks the tears are for Danielle? Well, whatever works to soften this Brunhilde. She gave another swipe at her eyes, sniffled, and said, "I'm fine."

Zazzi put out her cigarette, went to a door marked EMPLOYEES ONLY, and passed through, leaving it ajar. Win immediately followed with Kendra several paces behind.

Two steps in, Kendra heard a bang and leaned around Win's shoulder. There was nothing to see but a long corridor with six closed doors, terminating at an exit at the far end. All the doors were fitted with sliding bolts on the outside. Stained and faded wallpaper in a floral print covered the walls and the high ceiling evoked a Francis Bacon painting: peels of mauve and mustard paint hanging down in strips like flayed flesh.

"Where did she go?" whispered Kendra moving up behind him.

"Out the door at the end," said Win. He put an arm out to stop Kendra from going around him. "We have to check these rooms, because the far door has to be the way out."

"Yeah, and the way out sounds good to me."

Win rapped firmly on the first door on his left. The sound

ricocheted uncomfortably in the confined space. Kendra moved back to give room in case a gun-toting gangbanger charged out.

"Where you going?" hissed Win, frowning at her retreat.

He slid off the open padlock, opened the door and stepped in. Nothing happened. When he beckoned, she came to join him in the doorway.

The tiny room was windowless, with bare walls that had once been white. The only light came from a child-size plastic lamp resting on the bare floor adjacent to a narrow mattress covered with a filthy pink sheet. An overpowering fruity smell came from an air freshening pod stuck to the wall. With a sinking heart, Kendra took in the rest of the room, bare except for a plastic chair and matching table. The only signs of occupation were a half-used roll of paper towels, a hairbrush and the nub of an eyeliner pencil.

Win continued down the hall and opened doors until they'd seen all the rooms. Similarly furnished, all were devoid of personal belongings except for the second room's bag of dirty women's underwear and the empty bottle of painkillers in room four.

The place reminded Kendra of flophouse photos she'd seen in the newspaper except here the locks were on the outside, giving her a definite opinion about the business Zazzi was really running. Was that why Win didn't want to have the police search for his sister? Where was she, and where was Elias?

"This doesn't help," said Win in a low voice. "Let's go out this way."

Kendra winced as Win pushed the bar that said CAUTION: EMERGENCY EXIT ONLY but no alarm went off. She hung back as he propped the door open with a bent knee and leaned out to pick up a brick from the ground to use as a makeshift doorstop. Suddenly, he pitched backward, out of sight. The door began to close. A second later, a meaty hand stopped it. Paralyzed by shock, Kendra watched the man from the Soriano's house step in. He was pointing a gun at her.

"Lookie here, a bonus prize came out of the piñata! Let's go to the party room." The big thug grabbed her roughly by the arm, yanked her into the nearest room and gave her a mighty shove. Her right palm scraped painfully over a rough patch in the linoleum, right before her shoulder and hip hit the floor in tandem. The body slam knocked the can of pepper spray out of her pocket. Before she could grab it, he pressed her on to her stomach, and pinning her down with his legs, bound her hands and ankles with zip ties. She felt his fingers move to her armpits and grope at her breasts. In a panic, she tried to twist from his grip. He laughed and dragged her into a sitting position with her back against the wall. As she strained against the bindings, he swooped up the pepper spray canister and said, "Be right back with the cake and punch, heh-heh-heh." Retrieving his gun from the back of his waistband, he went out.

She'd been set up! From the get go, there had been something fishy about Win's plan to come here. He'd probably show up in a minute holding a gun of his own. Kendra wished she had one too so she could shoot both of them!

There were footsteps in the hall, followed by muttered curses, and suddenly, Win fell into the room and lay sprawled next to her. He held his head in both hands, moaning softly.

Their attacker came in, this time joined by Zazzi, who manacled Win's ankles and wrists, then pawed through his pockets for his cell phone. She took Kendra's also. "Elias, you want me to get rid of these?"

"Yeah. Now get lost."

Zazzi left them. Elias leaned against the door jam, rolling the can of pepper spray in his left hand and using the other to leisurely scribe a line in the air with his gun, with Kendra as point A and Win, point B.

Kendra meet Elias, she thought bitterly. What did he want with her? Did he kill Reyna and intend to get rid her because she could connect him to the girl's disappearance?

Elias directed a smug smile at Win. "Like how your fancy boxing moves matched up with my Glock?"

"Take these things off me and try it again," Win growled through lips contorted in pain. Blood streamed from his nose. He attempted to get to his feet, but tipped over, landing on his back.

This elicited a snort of contempt from Elias, who turned his attention to Kendra. She didn't understand the dynamic between Win and Elias, but now doubted Win had knowingly set her up. She'd blundered into trouble willingly, just as she always did.

"So, lady, we meet again. We ain't been properly introduced. Elias Carmona at your service, and under other circumstances, I'd ask, 'What can I do you for?'"

Win coughed. A bruise forming under his right eye framed the accusing look he gave her, like she'd betrayed him by not saying she had already met Elias. Even though she hadn't known that until now, she stared a message back: Two can play the deception game.

"When I saw the Mustang parked down the street I sent our other guests home so we could party in private. See you got it running again, eh? Guess you didn't get the message to mind your own business. I told Win to take care of you, but he got other ideas, and here we are."

In a night of surprises, this one was least expected. Elias knew the car, must have planted the M1000s. What motive did Elias have to go after her unless it had something to do with Reyna?

Elias jerked the gun barrel in Win's direction. "Hey Win, did you know I already met your girlfriend? I gotta agree, she ain't half bad for a teacher." Elias ran his eyes over Kendra's body like a child trying to decide where to start licking a Dreamsicle.

"Leave her alone," said Win without conviction.

"You gonna stop me?" Elias turned back to Kendra. "You wanna proofread my letters, baby? We could do some kinky stuff with red ink."

"I don't know what you're talking about," Kendra snapped.

"Maybe not," said Elias, "but you seem to get around."

"I don't know anything about you and I don't want to. If you have issues with Win, work it out with him and let me go!"

Elias tucked his gun into the back of his pants, lit a cigarette and pointed the end at Win. "Issues. I like that, sounds so...teachery. So, Win, tell me, did you come here because you have a beef with me, like the lady says? Sorry kid, but I don't owe you. I had to spend your share, and more, when I had to restart this whole operation after you let all the chicks run off. Too bad how things worked out 'cause I always liked you. Really, you shoulda left town. The cops were at West Ridge asking about you and your friend Rhus." Elias took a drag of his cigarette and smiled at Win with what appeared to be genuine affection.

Given the situation, Kendra had to wonder if Elias was off his rocker. Which made him more all the more dangerous. And he knew Mr. Rhus. Maybe he killed him, and thought she'd seen him at the house!

Win whispered something or maybe the sound came from his sniffling at the blood still trickling from his nose.

"What's that, Win? I can't hear you. But I got a question," said Elias. "If you wanted to get your visa back, why didn't you just ask Mr. Rhus for it nice?"

Win found his voice. "Shut up, you dirt bag. You probably killed him yourself. What have you done with Sandi?"

Kendra knew she was missing a few pages of whatever drama was playing out, but several serious crimes were definitely involved. Elias didn't seem to care how much he said in front of her. Did that mean he was going to kill her?

Elias clicked his tongue and gave a very fake sigh. "She went out freelancing. Dumb move on her part. Last I heard she was in the morgue. Did you try looking there?"

"I don't believe you!" shouted Win.

"Believe what you want. She ain't here."

Win scooted toward Elias and tried to kick at him, but the big man swiped a foot out and kicked Win flat.

"Party's over, kids. I'm leaving before I lose my temper and do something I ain't got time to clean up. Remember, Win, if the cops find me, they'll put you in the cell next door. The difference is, I'm already friends with Bubba Badass and you're not."

He paused for a moment with his hand on the doorknob. "If you really wanted Sandi, why didn't you have teacherlady here ask Carol Goodman about the little whores at Standard High? And what happens to them when they get out of line."

Kendra's demand for an explanation bounced off Elias's back as he strode from the room, shutting them inside with a nasty chuckle. Kendra slid toward the door but gave up when the bolt engaged.

She turned on Win, trembling with pent up rage. She wanted to give him a second black eye. Unfortunately, her hands were tied. And maybe he was already in enough pain. "I wish he would've shot you. You've known all along where Sandi went but you don't really care. You really came here to get money! Why did you have to drag me with you? None of this is my business!"

Win groaned. "No, you're wrong, I don't know where my sister is, honest. I thought she might be here, and you could help...."

Deadly Traffic

"Oh please! You don't think I'm dumb enough to believe that. You're as filthy as Elias. No wonder you didn't want to have the police find Sandi. You didn't want them to find you either."

"I know this looks bad, but…"

"Don't feed me any more of your lies. As soon as we get out of here I'm staying as far away from you as I can get."

"But you might still be able to do something—if you really do care about the kids you teach. You heard Elias, he said to ask Carol at Standard High—"

They both looked up at the sound of the lock snapping open. Zazzi stepped in. She moved in on Kendra and flicked a switchblade open. Kendra let out a feral shriek and kicked her hogtied feet at Zazzi, who jumped to the side and laughed. "You are trouble. I can see why he told me to shut you up, but I want no part of that." She sliced through their restraints, saying, "I'm gonna cut you loose, both of you. Keep your mouths shut and don't ever come back or he'll do you like he did those girls."

Chapter 36

Saturday, October 23

Detective Howard stood in front of Kendra's bookcase. After running her eyes over the eclectic collection of books, she proceeded to check out every inch of Kendra's living room. Kendra itched to ask her if she wanted some decorating tips. She had no doubt Howard lived in a studio apartment with white walls, vertical blinds and furniture left over from a dead relative. Meanwhile, Detective Tapia took a seat on the couch, opening his notebook as he settled in. Kendra believed it was full of doodles, its only purpose to intimidate the people he was questioning.

This time, it wasn't working. Kendra was irritated, yes, but not anxious. Did one actually get used to home visits by detectives? If this engagement marked the end of her cop-o-phobia, as Maretta liked to call it, all the better.

She had already gone to the station and signed a statement about finding Mr. Rhus, and had the unpleasant one-on-one with Howard. Yet here they were again. Fortunately, they seemed not to know where she'd been last night. If they did, she would be getting a ride back to the station with them right now.

"I don't know what you want with me this time, but can we get it over with fast? Walking dogs all day is tiring and I want to make dinner," said Kendra.

"Dog walking all day? What about last night? Howard asked. "We came by but you were out."

"I had a date." Some date. Threatened, knocked around, and Win didn't even bring me flowers.

After Zazzi's rescue the night before, Kendra drove back home, relying on Win's eyes when she needed to. She trusted he'd keep her from driving off the road for his own self-preservation, but didn't trust him enough to let him drive her home.

He jumped out of the car before she'd even cut the motor and sprinted away without a parting word. She went straight inside to soak her bruised body. Ten minutes later she heard his Honda rev up and roar away. For all she knew he hadn't returned home since. Perhaps he'd taken Elias's advice and fled to avoid being questioned or arrested, but in spite of Win's duplicitous behavior, she didn't believe he was a killer.

"We got a report today about an incident involving your car," said Tapia.

Kendra sighed. Too bad it hadn't taken longer for them to make the connection. "I filed a police report on that."

"We thought you might have something new to add." Tapia spoke with the characteristic slowness that made Kendra want to shake him like a rag doll to make him talk faster. Then he'd leave faster, too.

"No, it's all there."

"Where do you think you picked up that little bomb?"

"Don't know. The car's usually parked right out front. Are you going to catch who did it?"

Looking out the bay window, he said, "No fingerprints to tell us anything. Might be a good idea to keep an eye out in the future."

"Trust me, I will."

"You live in an interesting neighborhood. Seen anything suspicious?"

"This is a pretty quiet street." Except for flying rocks, she silently appended.

"We interviewed one of your neighbors a few days ago," he went on, searching her face for a reaction.

Kendra bit down on the inside of her lip. Win must have been Howard's unnamed source. Another favor he'd done her. Still, Tapia might just be fishing. She let his comment go unanswered.

He opened a 10x12 envelope, pulled out several sheets and handed them to her. As she stretched out her hand to receive them she saw his eyes flit over the large bandage on the heel of her hand.

"What happened there?"

"I tripped and cut it."

She fussed with the pages to put it out of sight. The copies showed rectangular images the size of photo ID cards. She needed stronger light or a magnifying glass if they expected her to read the tiny type. Couldn't the police afford a copier with an enlargement feature?

"Recognize any of these people?" asked Tapia.

Kendra stepped to the window both to both take advantage of the light and put her back to her uninvited guests. Due to the poor quality of the black-and-white photocopy, and the style—an intricate, engraved pattern reminiscent of paper money—the word VISA on the upper border was nearly illegible. No wonder she hadn't seen what these were at first glance. Her pulse roared when she flipped to the third page and saw Win's picture. After that, it took only a second to notice that all three documents on the page bore the same last name. Win's whole family?

"Well, this guy lives next door," she said, holding up the page and pointing to Win's VISA.

"What about the two females? Do you know them?"

"No, I've never seen them." That, at least, was the whole truth. "Why are you asking me? What have they done?"

"Take another look. Maybe you've seen them around." Tapia put on the encouraging tone he took when he wanted to call a ceasefire.

It didn't work and even if it did, one word from Howard would load the catapult again. She bought herself another moment by pretending to study the IDs. Her brain was firing on overload: dead man, bomb, missing girls, Win, Elias, Zazzi, visas, Linc who was Mose...and now?

"No, I don't know them," she repeated."

The detective took the papers from Kendra and pointed at the photo above Win's. "This girl goes to Standard High, Special Ed. student. Not one of yours, I take it?"

No, Win's sister is not my student. "Don't know her. She could be new this semester." She sat on an ottoman and waited for more. There was always more.

Tapia opened his notebook and leafed through it intently, like he was looking for a hundred dollar bill in a stack of ones. Kendra wondered if it was the same notebook he'd had last year, or if he used a fresh one for each case. She envisioned a tall cabinet in a corner of his living room, jammed full of his little notebooks, probably aligned neatly in chronological order, or would it be alphabetical? Was there a Mrs. Tapia who dusted them once a week? She didn't know a thing about his life, but here he was, insinuating himself into hers once again.

Deadly Traffic

Leaning against the fireplace mantle, Howard asked, "What do you know about Mr. Rhus's law practice? Did you meet any of his clients?"

"No," said Kendra.

"Any of the household staff?"

"I told you, Detective, I didn't really know him. I went to his house to walk the dog a few times, and he was the only one I ever saw there." Kendra wiggled her shoulders to relieve a growing knot between her shoulder blades. Were they back to square one again?

Tapia finally surfaced from his notebook. "The night you found the victim, you said you checked to see if he was dead. Have you recalled anything from that night you didn't tell us before?" he asked.

"It keeps replaying in my head, but nothing new has come up," said Kendra.

Tapia picked up another envelope and pulled out two 8x10 photos, setting them on the coffee table in front of her. Kendra gasped at the sight of Rhus's corpse, harshly illuminated by the camera's flash. The second photo was a close up of the man's right hand. Lying in the palm was an oblong piece of stiff paper or maybe thin wood, decorated with some sort of foreign script. A thin red cord trailed from one end, over and across the lifeless fingers to the floor.

"I don't remember seeing this," Kendra said slowly, "but I could have missed it. I was freaked out." And thanks for a new, horrible image to haunt my dreams.

"Think back. Maybe you didn't see it, but if you felt for a pulse, do you remember touching something in the hand?" prodded Tapia.

Left hand? Right hand? Kendra didn't remember and she refused to look at those photos again. "Is it important?" she asked, wondering if she'd really overlooked something vital to the case.

Tapia apparently didn't think Kendra needed to know. He gathered up the photos and exchanged a look with his partner. "If you do recall anything else, please let us know."

He headed for the door, but Howard paused again in front of Kendra's book collection. Before Kendra knew it, she heard herself say, "Would you like to take out a book? I have the

175

collected works of Gore Vidal."

"Who's that?" asked Howard.

Kendra didn't bother to answer, but thought she heard a choked off laugh from Tapia as she ushered them out. For several excruciating minutes they just sat in their car, probably comparing notes on how many lies they thought she told them. In truth, she might have learned more from them than she'd given. She had a whole list of new questions. And she knew who had the answers.

Chapter 37

Sunday, October 24

They'd walked more than a mile, but Jackson seemed keen to keep going, so Kendra decided to ignore her tired feet a while longer. Halfway around the block again should make him happy, especially if she took him home through the alley where he could visit a neighbor's dog through the fence. Poor Jackson deserved to be spoiled after what he'd gone through. She wished someone felt that way about her.

They'd reached her back gate when Jackson's ears perked up at a scraping noise coming from the right. She turned and saw Win standing at one of the dumpsters behind his apartment building. He'd finally returned! She allowed the dog to lead her over there. Win didn't look happy to see her, but gave Jackson a perfunctory head rub. Satisfied, the Lab began a careful examination of a pair of large cardboard boxes at the foot of the dumpster.

If she confronted Win right away, he might get defensive and refuse to talk to her. "Glad to see you're okay," she said with a warmth she didn't feel. "Did you find out anything about Sandi?"

He looked everywhere but at her. "No, not much. How you doing?"

Like he cares? It didn't matter as long as he gave her the information she wanted. Pulling Jackson along, she moved a few steps to the walkway and watched him pick up and dump the boxes. There was a smell of patchouli before the much stronger smell of rotting garbage took over again. Just like Win, enticing on the outside but corrupted beneath.

He slammed the dumpster lid and finally looked her in the eye.

In spite of herself, she said, "Your black eye looks awful. Does it hurt? I still have some scrapes and bruises. Next time, remind me to get thrown down on a nice thick carpet."

"Sorry about that." For a brief moment, she read something like regret. Wordlessly, he broke eye contact and headed for his apartment. Jackson started to follow and Kendra happily let the

177

dog act as her entrance ticket.

Win let them in, but once inside he seemed to barely register their presence. Kendra had never seen him act this jumpy, not even when Elias was pointing a gun at him. From his twitchy movements and the way he moved his jaw, he showed signs of being on coke or amphetamines. She could imagine him and Elias as drug dealers, but Mr. Rhus didn't fit that pattern unless he was the big boss and kept his hands clean. Until someone got very, very pissed off.

The apartment was a maze of cardboard boxes and bulging plastic bags. Clothes still on their hangers covered the couch. Unmatched socks marked a path on the floor from an open suitcase to the bedroom. Win went into the living room where he began hunting through boxes like he'd misplaced something.

If she wanted to talk to him she'd better be quick because Win was obviously moving—running away, more likely. Time to go for the three point shot. "Are you taking your mother with you?" she asked.

Win spun around with a roll of sealing tape in his hand. He really looked at her for the first time. "What do you mean?"

"The cops were at my house yesterday, asking about your mother." Kendra let the edge stay in her voice.

Win unstuck the a tangled length of tape from his fingers and wadded it into a ball. "You're pissed off. I deserve it, I guess."

"I'd like some information, but don't know if I should waste my time asking because you'll just feed me more crap."

"No, ask me whatever you want, I owe you that much after almost getting us killed. I promise I'll tell you the truth." He made himself a place to sit on the arm of the couch. His feet tapped nervously like they wanted to lead their commander away from the battlefield.

Kendra unclipped Jackson from the leash and went to face Win. "The police are looking for both your mother and your sister. But you knew that."

"I had an idea what happened to Sandi. But please believe me, I don't know where either one of them are. I didn't bring up my mom because it has nothing to do with Sandi."

"Really? What I think is, you don't want the police to find either one of them because you are part of the reason they're both missing."

Win shook his head. "You're wrong."

"Did you tell the cops I know your family?"

"No." He picked up a shirt from the couch and fiddled with the buttons.

"You told them something. How did my name even come up?"

"It wasn't my fault. The female cop started asking me things about Mr. Rhus and, well, it's not a secret you found his body."

The one thing she could count on was every time Win told her the truth he held a good chunk of it back. She needed to map out the connections between Win, his family, Rhus and her recent string of misadventures, but the pointer of the compass spun around like it had been dipped in the same drug Win had taken. To validate one of her basic assumptions, she asked, "Why are homicide cops interested in your whole family?"

"Mr. Rhus, me, my mom, we all worked at West Ridge."

So, his mother worked there as well. Just another tidbit he neglected to tell me. Did his mother work for Zazzi, too? "I think the cops are interested in your family for other reasons besides a West Ridge connection. You knew about Zazzi's and you were getting money from Elias. How long were you involved in the sex trade with him?"

"I wasn't."

"When you asked him about Sandi he said she was freelancing and it got her killed. You don't deny you knew what Elias was doing?"

"No, no, see…Elias started doing that and I figured he took Sandi…"

"So you knew what he was doing and you never turned him in?"

Win blinked several times in rapid succession. "Yeah, okay. I knew. I wanted to turn him in, but he was my boss at West Ridge."

"Is that your justification? You do everything your boss tells you to do? Did Elias also ask you to kill Rhus?"

"No! He didn't ask and I didn't do it," said Win. "I'd never kill anyone! Look, I wanted to stop Elias a long time ago, but he would have had me fired and then my visa wouldn't be good anymore. I didn't want to become illegal and get deported. I never thought he'd do anything to hurt Sandi."

Win actions couldn't be explained away by his fear of

deportation. They showed he cared more about his dirty money than his own family. How could she have been so wrong about him? Prostitution, drugs, who knew what else they were into? Did all three guys have mob connections? And now, Rhus was dead, Reyna was dead, Win's sister and mother were missing, and Win intended to run.

"You didn't care either what Elias might do to me. Or did he ask you to blow up my Mustang?"

"Huh? What do you mean blow it up?"

Kendra detected real puzzlement and decided not to pursue the subject. More important things were at stake. She hadn't found Reyna in time, but she might be able to do something to locate Sandi and keep other girls safe as well. "Never mind the car," she said.

Win took that as a dismissal and jumped up to sort through a box of magazines as if his life depended on finding a back issue of Cycle World.

"What did Elias mean about asking Carol Goodman at Standard High?"

"I have no idea. I just know Mrs. Goodman is Sandi's school counselor."

The off-hand way he threw out the remark brought her within a heartbeat of picking up the roll of tape and hurling it at his head. "Why didn't you tell me that before? You know where I teach. I could have helped you if I'd known."

"I went down that road myself, called over to the school. Mrs. Goodman refused to talk to me. Probably 'cause she's the one who helped place Sandi at the Cap Home in the first place. Sandi hated it so much she ran away and that doesn't make Mrs. Goodman look good."

Kendra filed this information for later. She was about to ask why Sandi had been placed there when a metallic ringing sound came from the kitchen.

Win called out, "Jackson! Playing your dish washing game again? Come here, boy."

Jackson obediently padded toward them. Kendra had a flashback. On the one occasion she had allowed Jackson inside her house, she learned the hard way he loved to nudge pots and pans off the stove. How did Win know about the dog's habits?

Jackson propped his chin on Win's knee. The Lab was shy with strangers, but not with Win, who began to scratch the dog's ears just the way he liked it. Suddenly, Kendra made the final connection. Win had known Rhus much better than he let on, and had gone to great lengths to cover up the fact.

She flashed back to the murder scene, to all the passports in Rhus's office, and to the photocopies the cops had shown her, one of them Win's. Rhus must have provided documents for his whole family and many others as well. She'd never considered that someone would commit murder over a passport, yet Elias had accused Win of doing just that. Denial or no denial, Win might have killed Rhus, either because of a problem with his precious visa or for some more personal reason. And here she was, sitting in his apartment!

"Jackson must be hungry, I'd better take him home," she said. She went to the kitchen and snapped on Jackson's leash. Win didn't say goodbye when she left.

Chapter 38

Maretta snatched the desert menu from Kendra's hand, setting the laminated card on a vacant chair out of Kendra's reach. "Kendra, do you have to fan yourself with that thing? Calm down before I ask the waitress to bring you a bib with your vanilla-apple tart."

"Can you blame me for being jumpy? I feel like I need to look over my shoulder."

"I'm the one who should be nervous after listening to your hysterical phone call. You know what I'm going to say next, don't you? Did you call the police? No, of course not. Why am I even asking?"

"I'm afraid they're going to think I was holding back. I didn't know Win knew Rhus on a personal basis, not until I finally realized his dog wasn't acting shy with Win. That just shows how stressed out I've been. I'm usually tuned in to animals. And I didn't know much about Win's family either, at least not what counts. The detectives will think I'm making excuses to cover up consorting with criminals and a homicide suspect!"

"Consorting? I thought it was a fake date you planned."

"A poor choice of words, okay? The date, as you call it, never even came off and you can tell me some other time how stupid I am. The thing is, I have no proof of what Win's really been doing and I have a hard time seeing him as a killer. What if he's innocent?"

She broke off as the server appeared with two coffees, Kendra's ice cream tart and a wedge of Dobos torte for Maretta. Kendra looked at the pie, knew she wasn't going to touch it and pushed it toward her skinny friend.

With the waitress out of earshot, Maretta put down her fork long enough to say, "Innocent is not a word I'd use to describe Win. Going by what you've told me—which I hope is everything—he could have committed several different crimes. Does it matter at this point what he's arrested for?"

"Murder is different and you know it. What if he gets charged on my say-so and I'm wrong?"

"Give the justice system some credit. Innocent people aren't always prosecuted, and the guilty often go free as well, as you should have learned from your past escapades at Standard High." Maretta wagged a school schoolmarmish finger at Kendra.

"I don't feel bound to help Howard and Tapia do their jobs. If they're any good, they'll arrest him without my help. I'm more interested in locating Win's missing sister before she ends up like Reyna. I bet we can find her."

"I'm not liking the plural pronoun."

"Hear me out and then decide, okay? Win's sister goes to Standard High."

"She does?"

"I just found that out. Win said he called Carol at school but she wasn't helpful."

"Carol Goodman, the counselor?"

"Win told me Carol helped place Sandi into foster care. I wish I'd have known. Remember, the day I went to the Cap Home and Reyna told me her roommate had run away? I bet the roommate was Sandi. I feel horrible. I never even asked Reyna for her name."

Maretta groaned. "I'm afraid to ask, but what's Sandi's last name?"

"Ni. Her name's Sandi Ni."

"I know her, she's in one of my classes! She enrolled this fall and was quickly transferred to Special Ed., largely due to Carol's insistence."

"When's the last time she came to class?"

"I'm not sure off the top of my head, maybe two weeks ago. She's not on my homeroom list. I did call the Cap Home about her absences, and after a five minute run around the House manager finally admitted she'd run away. So I went to see Carol in the counseling office."

"Because you knew she put Sandi in Special Ed."

"No, because Reyna had run off by then, too, and Carol had a relationship with both girls, especially Reyna. I thought Carol might have heard something during one of their counseling sessions that might reveal where the girls had gone."

Kendra leaned forward. "What did Carol say?"

"She acted defensive, like I blamed her for not doing enough to intervene before the girls disappeared. All she'd tell me was Reyna hated living at the Home, but never talked about running away."

"I have a gut feeling Carol knows more than she says. Don't give me that look. She doesn't have to be holding back for an evil reason. Reyna and Sandi got involved with some tough characters. I don't blame Carol for being scared. You'd understand if you saw those rooms behind the hair salon."

"Your description is enough, thanks. But if Carol had suspicions, why not report them?" Maretta spooned up some of Kendra's half-melted ice cream, then set it down with a frown.

"We don't know what she did or didn't do. If she only had suspicions and reported them perhaps she wasn't taken seriously. Or she hasn't followed up because she doesn't want a pistol pointed at her head," said Kendra, shaping her hand into a gun and pointing the fingers to her temple. "Suppose she's being threatened…."

"Because she's involved?" Maretta's eyes narrowed.

"Ah ha, I'm not the only one who sees the dark side in people. After last year, neither of us gives a pass to anyone on the basis of their professional status."

"I just thought of something. Is Sandi's family here illegally?"

"They've got visas. Whether they're valid or not, I can't say. What's your point?"

"Don't you think it's odd that we know of four girls, three with known connections to our school—all children of immigrants—and two are dead and two others have disappeared within the last few months?"

"Win's mother went off somewhere as well. Still, we shouldn't jump to conclusions," said Kendra. "It could all be coincidence."

"I'm not jumping to conclusions, but it's something to keep in mind. We don't want any more mysterious disappearances, or deaths."

"So, you'll drive me over to Carol's?" Kendra felt certain Maretta was hooked. "Do you know where she lives?"

"I already looked up her address," admitted Maretta. "I was vacillating on what to do. Now, you've convinced me to go."

Chapter 39

"I'm glad I checked Carol's address, because I've only been here once and some of these streets really curve around," said Maretta, locking the car. "Nice neighborhood. Expensive. Her divorce must have worked out well."

Carol's cottage style house sat well back from the street behind a garden of wild flowers, most of which were past their blooming season and gone to seed. A strong breeze carried the smell of an unseen outdoor barbecue, making Kendra's stomach grumble. She regretted not eating the pie.

Maretta led the way under a trellis flanked by garden gnomes, holding out an arm to warn Kendra away from the sweeping tendrils of a thorny wild rose bush. From there, a flagstone path zigzagged toward the side of the house. "This way. Carol uses the side door, at least she did at her Christmas party."

"I'm glad one of us was invited," said Kendra acidly.

"Aren't we touchy. Your month-long feud with the counseling office wasn't a good basis for an invitation, you know. Don't worry, I'm sure Carol's forgotten about it by now."

"You take the lead, just in case," said Kendra, deliberately trailing behind.

When they reached a raised brick patio Maretta stopped abruptly and held up a hand as a stop sign. She looked past a row of small fruit trees to an open window a few feet beyond. "Shh. Wait."

A woman with a high voice spoke slowly with a heavy accent. Kendra caught only the last words, "...arrest my son."

Carol spoke. "You came to me when you needed help with Sandi. Why don't you trust my judgment now?"

"I did trust you. To put her in the good home, and look what happen."

"I'm not to blame because she ran away, and neither are you," Carol insisted. "You came here for advice. Now take it. I'm trying to keep you from doing something you'll regret. I know how the system works."

Interesting, thought Kendra, sneaking closer to the window. She pointed to her ear to show Maretta what she wanted to do.

"You know nothing," said the foreign woman, suddenly angry.

"And you're full of secrets. To be honest, your attitude offends me. I've already done more for you than I need to. Usually I don't give out my home address," Carol said stiffly.

"I am sorry. I respect your advice, but I want to turn myself in now. Why is Win pay for my mistake?"

"The cops will figure out you're lying."

"No, I touch. They get my fingerprint."

Kendra leaned closer, banging her head on a branch, then froze in a panic fearing she'd been overheard, but the two women were wholly focused on each other. She sensed, rather than heard Maretta creeping up to join her near the window.

"What do you mean you touched things?" asked Carol.

"In Mr. Rhus office."

"Of course you did. You cleaned his house."

"No, I come from the cleaner store with his shirt and I go to his office, to tell him. I see him on the floor. Dead. Blood on him, on the floor." The woman's tone was odd, angry. Kendra didn't think it could be attributed to her inexpert English skills. It was almost as if was blaming the man for inconveniencing her with his untimely death. Or she thought someone would make her clean up all the blood?

Carol didn't seem to notice. "Well, under the circumstances, it's only natural you touched things, you were shocked. Of course your fingerprints are all over the house. Why worry?"

"The lethpwe, I put in his hand."

"Leth...is there an English word for that?"

"I do not know. Mr. Rhus buy many lethpwe, put them on the wall to look at. In my country they are good luck charm, to scare evil spirit. I see him, the blood. I know the gods are angry. I get lethpwe off the wall, put in his hand...." The woman's voice faded.

Carol brought her guest to a sofa closer to the window and Kendra had to duck behind a bush to avoid being seen, but not before she got a glimpse of the foreign woman's face. She'd already seen it on a visa. Win's mother.

"They can't convict you on evidence like that, Thida."

186

"Rhus a rich man and I am nothing."

"This is America. It's different here."

"I did not call police. I run away."

Carol's voice was gentle, but imperative. "You were frightened. Look, the police might find your fingerprints on that thing, I see that. But you could have easily touched it while you were cleaning or something. Can't you see? There's no reason to turn yourself in for something you didn't do."

"I give Win time to go far away. That is all I want."

"Look, if you insist on turning yourself in, do it like this. Tell the truth about how Roger Rhus abused you in every way, and say you killed him in self-defense. You've got the bruises to prove it. That scumbag deserves to have his reputation ruined, although he didn't deserve to die. Even if the police charge you with murder, after what he did to you a jury won't convict you. I'd vote 'not guilty' in a minute."

"Why you wait to tell me my Sandi is dead?"

Kendra reeled back and almost lost her balance. She felt Maretta pull on her sleeve and shook her head in refusal.

Thida continued, "Now I do not care what happen to me. Win has the whole life to live."

Maretta gave another yank that almost sent Kendra to the ground. Meanwhile, Carol and her visitor were on the move. Their voices faded and a door clicked shut. She felt another tug on her sleeve, and this time, obeyed. The rest of this game wasn't going to be viewable from the outfield anymore, and she didn't have the guts to go in and confront Carol. Did it matter? Sandi was beyond saving. They would have to pass on the rest to the police.

After Maretta unlocked the car, they sat in silent misery. Maretta hugged the steering wheel, with her forehead resting on one arm. Kendra sat sidesaddle, her feet planted on the curb, taking slow breaths to calm her heart. When did Sandi die, and how did Carol know about it? Elias said to ask Carol. Was Sandy still alive when he said that?

Somewhere down the block an engine started and a man yelled out something about extra cheese and anchovies. A dog barked. Someone was blaring a ballgame on TV. The sounds could have been the soundtrack of a 1950s TV show. Kendra looked up and down the street. Why did these every day, benign things seem jarringly out of place to her, almost surreal? She'd fallen out of her own, normal life into a frightening, dangerous world where she'd failed to save anyone. And had almost lost herself.

Kendra looked at Maretta, whose shoulders shook with sobs, and regretted getting her into this. Maretta's life wasn't a series of mishaps because she knew when to draw the line. Kendra kept trying to be like that, but she always had to have an answer for every question no matter what it cost. She thought about Elias and shuddered.

Maretta sat up and broke the silence. "Looks like your friend Win's a murderer."

"He's not my friend. I don't know why he killed Rhus, but I'm sure he didn't kill his own sister. I'm sure Elias killed Sandi. Maybe if I'd done something sooner…"

"None of this is your fault, Kendra. You're lucky you didn't get hurt. If anyone could have done something for Sandi it would have been Carol."

"I know but I can't help feeling—"

Maretta took out her phone. "We can talk later. Right now, I'm calling the police."

Chapter 40

Kendra looked into the shopping bag to verify the contents. Whole milk not skim. Good. The 32 ounce carton felt as heavy as a bowling ball dangling from her hand. She should have accepted Maretta's offer to wait while she shopped at the tiny corner store, but Maretta needed to get home and she only had two blocks to walk from the store to her house. A short and pleasant walk when she wasn't exhausted and aching.

She crossed the street to avoid a gardener wielding a leaf blower. The fumes went right to her head, making her feel as insubstantial and useless as the gutter trash he was blowing down the street.

As she turned in at her house and mounted the first step, someone came up behind her. She wheeled around, mouth open to scream.

"Kendra, it's me. It's okay."

The scream turned into a choking sound. Their eyes met. Her words came out through clenched teeth. "What are you doing here, Brian?" Of course, she knew. He was there to teach her never to assume the worst wasn't yet to come.

"I came to say goodbye."

"We did that months ago, remember? Do I have to get a restraining order to keep you from bothering me?"

"No. I'm going away. For a long time. Didn't you read my note? In the flowers I sent you? I told you all about it."

Kendra took out her keys. Either to jam them in his eye or to unlock her front door, Brian's choice. He read her intent and hurried to explain. "I enlisted in the military, the Air Force. I'm going to basic training tomorrow, starting a new chapter in my life."

"Good luck, then."

She mounted the four steps to her porch and had reached her door when the ramification of his words sank in. The date with Win had been unnecessary. Win's lies, Elias and his gun, Zazzi and her house of horrors—she could have avoided all of it. If she

189

hadn't been too pigheaded to read Brian's gift card. The horrible absurdity welled up inside her and she began to laugh. And laugh. At last, she leaned against the door, shaking her head at her own folly.

"Kendra?"

Brian was staring up from the sidewalk. He had his head cocked, examining her like she was a cat up a tree in need of rescue who might claw him to death if he tried.

"I wish you all the best, Brian. Good night," she said with finality.

"I won't bother you again, Kendra. But I'll be there for you if you ever need me."

Kendra slipped into her house and said to the closing door, "Not in a million, trillion years."

Chapter 41

Kendra found Bobbins pacing the front hall, meowing with hunger. Cuddling the cat to her chest she carried him to the kitchen. What comfort this loving fur ball provided. If he hadn't been so distressed she would have continued to hold him, but he didn't want love at the moment, he wanted food. Jackson barked and pawed at the back door. He was hungry too. It was an hour past their dinner time.

She and Maretta had spent far too long debating what to say to Detective Tapia, or how to frame a message if he didn't take the call himself. It wasn't until after Maretta finally made the call and left their message that Kendra remembered her responsibilities. If anything could force her to stop rushing into trouble, it would be the knowledge she'd neglected or caused distress to her cat. To make up for her guilt, she gave Bobbins his food, dribbled with a few drops of the milk she'd just purchased as a special treat. She filled a bowl of dog kibble for Jackson and had her hand on the switch for the outside light when she saw something that made her keep the darkness. Someone was walking furtively alongside the building next door.

Kendra put the dog's meal in front of him, crossed her yard and stepped into the back alley. Win's motorcycle wasn't parked in its spot. She stood in shadow and watched as a woman stopped at Win's apartment, unlocked the door and rushed in, leaving it ajar. Kendra sidled up closer. When the bedroom light came on, it revealed a stripped down bed, part of a dresser, and the rear view of a short, pathetically thin girl darting around in a frenzy. She appeared to be holding something in her hand.

The girl bent and lifted a corner of the queen sized mattress. In spite of her undernourished appearance, she had no trouble lifting it, and held it that way for several seconds, blocking Kendra's view of her other hand. When the girl let the mattress fall back into place, both hands were empty. She suddenly turned and looked behind her, and Kendra met the eyes of a dead girl.

Kendra didn't believe in ghosts. She almost called out her

name, then held back. The girl looked right at her but didn't seem to register Kendra was there. Her half-open mouth, heaving chest, and the wild look in her eyes warned Kendra to be cautious. Yet the girl had a key to Win's door, making her impossible identity possible. If she had a key, why sneak in? And what did she hide under Win's mattress?

Kendra edged through the door of Win's apartment before she'd even made a conscious decision to go there. Most of Win's belongings were gone. The living room held only the furnishings that came with the apartment. Three open boxes sat on the kitchen floor and a jumble of utensils and dishes littered the big table and the counter next to the sink. Busy rifling through one of the boxes, the girl didn't notice Kendra's entrance.

Up close, she looked no older than fourteen. She had shoulder length, black hair streaked randomly with gold, a round head with a square chin and Win's nose and mouth. Her midriff top revealed the lines of a garish tattoo, almost obscured by a mass of bruising that descended below the waistband of her skirt. More bruises crawled down her legs. Surprisingly, her feet were bare. Kendra knocked lightly on the wall.

Startled, the girl turned around, her lips twisted into an angry scowl. "Who are you?"

Kendra had a question of her own. "Where have you been? People have been worried, looking for you."

"So? What's it to you?"

"I'm a friend of your brother." Kendra didn't know how else to put it.

"Yeah? Where is he then?"

"Out looking for you, or maybe hiding from the police. They're looking for him."

"Not my problem." She bent down to root through the contents of the box.

"They're also looking for your mother. About an hour ago, I heard her say she's going to turn herself in for murdering Roger Rhus."

Sandi continued her treasure hunt. "I don't care what she does. She's a rich man's whore."

"And if she's innocent?"

"Guilty either way. She should have killed him a long time

ago, but she only cared about his money, not what he did. She let him send me to the Home so she could stay with him. He deserved to die."

"What makes you say that?" Kendra asked, as much to hear the answer as to give the girl a chance to unburden herself.

But instead, Sandi said, "I'm glad he's dead, I wish he could die twice."

"Shoving a knife into someone's chest doesn't solve problems, it makes more."

Straightening up, Sandi took a step toward Kendra. "What do you know about the knife? Who are you?"

Kendra looked into her eyes. The dilated pupils were those of a trapped, angry wild beast. One who'd lost everything and had nothing to lose. "I have been trying to find you, to help you."

"I don't want to be found. Especially by my brother." Squinting, Sandi went quiet and looked Kendra over as if seeing her for the first time. "How come Elias didn't take you, get you strung out, put you to work? Tell you his lies—how he'd get you a job dancing in a club, how he knew people who could make you a big star."

Sounds about right, thought Kendra, who could see how a lure like that might attract a certain kind of girl. It was too late for Reyna, but Sandi still had a chance. What were the right words to say? "Is that what he told you?"

"No, I see. You're too old. He wouldn't want you. I get it, you're working for Elias like Zazzi does and he sent you here to find me."

"No, no. He almost shot me. He only let me go because Win was with me."

"Then you're working with Win, and you worked for Mr. Rhus too."

Sandi lunged forward and gave Kendra a violent shove. Kendra fell backwards but strong hands caught her before she hit the floor.

"Kendra," Win whispered as he put her back on her feet, "what are you doing here? Get out before you get hurt."

She whispered back, "I can help. I've dealt with troubled girls and she's already mad at you. You'll just make things worse."

"No. You don't belong here. Get out." He pushed Kendra

Mickey Hoffman

roughly toward the door. The roughness of his thrust jolted her back to their experience at Zazzi's and to his mother's incriminating words. What would he do if she left him alone with Sandi? Kendra stayed.

Win took a few steps toward his sister, who quickly backed into the kitchen. Holding up his hands in mock surrender, he said, "I didn't know if you were alive or dead. Do you have any idea how worried I've been?"

"Don't even try your phony big brother routine," said Sandi. "And don't pretend you didn't know where I was. You sold me to Elias, didn't you?"

"You're crazy. You ran off like you always do. How's that my fault?"

"You wouldn't help me. I told you I wouldn't live in that stinking home. You and mom, you don't care what happens to me as long as you don't have to watch."

"You're wrong. I do care. I warned you about Elias."

Sandi's eyes half closed like she'd folded into some internal space. When she spoke again, it was with a very different, little girl voice. "Elias promised me a place to live, lots and lots of money, nice clothes."

Even Kendra, who'd taught kids with mood disorders, was shocked at the abrupt personality switch.

"When you found out the truth, why didn't you come to me for help?" Win asked.

"You? You're the one who brought him the drugs he made me take."

Win shook his head and sighed like he felt he felt helpless, unable to combat her fantastical charges. "I didn't know Elias gave you drugs, I didn't know he had you in the first place. I've been trying to find you for days. "

"Days…" Sandi chewed on a fingernail. "I went out to make some money of my own. Money I wouldn't have to give Elias. I remember being on the street, and then I woke up in the hospital. They said maybe I got thrown out of a car. My head hurt bad and everyone kept asking me who I was. I didn't tell them because they wanted to put me away for good. But we got away."

Win's reaction showed shock and confusion. "We? Who's we?"

194

The answer came unexpectedly. Sandi looked to her right at the empty living room and whispered, "Not now," as if voices were calling to her from there.

Wow, she's been through hell, thought Kendra. The hallucinations could be from hitting her head during her accident, drugs, or other unknown causes. Where has she been hiding out all this time? She's obviously half starved.

Win moved to take Sandi in his arms, but she let out a cry of fear, drew back, and threw a coffee mug at his head. It hit the wall behind him and fell to the floor in a shower of plaster dust. "Don't come near me."

Win got the message. "Okay, okay. I won't touch you, but at least tell me where Mom is. Have you been staying with her?"

The mention of their mother brought back the other Sandi, focused, spiteful and aggressive. "Isn't she with you? So you can both cry over Roger? Be sure to tell her he wanted me more than her. Yeah, he wanted me bad. He used to sneak into my room all the time. He just wouldn't pay money for it."

She reached back to the table and a serrated knife appeared in her wavering hand. "I made him pay for that, and if you come any closer, I'll kill you too."

Chapter 42

As Kendra took off for the door a shout came from outside, "Police. Nobody move!"

She dug in her heels too late to avoid a collision with an oncoming barrier of blue: two uniformed officers with Tapia and Howard close behind. Staggering back, she grabbed at the arm of the closest officer. She realized her mistake when a hard hand yanked her away and spun her face forward into a wall. A stunning pain wracked her nose and mouth as her vision tunneled toward blackness.

A deep voice said, "I'm taking this one in for assault."

"For now, just keep her out of the way," said Tapia.

Assault? Kendra heard a soft whooshing sound and realized it was the sound of her jeans sliding along the floor. She opened her eyes to find herself on the floor, handcuffed and propped against the back of the sofa with her feet pointing toward the kitchen. The officer who'd pulled her aside stepped back and ordered, "Don't move."

She started to cry, from both the pain and injustice. She'd only grabbed at the officer to keep from falling.

Tapia and Howard stood in command positions, framing the exit with guns drawn. Kendra's captor left her and went toward Win's bedroom while a second officer finished cuffing Win's hands. Tapia and Howard moved aside just enough to let them take Win outside.

Kendra felt a hot wetness on her chin. She ran her tongue over her teeth. They hurt but they were all there. She reflexively tried to put a hand up to wipe her mouth and got an instant reminder of her restraints. An attempt to wipe her cheek against her right shoulder increased the pain in her head, as did the sound of doors slamming elsewhere inside the apartment. Another cop stood alertly on the stoop outside. How many were there? The situation must be even more dangerous than she knew—a cache of drugs or weapons hidden in the house perhaps? Or were the cops just being cautious? She started to shiver.

Deadly Traffic

From the far end of the living room Kendra's captor called, "All clear," and came back to stand at Kendra's right. Tapia took up the inside position near the kitchen with Howard to his left, closer to Kendra.

Sandi now held the knife in both hands, scribing a large X into the air like she was crossing out something in front of her that only she could see.

Detective Tapia ordered, "Drop the knife."

Kendra looked from gun to gun to knife, and the impossibility of the situation hit her. She watched with horror, bracing herself for gunshots.

With Sandi zoned in on Tapia, Howard slowly worked her way to the other end of the big table. What was Howard doing? It looked like her current path would take her into Tapia's line of fire, but she must have something else in mind. Kendra didn't want to see a gun go off no matter what. She gave a hiss to get Howard's attention to warn her in case the cops didn't know they were dealing with a mentally impaired girl. Howard either didn't hear or chose to ignore the interference.

Tapia said, "Sandi, you're safe now, put down the knife."

Sandi seemed to focus on Tapia for the first time. "What's the matter? Afraid of a girl? That's what Roger called me, his pretty girl, when he invited me into his office. And then I stuck him in the chest."

"Sandi, set down the knife and we can talk," said Tapia in a flat voice.

He took one step toward Sandi, but she pointed the knife at his gun like the weapons were equal.

"You want to talk?" Sandi replied in a higher, sing-song voice. "Dirty talk costs ten bucks. You want more? Fifty dollars and I promise me and my friend will make you feel real good."

"I don't feel good about your knife, Sandi."

Sandi laughed, drew the blade of the knife across her left palm and licked the fresh wound. "I like to cut myself, see? The doctors told me it's bad, but I like it." She slid a thumb under the leather bracelet she wore and unsnapped it.

Kendra's eyes were glued on the white wristband that seemed to fall in slow motion to the floor. When she looked up again, for just an instant she saw Reyna instead, holding out her arm to show

197

off a similar leather band. The image dissolved as Sandi flexed her hand so the inside of her wrist pointed at Tapia's gun. Then she angled the knife so the point pushed into her forearm.

Kendra's minder aimed something at Sandi. It looked like a gun but had yellow markings on it. A Taser? She suddenly knew what to do. Somehow, through numbed lips, she called out, "Sandi, can you help find Reyna?"

Simultaneously, the Taser went off. Sandi dropped to her knees. The knife clattered to the floor. Howard sprang forward, kicked the knife away and held Sandi on the ground while Tapia cuffed her wrists and removed the Taser darts. Then Howard led her out into the night.

Kendra tried to get to her feet, but the floor seesawed beneath her and she fell back against the wall.

"I think you'd better come with me, Ms. Desola," said Tapia. The harsh edge in his voice made her teeth chatter. Yes, she deserved to be punished. One girl dead, the other's life gone down the toilet, and what had she done to stop any of it? She might even have made things worse.

Tapia ushered her toward the door. Her legs gave out and she fell against him. "You need medical attention?" he asked.

She shook her head, blinking to see through the haze in front of her. A man appeared out of nowhere. She knew him and let out a cry.

"Detective, is she under arrest?"

"Not at this time, no." He unlocked her cuffs.

"Then I'll take care of her, Detective. I'll make sure she shows up at the station first thing tomorrow."

Lincoln the emancipator put an arm around her and led her home.

Chapter 43

Monday, October 25

The coffee maker sputtered and spit the last drops into the filter basket. The tiny sounds echoed like mini-explosions in Kendra's aching head. She watched from the kitchen door as Linc gathered up a sugar bowl, spoons, two mugs and carried them to the table. "I wouldn't put the milk down there, not if you're planning on having any," said Kendra hoarsely. Her throat hurt, her vocal cords didn't seem to be working and her lips felt thick and crusty. She had gone to bed the night before—or was it this morning—without even an attempt to bathe.

Linc took the milk away, poured some in his mug and returned it to the fridge. "Does your cat always sleep on the kitchen table?"

"Only after breakfast. He's like clockwork." She leaned over Bobbins, stretching out a hand to pet him, but she didn't have the energy. She gave up and plopped on the nearest chair instead. "I'm so tired I could sleep on the table too. I need two more aspirin and a lot more sleep. How can you be so chipper?"

"I'm as chipper and sunny right now as one of your Klingon warrior heroes. After I tucked you in last night, I went and met with your detective friends for hours. It was almost four a.m. when I got back and crashed on your couch. Why don't you train the cat not to demand breakfast at six-thirty?"

"You're welcome to try. Now that you fed him, he's sleeping. I'm going back to bed." She got up and started to shuffle toward her bedroom.

"Don't even think about it until you explain yourself. Sit down. Have some coffee."

"No way, not with my mouth swollen. It hurts to talk, too." Maybe she could postpone this conversation.

"I'll fix you an ice pack. Remember the time we got into a fight over my model plane and I gave you a fat lip?"

"I wanted Dad to punish you but he decided we were both at fault for fighting over a piece of plastic." She put a tentative finger

199

to her mouth and asked, "How bad does it look?"

"Let's just say you won't be putting on lipstick for a day or two." He handed her a plastic bag filled with ice cubes. "Hey, I've been meaning to ask, where are your glasses?"

"I had Lasik surgery. Long story."

"Knowing you, I'm sure it is." Linc pulled a long face.

"Tell me how and why you turned up at Win's last night. If you hadn't saved me, I'd be in jail right now. I don't understand why you were there or why Tapia let you take me."

"I only got you a temporary reprieve. You have to report in and do a lot of explaining. Why don't you practice for it right now?"

"I'm in pain and my mouth is gonna be frozen shut." She put down the bag of ice cubes and swapped it for the towel Linc held out to her. "Ouch!"

"Use the ice."

"The ice hurts…"

"Okay, okay, since you're giving me your pathetic, orphaned baby seal routine, I'll go first, but you're not going back to bed until I hear your side of things. And I mean everything."

"Deal. Go ahead."

"A bit of background first. I meant to follow up after I texted you, but I discovered someone was tailing me. For your safety, I didn't want them connecting me with you.

Puzzled, she asked, "My safety?"

"When I left you that message, I had no idea you knew anyone from West Ridge. I was totally blown away when you showed up at the river with Win."

The ice bag clinked as she knocked it on the table in rebuttal. "Not as shocked as I was, Mr. Mose. When you didn't call me the next day to explain, I was sure you were doing something illegal, but Win said you were just an ordinary kitchen boss."

"He's a fine one to trust. You do have the knack of making things impossible for yourself," said Linc with a degree of tenderness.

"Well, maybe if I had a big brother who was around to help me—sorry."

"No, you're right, I could have handled things better. I just wasn't sure what I could tell you or how you'd take it, knowing how you feel about cops."

Kendra opened her mouth to speak, but he motioned for her not to interrupt.

"At the park that evening you popped out of the trees like a wood nymph. I almost lost my cool and had to wing it the best I could with Win there. I couldn't tell you I'm a government agent. I work for the Investigations Office of ICE."

"Huh?" Kendra fell into a stunned silence. Agent? Ice? Her eyes went to the ice pack. She pressed the pack to her throbbing forehead. She must have heard wrong. "What ice?"

"It's a government acronym for Immigration and Customs Enforcement. Used to be the INS."

"Yeah, you're right. I'm not taking this well. I could kill you for not telling me."

"Give me a break, Kendra. I never dreamed you were anywhere near the investigation. I wasn't happy about your friendship with Win, but I knew he wasn't violent. I figured you'd be okay for the next few hours. I left you a message the very next day. Didn't you get it?"

"No. I lost my phone later that night and things were…I didn't have a chance to buy a new one."

"If things had gone the way I planned Win would have been under lock and key by Friday night, and the entire case would have been wrapped up. Turned out to take a little longer."

"Win didn't murder Rhus, you know."

He gave Kendra a look that showed disapproval of her advocacy. "I know now, but I wasn't involved in the murder investigation. ICE has been trying to nail the top players in an extensive document fraud network with connections in the U.S. and several foreign consulates. West Ridge attracted our attention because they made a sudden and complete turnaround from years of hiring undocumented workers to a new practice of importing dozens of foreign workers on a visa program. I'm not allowed to give you details. Probably shouldn't have told you this much."

Kendra thought a moment. "I saw a lot of passports in Rhus's office and wondered what he was doing. Were they all phony?"

Linc frowned. "Some were. Many had been stolen from their rightful owners. I was inserted to work undercover at West Ridge a few months ago. The CEO there agreed to hire me after we

201

presented him with a less pleasant alternative. I uncovered evidence that Rhus was dirty, but I didn't have enough to arrest his government contacts as well and shut down the whole enterprise. Then Rhus got himself killed, a major setback to the investigation."

"And then I stumbled into the mix," said Kendra with increasing distress. With every revelation, she was becoming more aware of the seriousness of what she'd blundered into.

"You have no idea how surprised I was to see you come out of those bushes. Talk about having to play a role, nothing in my training prepared me for a situation like that."

"Your name change, is that part of your role playing? How did you come up with a name like Mose?"

"I picked that up in prison. The guys in my cellblock made fun of me. The only Lincoln they'd ever heard of was Abraham Lincoln, so some guys started calling me Mr. President, or Dead Abe. One day, one of the black inmates, the shotcaller, ordered everyone to stop making fun of me because Lincoln freed the slaves, just like Moses freed the Israelites. From that point, everyone called me Moses, then it got shortened to Mose. I got to like it and decided to keep it. Do I have to tell you where Grant came from?"

"No, I get it. So what did Win want from you, really?"

"He asked me to get him a copy of his visa from the files at West Ridge. He lied about why he wanted it, but I thought I could play along and get some information out of him anyway."

"Win told me you gave him an address where his sister was staying."

Linc looked at her over his coffee mug. "Not true."

In her virtual record titled Win the Charmer, Kendra mentally moved Win's assertion from the "Probable Lie" to the "Big Whopper" column. "Can you tell me what Win's visa had to do with any of this?"

"Rhus had gotten visas for Win's family. Originally, they entered this country illegally. I'm sure there's more to it and I'm hoping Win will come clean and tell me everything."

"I'd love to ask him a few questions myself," said Kendra throwing down the bag of half-melted ice.

Bobbins righted himself and jumped to the floor in one

frenzied motion, drawing a laugh from Linc. He tossed the bag of melting ice cubes into the sink and brought her a bag of frozen peas as a substitute. "Lots of healthy stuff in the fridge. You a vegetarian now?"

"No, but I read a lot lately about problems in the meat industry, kind of put me off."

"As long as you're making lifestyle changes, can I make a suggestion for Round Two? How about following this advice: You don't need to solve every problem or answer every question."

Kendra started to wonder if he'd just called her a busybody when another thought hit her. "Elias. He's still out there somewhere. I think Elias was taking underage girls and—"

Linc cut in. "Yeah, I know. I heard the recording of Maretta's phone call. She made it sound like Elias Carmona killed Win's sister, and Win killed Roger Rhus."

"Well, that's what we thought. So, Carmona didn't kill Sandi, but what about the other girls from Standard High?"

"The cops are looking for him, so we'll see."

"How it is you heard the 911 call?"

"My agency and the local police had overlapping interests so it became a joint operation. ICE is handling the visa fraud and possible sex trafficking and the locals are in charge of the murder investigation. A team went to stake out Win's apartment after the call and since he's a valuable witness in my case, I went along. And there you were again, with him."

"Don't sound so pissed. I wasn't with him. I was already there when Win walked in. I was in my yard and happened to see a strange girl going into Win's apartment. I thought she might be breaking in, so—"

"You went to do what, watch? Tackle her? In what grade do you teachers teach kids how to dial 911?"

"Don't be sarcastic. I thought maybe she was his girlfriend and if Win was a murderer, she ought to be warned."

"Sister Kendra at work again."

"Don't give me that lecture. I know what you're going to suggest for Round Three: Help according to your ability, not your instinct."

"Better said than I could have. You're very lucky, as things worked out. I only wish I would have known earlier exactly what

Win and Elias were doing."

Kendra didn't think she deserved his censuring look. "And I would have liked to know what you were doing," she retorted.

"My excuse is better. Law enforcement agencies don't always share information with each other and never with civilians. Until recently, the murder investigation ran separate and parallel to the work my agency was doing, and I had only an inkling of possible forced prostitution."

"And I didn't know Sandi murdered Rhus until I heard her admit it," said Kendra.

"Same here. Sandi was found unconscious, carried no ID when she arrived at the hospital. They took her fingerprints in an attempt to identify her. Since it was a hit and run, they sent her prints in for an ID right away. But things don't happen as fast in real life as they do on TV, especially when the victim's from the—shall we say— less advantaged population. By the time her prints came back as a match for ones found at the crime scene, she'd run away from the hospital in spite of a concussion and deep bruising on the lower part of her body. The city police were looking for her while I was trying to keep tabs on Win and Elias, and the two cases came together. Now they have the murder weapon as well. She hid the dagger in Win's bedroom. Trying to frame her own brother, looks like."

"I'd never do anything like that to you, no matter how irritated with you I am."

He wiped a palm across his forehead like he was whisking sweat away. "I hope not."

"I just realized, something still doesn't make sense. Carol Goodman said Sandi was dead. If she believed it, why didn't she tell the mother sooner? If she didn't know either way, why would she lie?"

"The police took Carol in for questioning last night. I don't know the details except she admitted she was the one who found Sandi after the hit and run and made the untraceable 911 call."

"Untraceable? Like in spy movies? You have to tell me the rest as soon as you find out!"

"You have to know everything. I almost wish you were a psychic so you wouldn't get yourself in trouble all the time looking for answers. I had a real fun time explaining your antics to my boss."

Deadly Traffic

"I'm sorry if I got you in trouble."

He pointed his teaspoon at her. "Well, Ms. Nuisance, today you'll have to make a full report of everything you know and when you knew it."

Kendra let out a long sigh. Bobbins comforted her by jumping to her lap and rubbing his head against her arm. Then he jumped on to the table where he began to lap at droplets of water left from her ice pack. This is what counted, being at home safe, talking with her brother, holding her cat. The events of the past few days seemed to recede, seem less frightening, but one of the impressions refused to go.

"What about the sex trade? Sandi thought both Win and Rhus were involved with it, but she isn't what I'd call a reliable source."

"Can't say about Win. At this point, I have no evidence linking Rhus with prostitution. He'd actually been heading in the opposite direction, toward more skilled...workers. We were investigating the process behind several teachers and nursing professionals he brought in recently. Judging from the care he took to avoid detection, I doubt he ran prostitutes. It's too risky a business. Don't look at me like that. Rhus was ruthless. I believe he knew what Elias did, but chose to look the other way as long as he couldn't be directly connected. To answer your other questions, from Win's behavior, I think he might have been coerced into helping, either by Elias or Rhus for any number of reasons, the visa being a strong one."

"He sold his own sister for a visa? I might sound naïve, but that doesn't sound like Win."

"Perhaps there were other reasons. Who knows what happened to his family on the road to getting those visas, or what price they had to pay?"

She picked up Linc's empty mug and got him a refill, adding the milk, and passing him the drink before Bobbins noticed his missed opportunity. Her legs felt tired from the round trip from table to fridge. Why did she always want to wait on him? "You think Rhus might have been holding something over them?"

"People think of undocumented foreigners as criminals, but often they're victims as well. Foreign workers brought in using perfectly legal channels are sometimes turned over to bosses who treat them like slaves, including forcing them into the sex trade."

205

"Hmm, I think maybe Win's mother was being coerced. I heard her say she was being abused by Rhus."

"Thida Ni lived in Rhus's house, supposedly as his housekeeper."

Even though Kendra thought she'd become immune to Win's multi-faceted notion of honesty, she was stunned by this bit of news.

"You didn't know? I assumed you'd have picked that up," said Linc with a touch of surprise.

"Win never said, and your detective friends didn't tell me either when they showed me her photo."

"They don't usually share information about suspects."

"Well, now I understand something. Thida said she was going to confess to the murder and Carol told her to claim self-defense because she had the bruises to prove it. I don't think Thida really knows anything about the murder. She believed Sandi was dead and Win was the killer."

"In that case, Thida might be eligible for a special type of visa reserved for immigrants who've been victims of abuse."

Kendra frowned. "My god, Rhus was a monster. How could Win not know what his mother was going through?"

"I've seen reports about foreign nannies and housekeepers being held like slaves, and the abuse went undiscovered for years. Their employers went to unbelievable lengths to hide it. In one case, a nanny was taken on outings and forced to smile and pose for photos like she was having the time of her life. Then the abuser actually mailed the photos home to her family to prove to them how happy she was in her job. Meanwhile, he was raping her on a regular basis and feeding her with scraps from the family table."

"I don't think Win went through any of that. He had his freedom, seemed to be happy, with no reason to kill Rhus. Then, Maretta and I heard his mother say she was going to make a false confession to protect him. It was quite a shock."

"And you still went over to his apartment an hour later. What am I going to do with you?" Linc asked helplessly.

"He wasn't home—not when I went over. Anyway, now we know Win wasn't the murderer after all."

"Oh, that reminds me. Win said something weird to me when they were taking him to the patrol car. He said, "Tell Kendra I'm sorry for everything, even the rock."

"What?" Kendra looked at the back entrance, then at Linc, who was watching her with some amusement. She scowled. "What's funny?"

"The way you squawked, the look on your face."

"Well, I'm a total idiot. The door, even the effing door."

"A door is a door is a door," Linc paraphrased. "Mind telling me what you're talking about?"

"Only if you stop doing Gertrude Stein parodies. All right, see, it goes back to how I met Win. I heard a crash and ran outside. He was standing on my front porch, said he heard a noise and came running." She pointed to the back door. "Turned out someone threw a rock through the storm door. When I went round to the front again, I found Win on the porch, holding my mail. He gave me a dumb reason why he was there."

Kendra still intended to avoid telling Linc about her two encounters with Elias and the creepy reference he'd made to letter writing. She'd have to tell the detectives, but maybe she'd luck out and the two agencies would renew their mutual stonewalling or rivalry or whatever, and her brother would never hear about it. And would she ever live it down if Linc found out about the damage to his Mustang?

He sipped his coffee. "I hope you're not done because you're still not making sense."

"Sorry. Later, when I looked through the mail, one of the letters was from the State Prison, which didn't make sense to me either, until now."

"The State Prison?" Linc glared at her, rubbing the bridge of his nose like he did one time in their childhood when he was debating whether or not to drag her before their father to confess to breaking the grandfather clock.

Twenty years later, she felt the same foreboding. "I'm not sure I can explain it. I think Win and Elias were partners. I bet the letter was for Win—no, it still makes no sense because the letter wasn't addressed to him, it was addressed to my house but not to me either."

"It makes sense to me. Inmates use drop boxes sometimes. Win was using your mailbox so he wouldn't be connected to Elias that way. Did you save the letter?"

Mickey Hoffman

"No, I sent it back unopened."

"Make sure you include those details in your statement tomorrow. Perhaps the letter's still sitting around at the prison. It could be valuable evidence."

Kendra suddenly needed to curl up with Bobbins and have a full-out, pity party. She'd been used from the moment she met Win. When he offered to fix her door and invited her for pizza, was he just trying to get close to her? To find out if she read the letter? It had to be. Had he ever actually liked her? At least he said he was sorry....

"Hey, don't look so down in the dumps. If not for you and Maretta, we wouldn't have shown up at just the right time to catch the killer confessing. We heard everything from outside the apartment right before you decided to crash into Detective Tapia." At the memory, Linc started to laugh.

Kendra extended a leg and kicked him in annoyance. She had a big fat lip and he was laughing. Big brothers never changed. "You guys waited long enough before coming in."

"Don't go there. You should have reported days ago what you're telling me now. Even if you convince the investigators you weren't working with, or protecting, a bunch of criminals, you could still be charged for withholding evidence."

Kendra couldn't look him in the eye. She didn't want to hear what he'd say if he knew everything. "Okay, I made things worse for myself," she admitted, "but I didn't want to jump the gun and get any innocent people in trouble."

"How long are you going to carry that old baggage around?"

She held the towel to her forehead so he couldn't see the tears come. "You don't know what it was like after you went to jail. It got ugly. Mom bought all their lies and said you were guilty—that the drugs and the gun they found in the apartment were yours—and you deserved what you got. Dad disagreed and they fought about it all the time. They didn't even notice I existed anymore. Sometimes I envied you for being in prison, away from them. Then they divorced and our family fell apart, all because of the police. And none of the cops ever showed the slightest bit of remorse for planting evidence on you or for screwing up our lives. How can you be one of them now?"

"It didn't happen overnight," said Linc slowly. "The short

208

Deadly Traffic

version is, prison was scary, especially at first, but I learned how to fit in—I had to if I wanted to survive. The guys in my cellblock were mostly in for drug dealing and armed robbery. They were a long way from the kind of people we grew up around. Anyway, to keep myself from winding up like them I worked hard to suppress my anger by studying different types of crime. I looked into cases like my own to see how they'd been adjudicated and learned a lot. But by the time I was cleared, a free man again with my record wiped clean, I'd lost track of my life, of myself."

"You sure lost track of your sister." At Kendra's peevish tone, the cat raised his head and squinted at Linc.

"Don't you two gang up on me. I know I haven't been good about keeping in touch, but I had to get my head straight first. So, to do something mindless for a while, I went up north and got a job in a logging camp. I didn't have any experience, but they were willing to hire anyone who didn't mind losing a foot or hand. After that, I moved around for a while and wound up in Denver."

"Doing what?"

"I got a job in a big box store. I'd been there a few weeks when I got a text message from my attorney, who'd taken a liking to me, kind of kept tabs on me. He thought I was wasting my education. He kept offering suggestions about things I could do with my life. Apparently, the warden told him how I rescued another inmate and he was impressed, so he—"

"Stop. I want to hear about the rescue."

Linc frowned slightly. "You never stop, do you? Okay, okay. One of the inmates, a middle-aged guy named Paul, was a bit slow. What do they call it these days, intellectually challenged? He probably shouldn't have been put in with the general population. Anyway, a guard was supplying illegal drugs to the inmates and using Paul to deliver them. Poor Paul thought he was handing out cigarettes. Then, one day, one of the packs came open in Paul's hand and a red pill came rolling out. He picked it up and called over to the guard, 'Hey, what's this?' Half the cons in the dayroom saw, including me and a bunch of gang members. The next day, I heard whispers someone ordered a hit on Paul. So when I got to my shift at the library, I snuck a note out to the warden."

"Didn't that put you in danger, too?"

"Some." Linc made a sour face. "I couldn't let someone kill

209

the poor bugger, could I?"

"I could say something about sticking one's nose where it doesn't belong doesn't just apply to me," said Kendra laughing.

"Don't." Linc held up his hands. "Anyway, the warden figured out who sent the note and moved me to a segregated unit, away from the others."

"They should have released you for what you did."

"It doesn't work that way. But my good deed paid off when my attorney heard about it. He suggested I look into a career in law enforcement, said I might actually be able to turn my research and 'experience' into something useful. So here I am."

"You told me you were working in a warehouse in Indiana," she complained. "What was all that about?"

"I was in Indiana for a while, really, getting field experience. Eventually, I got assigned here. This was my first major case. I've been working around the clock.... How was I going to know my sister, 'Miss Hap,' would end up in the middle of things?"

Kendra grimaced at the mention of the name of her high school girls' club, the Miss Haps. "Okay, Linc, let's call it even for now." She put out her arms. "Can I have a hug?"

Chapter 44

Monday, November 1

Thida waited until most of the passengers left the train, then stiff from days of train travel, slowly descended to the platform and followed the stragglers into the main terminal. She had never been to an American city as big as New York, or any place as cavernous as Penn Station, but she'd seen train stations before and knew what to look for. With the mass of travelers milling around she felt anonymous, safe. The diversity amazed her, the languages she heard but didn't recognize; even Los Angeles wasn't like this. She looked longingly at a juice bar and almost stopped to buy a drink, but thought better of it. What if she missed him?

She spotted the big departure board where he'd told her to wait and finally saw him. She picked up her small tote and ran toward him. They met half way and she felt his strong arms encircle her. She wanted to stay like that forever, but he pulled away and frowned.

"A short ride to New Jersey, and we are home," he said. Shifting to Burmese, he asked, "Where is Sandi?"

"Things did not go like we planned, Daw. I exchanged the stones for cash and hired your man, the one you call Crane. He came and opened the safe late at night when I was…with Mr. Rhus."

Daw made a hissing sound. Thida gently put her fingers to his lips before continuing, "I had to be with him then, for the alibi. Mr. Rhus slept late the next morning. I took my things and sneaked out to meet Crane to get the money. He had the money but he forgot the IDs. I waited to go home until I thought Mr. Rhus would be out. But he never went anywhere, I found him in his office, murdered. I was so scared. I thought Crane did it. I threw things around to make it look like there was a fight. Then I took the IDs and ran."

"What about Sandi?"

"She did it," said Thida, her voice trembling.

211

Daw almost dropped the tickets he was holding. His eyes moved frantically, worrying they'd been overheard, unlikely as it was anyone understood their language. "What do you mean she did it?"

"I do not know. She ran away from that Home. I could not find her. I did not know she killed him until they arrested her and I saw it on the news. I think she went to Mr. Rhus's house on Sunday, but I don't know why."

"What will happen to her? Does she have a lawyer?"

"She will have one. This is America. And the school counselor, Mrs. Goodman, is going to help her. She told me everyone knows Sandi has something wrong in her head. Because of that, and her age, she will be sent to some kind of special hospital instead of jail. She will be safe there. Maybe they can cure her."

"And even after all that, Win still would not come with you?"

Thida grabbed Daw's arms tightly and began to cry. "They arrested him, too. I could not find out why. I had to hide. The cops were looking for me, too. I knew he would land in trouble when he refused to go to school. I told him not to work for Mr. Rhus." She hung her head. "I do not know what happened with our children, Daw. Was it a mistake to come to this country?"

"It is not your fault everything did not go like we planned." He pulled her into her arms again and rocked her while the relentless stream of commuters hurried past, wholly contained in their own life stories, rushing toward their own destinations.

After a while, Daw whispered, "Did you get what we need?"

"We'll be fine," she assured him. "We have the $50,000 and many IDs. Enough to make a new life."

Mickey Hoffman was born in Chicago, and attended public schools where she acquired the strong suspicion that some of her teachers might be human. She wasn't able to prove this fanciful thinking until much later, when she became a high school teacher herself.

Before landing in the halls of academia, she worked in a variety of jobs, including computer typesetting and wholesale frozen fish sales.

The author is also a printmaker and painter and resides on the West Coast with her long suffering mate, eight marine aquariums and a very large cat. Mickey is also the author of School of Lies, the first Kendra Desola mystery.

School is murder if you are not a particularly good student. It's also murder if you are a manipulative, coercive vice-princi-whom everyone would like to see dead. The problem is the person whom the police suspect of the crime is our innocent heroine.

Available from Indigoseapress.com